Privacy Wars – Book One

By Terry R. Cooper

The Chelyabinsk Pandemic bacteria of 2038 ate concrete as well as bones, destroying most buildings, dams, and sewers. Three-quarters of the Earth's population perished. Two hundred thirty years later, Elites live in 548 closed cities in the Northern Hemisphere. Imperfect humans are exiled to the Southern Hemisphere, and everyone else scrapes a living from the food grower industry in the North. Government has been replaced with a triad: elected officials; a single global company; and the android police force, Pandera.

Happy Birthday

February 29, 2366—Richmond, Virginia

When the spiderlike struts settled onto the smooth bedrock of the bunker floor, Ady popped the airpod hatch and scrambled down the ladder. She ran, skipped, and jumped across the bunker lab towards the control panel, pumping her fist in the air with joy. She skidded to a stop next to Bo, who stood grinning at her.

He stroked his salt-and-pepper beard. "I would say that was a very successful test flight, especially in the confines of this bunker. Congratulations!"

She pulled off her skullcap, freeing her long auburn mane, and bear-hugged her grandfather as much as her smaller frame could grasp. After a moment, she said, "Thank you, thank you, thank you, for helping me. I love you so much, Bo."

"Well, Ms. Ford, you certainly pay homage to your lineage!" He pointed at the control panel. "Not a single wiggle in the gravitational waves."

They stood smiling at each other for a long moment. She felt tears welling. She hugged him again and buried her face in his shoulder. "I'm so lucky to have you." She stepped back and looked into his gray eyes. "And lucky to have your DNA."

He smiled and nodded. "Along with your mother's improvements."

"Natural and unnatural," she said. They both laughed.

He stood and looked at the airpod for a moment. "Incredible, Ady. It's not just the grav-wave propulsion. You fabricated and built every single part."

"With your lab and assistance. You fab'd all the skin panels and struts."

Bo waved a dismissive hand. "From your specs, plus Ellis did most of the work." He turned to the control panel vid and began tapping the panel. "It's been a long day. Let's shut down and get back home."

With today's success, Ady proved her creative and inventive skills both to herself and Bo. The myriad of small adjustments, overhauls, and inventions she had crafted in the last few years were precursors, she told herself. By the time her parents returned home, she'd have a hangar built near Bo's lab and would move the airpod there from the bunker. She could do real test flights then. Maybe they'd be home in time for her first untethered flight. As scientists, they'd appreciate how important her key invention could be, not only for Earth travel, but also potentially for space travel as well.

She wished there was someone else with whom she could share her success, though. A friend, a co-worker, or maybe even a lover…someday. She laughed to herself. Loneliness seemed inherent in her family legacy of key but unheralded contributions to humanity's betterment. All the way back to racist Henry Ford. Someone or some organization was always intent on discrediting or destroying them. So, she and Bo worked alone in their secret bunker, the only way to ensure their anonymity, and hence, their safety.

Ten minutes later, Ady unplugged the charging cable from the transport buggy and dragged it back to its rack in the bunker lab. "When I get time, I'm going to see if we can replace this old nitrogen supercooling system with a gravity wave modulator, too. This thing eats up nearly half of our power budget."

"It's been working alright for nearly three hundred years, Missy," said Bo. "Old man Rasp knew what he was doing."

As they accelerated down the tunnel, a voice from the buggy said, "Estimated arrival in 40.7 minutes."

"Thank you, Ellis," said Bo.

"If I may point out," Ellis said, "Adelya recently synchronized me into all the vehicle auto-drives as well as the computer systems in the bunker and the domicile. She also increased the speed of this transport by 41.2 percent. This trip used to take over one hour."

"Yes, yes, and now you babble at me from my grooming mirror to my workshop," grumbled Bo.

Ady tucked her hair under her cap. "I definitely created a monster." They rode in silence for a few minutes. "I'm glad I added a heater, though. Even though the tunnel stays at thirteen degrees, this used to be a chilly ride."

"Best mod you've made," said Bo, nodding.

She glanced at her wrist Linc and dipped her head. Her yearlong wait to see Anson again would end tonight. Her expectations were galactic, but if it didn't work out, she didn't want to worry Bo. She considered sending a vid to her parents to tell them about her airpod success, but the time lag to get her message to Europa had somehow dampened her desire to share with them. It took too long to get there, and their response would be even more delayed and anticlimactic. She'd pretty much given up routine communications with them, but she wished she had someone to share tonight's plans with.

"I'm going into Richmond tonight to see the Bacchus Festival," she said to Bo, "so I won't be home for dinner."

He smiled and looked at her. "Meeting someone special there?"

Before she could respond, Ellis chimed in. "Bacchanal: a crazed party with drunken revelry, ecstatic sexual experimentation, and wild music."

"Thank you, Ellis," said Bo. "I've been there, as you well know."

Attempting to steer the conversation away from her, Ady said, "How long ago was that? What was it like?"

"He last attended on March seventh, 2303. At that time–"

"Ellis, stop!" said Bo. "Reduce your conversational engagement ten percent until further notice." He scratched at his bearded jaw for a moment. "I'm sure she's right about the date, so I was fifty-nine then, not even middle-aged. Nearly sixty-three years ago. Doesn't seem that long," he mused.

"What was it like then?" Ady asked again.

Bo smoothed his beard and chuckled. "Raucous! But the Pandera police force pretty much left us alone back then." He proceeded to regale Ady with Bacchus Festival stories all the way to Virginia. Ady particularly liked the one about him meeting Wai-Wan, the love of his life, no matter how many times she'd heard it. It seemed to be Bo's favorite, too.

*****

The Krewe-Brew was an "ancient" bar instead of the typical self-serve vending style. The Krewe still had actual kegs of beer of their own making, and human bartenders. The one who served her tonight had a fake reddish skin tone and a shaved head. Ady spotted a nearly invisible tiny scar behind his left ear, a tagging scar from a tracking implant. If it was from Pandera, the android police force, he'd been incarcerated. Or he could have once been a Num, the common term for citizens of the closed cities. She couldn't see closely enough to determine if the tracker had been dug out. She frowned and waved the information out of her brain. The problem with noticing and analyzing everything was that sometimes your brain would fixate on trivial details that got through your carefully constructed irrelevance filters. She had more important things to worry about tonight.

Her focus shifted to a mug of this week's blonde ale warming on the worn walnut bar where she stood. It had been a whole year. Anson had surely forgotten her. Here she was, building gravity wave air vehicles by day, but camped in a Bacchus bar on her twenty-fourth birthday. She felt childish and disappointed with herself. Emotional attachments, men, even friends ate up your time, time you could be doing so much more. And yet, she'd felt giddy on the way to Krewe tonight. She wondered how Ellis would analyze her emotions, even though she knew an AI homebot was not the best place to seek emotional advice.

Krewe customers brushed against her repeatedly because it was so crowded. Someone tried to squeeze in between her and the woman standing next to her. "Sorry," said the guy as he bumped her again. He leaned into the bar and tried to attract the bartender's attention with a wave. She saw he had calloused hands and dirty fingernails, and no Linc on his wrist. The coarse fabric of his tunic sleeve was frayed and had faint red stains. He was probably a crop worker come to the city for Bacchus.

She scanned the crowd from the vid on her wrist Linc. She'd hacked into the Krewe's camera system a couple of years ago, mostly for fun, but it had come in handy as a behind-the-back spy on the patrons who approached and often propositioned her. She suspected the proprietor of Krewe owned the sex pod rental shop next door because their cameras were on the same net. She wasn't sure if Krewe's main business was drink, or a match-up platform for quick sex in the pods.

The agro-worker next to her retrieved his three drinks from the bar and slid off. As she sipped her beer, her third, she sensed someone else slide in next to her. But she didn't care. Three hours was a long-enough wait. Anson wasn't coming. She had definitely been wasting her time. He'd seemed different. Actually interested in her and what she had to say. But her memories of that night had aged and probably became embellished by her ego. Or her empty heart.

She closed the Linc vid and turned towards the throng to make her way to the exit. Something tugged at her sleeve. She turned back towards the bar as she tried to pull her arm away. She wasn't about to be pawed by some drunken crop boy. But before she could snap a warning, the person next to her clasped her hand and palmed a slip of paper into it. She looked up at him, but his tunic hood was up, and he had already turned and was melting into the crowd.

She headed towards the exit. Outside, she moved into the street, shoulder to shoulder with the meandering, drunken crowd. She threaded her way to a corner where lights were bright enough to read the slip. *Couldn't make it. Will contact you soon.* She leaned back against the building wall and closed her eyes. Her head tingled like it always did when she was stressed. Her shoulders slumped. She felt betrayed.

What did she really know about Anson? He was like a wisp of smoke, appearing and disappearing. When they'd met here last year, they immediately hit it off, and talked at an outside table for nearly five hours. That had been so much more fun than any ten-minute sex pod encounter. She'd been reliving that conversation for the last year, trying repeatedly to discern why she was so fixated on him. He was witty and intelligent, almost able to keep up with her intellect. He joked easily, and she'd noticed a dimple in his left cheek twitched when he was fibbing or teasing. She showed him how she'd hacked the Krewe's cameras. He showed her his double-jointed thumbs.

She chided him. "An anatomic anomaly doesn't equate to skill, talent, or intelligence."

"How about this: the Southern Hemisphere has half as much land as the North but has less than five percent of the population of the North."

"Interesting. I thought the South was nearly empty except for the Imperfects sent there. But still, just factual memory."

She smirked now as she had then, recalling his frustration when she beat him at his own "mental gymnastics" game. After some more flirting about comparative intelligence levels, he started calling her "Level 8" in a fake condescending tone. Grinning, he said, "Okay, Level 8, calculate the sum of the prime numbers under 100."

"One thousand sixty."

His grin faded a bit. "Okay, how about under one thousand?"

She crossed her eyes at him for a moment, and said, "76,127. But I doubt if Level 9 knows if that's correct."

His grin disappeared. She wondered if she'd hurt his ego and let the smirk fall from her face, but she gave him a chance to redeem himself. "Impress me with the sum of the first one hundred natural numbers. Your Level 9 is on the line."

He shook his head. "I don't know."

She stopped smiling. "I'm sorry if I offended you, Anson. I was just playing your game."

Anson nodded. "No offense taken. I was showing off and you kicked my ass." He leaned in and looked at her closely. "You're no Level 8."

She squirmed in her seat and examined her hands. Her life coaching to never reveal her true intelligence sounded alarms in her head.

"You didn't remember those sums, did you Ady? Not factual memory. You calculated them in your head."

She stared at him, unsure what to say.

Anson reached across the table and took her hand in both of his. She looked at their hands. Her pulse quickened as the warmth and roughness of his hands triggered a swirl of unfamiliar emotions. She suddenly had too much saliva in her mouth, and she swallowed before she met his blue eyes. He frightened her. Could he somehow see through her facade into who she really was?

"What's the answer, Ady?"

Startled, she said, "What answer?"

"Sum of first 100 natural numbers."

"Five thousand fifty." She blinked. Had she just blurted out the answer? Embarrassed, she pulled her hand away. "I'm sorry."

Anson stood, took her hand, pulled her up, and wrapped both arms around her in the best hug of her life. She wished it could last forever. Someone called out, "Rent a pod," and Anson stepped back. "Ady, I have to go. Let's walk to your vehicle."

Her heart fell. She'd made him angry, showed him up, and embarrassed both of them. With a few drinks in her, her damn big brain couldn't be contained. She liked this guy. He had a quick mind and an unmatched banter. She hadn't met anyone like him before and now she was near tears at the thought of ending the evening without him.

Unlike the "Rogues of Richmond," a term Ady used with Ellis for the men she met here, Anson checked box number two of her relationship checklist—intellectual and emotional sparring partner. At least he seemed to. As for box number one—companionship—she had hoped to find out tonight. At least get an intimacy score. That was part of companionship. The only part she'd found here so far.

He put his arm around her as they walked, telling her he was going on a trip and wouldn't be back until next year.

She stopped and turned to him. "Anson, I like you a lot. This has been unusually fun, but please don't concoct some cold fusion story to get rid of me. Just say 'see-ya' and I'll understand. That won't ruin the night or the memories like a lie will."

He put his hand on her shoulder and looked her in the eye. "What can I say to you to convince you this is not a lie? I'm stunned by tonight, at the odds of our encounter turning into what we've had in the last few hours. I want to see you again, tomorrow, and the next day, and the next. But I have a job, a very private job, and it means I leave tomorrow for a year."

She stared at him, wondering if she could estimate those odds, how to measure his truthfulness, and what to say about her sudden sorrow. "I don't have much experience with trusting people, other than my family. It's not that I've had bad experiences, just not many that counted." She paused for a moment, her mouth dry. That damned tingling was roaring in her head, too. "Your story sounds phony, Anson, but I'll accept it because you asked me to. If this evening meant anything to you, please don't bail on me."

Anson nodded and they walked on. She presumed he was going off world. If it was only for a year, it was probably the moon. He asked for her Linc contact, and she told him her public connection id. He told her he didn't have one and didn't use electronic communications, which made him both suspicious and mysterious. He also told her to immediately destroy any physical messages he sent to her so no one else could read them.

"Destroy them how?" she asked.

"If I send you a note on paper, after you read it, chew it up and swallow it."

She looked at his face to see if he was joking. No dimple twitched. "Seriously?"

"Please," replied Anson. "Security is important to me and to the people I care about." They reached her ground vehicle. "Interesting."

"It's called a convertible. Fold-down tops used to be popular a couple centuries ago." She ran her hand along the red fender. "I built it myself."

He smiled. "Of course." The smile slid away. "I may not be able to contact you until we meet here next year. But I'll be here, Ady, and I hope you will, too."

She couldn't make her mouth work, so she nodded. Anson leaned in and kissed her. It was way too brief, but it promised so much. And then he was gone, walking down the street for two blocks until he turned the corner and disappeared. She stood there a while longer staring down the street, reliving those last few hours at high speed, trying to remember everything. Her memories were all she would have for the next year.

Now, standing in the street shadows, she looked once again at the scrap of paper the stranger had slipped into her hand. She scanned the people around her. Pretending to cough, she brought her hand to her lips as she crumpled the paper and popped it into her mouth. After a few chews, she swallowed it.

Anson hadn't shown up, but he had acknowledged their planned rendezvous. A year-long trip could have complications, delays, schedule changes. At least he got a message to her. But why was everything so secretive? Passing a paper note. No electronic communications. Something was very off with him. Maybe that's what intrigued her—his mystery.

The packed crowd pinned her against the wall as they suddenly parted to allow a Bacchus Festival parade to pass through. She watched the characters on the floats with their lavish costumes and historical masks. They danced and cheered with painted smiles. The crowd cheered, too, as each float passed by blasting quad-sensor streams of audio, olfactory, light, and pressure, immersing you in the music. She wanted to dance and cheer, too. With Anson. She'd dreamed of sharing the street quad-streams with him. Without him, it was noise and sensory overload, which she ignored. She'd set her hopes on his promise and their journey to follow. It had turned out to be another solitary walk.

Drink 'n' Drive

Ady dozed as her ground vehicle drove along the dusky highway towards home. With the top down, her waist-length hair whipped in the cool evening breeze, dulling the buzz of the alert on the dash panel. Ellis, the autodrive, asked for instructions, but the sleeping Ady remained unaware. Additional alarms now flashed and buzzed. Suddenly, Ellis executed an emergency stop, deploying the restraints around Ady, and skidding to a halt after a loud thump sounded from the left front wheel.

"What the hell?" shouted Ady, as she struggled in the emergency restraint cocoon.

"Are you injured?" queried Ellis.

"No, Ellis! What did you hit?" She pushed at the restraints. "Let me out of here!" The restraints retracted and she pushed open the door. She stared at a lifeless feathered creature splayed on the blacktop. "What is that?"

Ellis replied, "My observations are consistent with *Branta Canadensis*."

Ady couldn't tell if it was breathing or not. "Common name? It has feathers. It must be some kind of bird."

"Commonly called a 'Canadian Goose,' if my observations of the creature are accurate."

"What's it doing here? And why did you hit it?"

"I repeatedly attempted to alert you–"

"Never mind," Ady snapped. "Open the storage compartment." A panel in the rear of the vehicle popped open. She approached the goose cautiously, trying to figure out how to pick it up.

"While your impairment from the bacchanal may be ignored, may I remind you that consuming, harboring, handling, or assisting any legged wild animal, which includes birds, is illegal, should authorities become involved."

"No, you may not. If we leave it here, there will be evidence you killed 'a legged wild animal' and I'll be the one in trouble." Ady slid her hands under the main part of its body and lifted the bird. It was soft and slippery, but surprisingly heavy. "If we take it home and dump it in the river, it will disappear. No one will ever know." She slid the goose into the compartment and closed the hatch.

"Home, Ellis," said Ady as she jumped back into the seat and closed the door.

*****

At home, the wrist Linc of Ady's grandfather, Bo, buzzed with high priority. "Is there a problem, Ellis?"

"We will arrive in 2.17 minutes. What appeared to be a Canadian goose tried to hit our vehicle or Ady directly. I tracked it from more than eleven kilometers away travelling at a speed of forty-two kilometers per hour. Natural geese cannot fly that fast. It originated near a hovering air vehicle that likely belongs to the Pandera police force. We avoided a direct collision by my evasive stop at the last minute. The goose was struck by the left front wheel and rendered lifeless. Ady retrieved the creature and put it in the vehicle storage compartment. The air vehicle has vectored directly to the house. We will arrive ninety-one seconds ahead of them."

Bo jumped to his feet and ran through the house towards the decontamination exit. "Rush her through decon when you get here. If it's their goose, they'll want it back. But I want to examine it." He'd never heard of Pandera using geese.

Ellis replied, "It can be moved to the Faraday isolation cage in your lab before they arrive, preventing any Pandera communication with the creature device."

"Good. Decon the vehicle compartment in case they investigate further. They won't want to lose their secret device, but they also won't want to reveal it. If it's not easily found, they probably want it to stay permanently lost."

A few moments later Ady's vehicle turned into the long driveway to the domicile. Ellis said, "Adelya, a Pandera vehicle is arriving in approximately ninety-one seconds. Your grandfather has selected a deception plan I am currently implementing. When we arrive, please exit, and decontaminate quickly. I have sent a full report to your Lync."

Ady skimmed Ellis's report. "For a goose? Pandera is gonna bust me over a goose? How do they even know?"

After the vehicle bay door slid open, the vehicle rolled inside. Ady jumped over the door and stood against the wall. Her grandfather's voice boomed, "Ady, decon immediately."

The bay door closed, and Ellis said, "Sixty-seven seconds until their arrival."

Ady pushed through the side door into the scrub room where she kicked off her boots and shed her clothes into the incinerator. She ran through the decontamination spray and quickly pulled on a black long-sleeved tunic.

Her grandfather was waiting when she stepped out of the scrub room. He stared at her and said, "You know nothing. You slept through anything

10

and everything. Understood?" Ady nodded. Bo pulled her into a hug. "And if things go badly, remember your training. Don't antagonize them."

She nodded. "I sure hope I don't need to use my training because of a damn goose!" She swept her hair back and clipped it into a long ponytail. "Doesn't make sense. There must be a part of this we don't know." She looked at Bo. "Hasn't been a great night. I'm sorry."

He nodded.

Ellis announced, "Pandera has arrived."

Bo walked to the front door. "What is your business?" he asked via the door communicator. He slipped an audio comm into his ear so he could listen to Ellis.

A too-cheerful male AI voice said, "Pandera business. We will examine your ground vehicle. Please open the bay door."

"Comply," said Bo as he stepped through the front door portal and stood looking at the Pandera vehicle hovering in the driveway. The bay door slid open, and a small ground bot rolled from the Pandera vehicle into the bay. Ady pulled up the bay video on her wrist Linc so she and Bo could watch. The bot opened a side panel on the vehicle and inserted a probe. A few seconds later, it withdrew and returned to the Pandera vehicle.

The same Pandera voice said, "Adelya Nichieu Ford, step forward."

She stepped around her grandfather and said, "What?"

"Why did you stop on your journey 3.7 kilometers from this domicile?"

"I didn't. The auto-drive did. I was asleep." She glanced at her grandfather.

After a brief pause, the Pandera voice said, "Your auto-drive has transmitted the journey record and confirms your account. Did you see anything on the road when you stopped?"

She slid her hands to her hips. "I was asleep. I didn't see anything!"

For nearly two minutes no further conversation or movement came from the Pandera vehicle. Ellis said in Bo's ear, "They are struggling to determine a course of action, as you predicted. Their communications indicate that the goose device has apparently been secret to parts of Pandera control."

A moment later a holo-vid projected on the driveway in front of the Pandera vehicle. It was an overhead video of Ady moving the goose from the road to the vehicle. Bo sighed and shook his head. He slid his hands into his tunic pockets.

The Pandera voice said, "Where is the legged natural creature we saw you pick up in that recording?"

She shrugged. "Inexplicable. I told you I was asleep the whole time. I don't even remember picking it up."

An android emerged from the vehicle and approached her. It said, "Are you Adelya Nichieu Ford?"

Ady's eyes widened. "Yes."

An immobilizer web shot out of the bot's hand and wrapped her arms, legs, and feet. "Adelya Nichieu Ford, you are guilty of illegally handling and interfering with a legged natural creature and attempting to deceive Pandera. You are sentenced to two years of service work on Mars outpost number three."

She tried to scream and run, but she knew it was useless. Immobilized and silenced. Mars. Two years. By herself. For a goose.

*****

Bo watched the vehicle ascend and fly off to the North.

Ellis broke the silence. "Based on the angle from which that video was recorded, it was not taken from that Pandera vehicle. There must have been a second vehicle not detected by my sensors. It was practically overhead."

"Indeed," said Bo as he clasped his hands behind his back. "Ellis, advise her parents, please." He looked down, scuffed the smooth paver stone with his worn black boot, and muttered, "Hope her DNA isn't flagged."

"Many Fords have been incarcerated, William. I'm sure Adelya will be fine and return to us unharmed. But I will miss her."

"Yes," said Bo as he looked skyward again. "Me, too." He went back inside and closed the door.

*****

As Ady lay immobile in the Pandera air vehicle, an image of her standing on the shore of the James River came to mind. It was her fourteenth birthday, she had returned home from Social, the one-day-a-week class where her classmates gathered in person. The E-droid who led the class had acknowledged her birthday and they celebrated with flavored ice bars for all sixty-two classmates at Hopewell Ed.

After returning home, Bo asked her to come to his lab. He said he had a birthday present for her there.

His lab was a hundred meters from the house atop the riverbank where, twenty meters below, the James River crawled towards the ocean like a sleepy southern caterpillar. A paved drive led past the lab and down the bank into the murky river where she supposed her ancestors had launched boats.

She glanced at the old wooden dock at the foot of drive. When she was six, Bo had taken her into the water from the dock, and over the course of a sweltering summer, taught her to swim. They had raced each other to the tiny islands just this side of the channel where they could watch some of the towboats up close. The *coup de grace* of her swimming summer was the swim from the islands back to the dock underwater on one breath. When she surfaced at the dock, Bo was right behind her. Once out of the water, he gave her an especially long hug as he congratulated her.

She smiled as she recalled her pride at her success, but more importantly how proud Bo was that day.

When she entered the lab, Bo had beamed at her and said, "Happy birthday and welcome to your birthright, Ady."

She smiled and said automatically, "Thank you, Bo." Then she frowned, puzzled. "What do you mean, birthright?"

Bo swept an arm around the area. "This. It's all yours now."

She looked out across the room, noting the chain hoist on the track near the roll-up door. There were exotic-looking heavy machines that she supposed cut, shaped, and crafted metal or other kinds of material. Vid screens, keypads, and electronics dotted the mostly-gray machinery.

"Let's take a ride," said Bo, stepping into a cleared area of the floor and gesturing to Ady to join him.

"Where to?"

"An ancient bunker."

"A bunker?"

"It's yours, too, now." The cleared area detached from the rest of the lab floor and began to descend.

"What's the bunker for?" she asked, staring at the floor.

"The government originally constructed it as a safe house for government officials in the event of nuclear war. But it was never used, and one of our ancestors, Jeremy Ford, purchased it and hid it for our family."

"Why?"

"Because we sometimes need a place to work or hide from folks, organizations, or governments who don't like us much."

She frowned. "I think all the kids at E-center like me."

"Yes, but there's Pandera, the Nums, the Coordinating Council…an endless line of people and organizations who would like to take this away. And it has a long, long history starting with folks like Rockefeller, Westinghouse, and Morgan. Our original benefactor was Henry Ford." The descending platform stopped, and Ady blinked as bright lights automatically snapped on. They were standing next to an underground train track where a small train car with a clear bubble front awaited.

"We call it a buggy," said Bo. "Seats eight in four rows. Has a seven-meter cargo bed. There's another one just down the track that can be connected to this one if we need to transport larger equipment." He waved in that direction. "And there are some older models beyond that, too." Bo opened the front door. "Please have a seat. I'll drive."

Bo climbed in and started the buggy down the track. "I'll give you the bunker background while we ride. Old Jeremy Clay Ford, great-great-grandson of Henry Ford, was buddies with Elton Rasp. Together, in 2061, they built the first Mars colonies using Rasp's tunneling technology. Jeremy had purchased the Greenbrier Resort, including this government-built bunker, in 2042. Rasp needed to prove his tunneling technology, so they cooked up a "demo" scheme to cut a fifty-mile tunnel from Norfolk to Richmond, mostly under the James River. The dirt and rocks from the tunnel were used to build a new jetty at the harbor entrance."

Ady pointed at the console. "Based on our arrival time and speed, it's a lot longer than that, right?"

"Yup. Instead of fifty miles, they cut just over two hundred miles—320 clicks—all the way to the bunker. There was little public understanding of tunneling at the time, so no one paid any attention to how long it took to build or how big the jetty grew to be. There was originally another entrance in Dillwyn up in the mountains, but it was sealed around 2100 when the state prison expanded. The entry near Norfolk Harbor was permanently sealed, too, after the tunneling demonstration took place. My lab, I mean *your* lab, was constructed by Jeremy to conceal the real entrance."

"How did they keep the tunnel a secret? And why?" she asked.

Bo shrugged. "Not really sure, but the six workers who built the tunnel with Rasp's tunnel machine were on the first mission to Mars in 2049 and they never returned to Earth."

"What happened to the bunker after Jeremy died?"

"His grandson, Hansen Lee Penn (HLP) Ford, and Rasp's granddaughter, Rokid Barbiere Rasp wed in 2048 at the resort. They became the co-heads of the combined Ford-Rasp companies and, as the story goes, they pretty much ignored the bunker. Fortunately for us, they were the last of our lineage of scoundrels, crooks, and racists who accumulated wealth at the expense of others. Their son and two daughters, disgusted with their parents' principles and behavior, moved to Mars in 2077 where they collectively oversaw the expansion of the Mars and moon colonies and planned the first manned missions to Jupiter's moon, Europa.

"Meanwhile, the bunker just sat here for nearly a century. Then, in 2138 when the pandemic started, Saad Ford and his daughter Onish, refurbished the tunnel with a maglev rail. They replaced the simple electric cars with three custom eight-passenger vehicles, and two materials transports, all of which could be linked as a mini-train. Cut the travel time down to ninety minutes.

"The Ford clan hunkered down in the bunker. The communications and power cables were 'repaired' with new technology, and the tower, about ten kilometers away, was rebuilt to include high-gain solar panels and satellite antennas. The stories say Onish saved the Ford clan and an equal number of close friends, employees, and their families. At one time, eighty-three people lived there, some for as long as nine years."

"How big is this bunker?"

"Just over ten thousand square meters."

"So it's a combination hideout and lab."

Bo nodded and shifted in his seat. His face softened. "There's something else I want to talk about, Ady. I'm sure you're well aware that you're smarter than your friends and most everyone around you."

Ady felt her face flush. She squirmed in her seat.

"There's a reason for that. Your mother Minda was a researcher at NeoHealth. When you were created, she secretly adjusted your DNA using intelligence enhancement techniques she had developed. A few months later, NeoHealth, which is mostly run by the Pandera AI's, reviewed her research, and deleted it. Minda was dismissed shortly before you were delivered to her and Vanessa."

Her mouth opened, and then closed. She looked away. "You mean I'm a freak, some kind of experiment?" Was that why her parents left for Europa when she was six?

Bo shook his head. "No, no, nothing like that. It boils down to this. When we're born, we have a certain number of neurons in our brain. It stays that way for the duration of our life. No more, no less. Minda found that the number of neurons correlates with mental capacity, or intelligence. You have about thirty percent more neurons than most of us."

She stared at Bo for a moment. "So, I'm an egghead and you've been coaching me to keep it secret all these years."

"More or less." Bo splayed his hands on his lap. "The fact that you were able to score almost exactly ninety-one percent on all your tests probably proves Minda correct. Your intelligence level is scored as eight, as you know. But you purposely steered that score to eight."

She nodded as she examined her hands. "It's like a mantra in my brain. Never reveal what you're really thinking or how much you know. Was that learned from you guys or did Minda slip that into my DNA as well?"

"Learned. Ellis—the Ellis in the domicile—assisted when you were a toddler. Minda even tried hypnotic suggestion. If NeoHealth or Pandera discovered your unusually high intelligence, we were afraid they'd exile you to the Southern Hemisphere to live with the other defective humans."

Ady sniffed and wiped her eyes. "So nobody really knows my intelligence level. Even Minda?"

Bo shook his head. "After you finish Education this year, it's not likely you'll ever be tested again. Vanessa, Minda, and I don't really need a number. We know you're smarter than us. We're anxious to see what you do in your Career training."

She frowned. "I know Minda's Career path, but what did Vanessa choose?"

Bo sighed. "Your grandmother and I probably drove her away from our technical career focuses." He shrugged. "As a child, perhaps seeing her parents arrested by Pandera multiple times scared her off. I don't really know. But she was all about people, relationships, and making the world a better place. I would say sociology would best describe her path focus. But in the end, she had the same Career path as you."

"What do you mean? I don't know what Career path to choose, and applications are due in a couple of weeks."

"Your Career was chosen before you were conceived, Ady," Bo had said. "You're a Ford."

*****

Ady felt a bump and realized the air vehicle had landed. The door opened and the android grabbed the webbing around her feet, pulling her towards him. He picked her up and carried her into a building. After a short walk down a smooth white hallway, he turned a corner into another hallway lined with doors on both sides. The fourth door on the left slid open. He carried her inside the cell and released the webbing, dropping her to the floor. He walked out and the door knifed shut, cleaving off all light.

She stretched and tried to look around, but it was total darkness. Although Bo had trained her for this eventuality, reality was more unsettling than the sims. She sniffed the air. A faint rusty scent drifted on the overwhelming disinfectant smell. It was the tranquilizer. They were putting her out.

She rolled onto her side, her eyes growing heavy. She had no choice. Bo's voice rang in her head. "Don't resist until you are sure of your escape."

Duck Duck Goose

After Pandera took Ady, Bo went to his room to change into his lab clothes. As he was dressing, a tone sounded from his Linc. "Yes, Ellis."

"Your vital signs indicate a likely emotional state that I am reluctant to interrupt, but a pressing matter outweighs my reticence to disturb you. If I may?"

Bo paused for a moment, and said, "Just a moment, Ellis." He finished dressing, grabbed his boots, and went downstairs to the study. He closed the door and walked to his desk where he picked up a tablet. He tapped a few instructions to Ellis. Momentarily, the lights in the room dimmed, a silent acknowledgment to his instructions. He sat.

A faint tone sounded, and Ellis said, "At your request, I have run a full assessment of all electronic systems and have not identified any intrusions, failed attempts, or other unidentified routines. Pandera is, however, attempting to monitor your Linc and our audio communications. Sensory jamming systems are now engaged within the domicile. Our conversation is secure and Pandera will not be aware I have jammed their reception."

"Thank you. Proceed with your report."

"The trajectory of the subject goose did not follow a natural path. Instead, it appeared to be on a collision trajectory from the time I initiated tracking at a distance of 7,392 meters. Its trajectory adjusted with my changes in vehicular speed. A collision was only avoided by severe evasive steps at the last moment."

Bo pulled on his boots. "Thank you, Ellis. I concur it's not a natural goose. Please open and vent the sub-tunnel to the lab. Also engage sensory jamming in the lab."

Ten minutes later, Bo approached the Faraday cage, which blocked any electronic transmissions to or from the goose. The goose, or whatever it was, lay inert in the middle of the two-meter cube. "Ellis, are there any electronic emissions originating from the subject?"

"No, and I did not detect any when it was approaching the vehicle either."

Bo scratched his beard. "What about laser guidance?"

"The vehicle sensors are inadequate to detect that spectrum."

Bo walked to a panel next to the cage. "Give me an infrared image, please." A few seconds later, the "goose" outline was painted on the panel.

The sharp lines that defined the array of varying densities confirmed it was not organic. "Scan for explosives or canisters, Ellis."

A few moments later, Ellis said, "What appears to be twin batteries at the approximate leg juncture location are still providing power to the device. The head contains a small device that could be an explosive."

"Clarify 'small device.'"

"It is spherical, 2.3 centimeters in diameter, and has three connection points to the circuitry. It is embedded within a gelatinous, spherical body approximately 5.72 centimeters in diameter."

"Impact protection," muttered Bo. "Any other curious or dangerous aspects?"

"Although physically still connected, the circuitry connection from the body through the neck to the head appears to have been severed. This is likely from the impact with our ground vehicle. The legs appear to contain antennae with some sort of small–" Ellis stopped.

The entire Faraday cage dropped through the floor and a blast door slammed closed to seal it below.

Bo watched the panel as video from below came on. Both of the "goose" legs exploded with what appeared to be something like red flares. They tried to shoot around the space but were so physically confined that they finally ended up in a corner burning out their red propellant.

Ellis said, "The containment field temperature has risen to 31.2 degrees. The oxygen content is now less than one percent."

The video view became obscured by smoke from the flares. "Vent the field into the river without any noticeable disturbance, Ellis."

"Underway. The object also contains a timer or clock. It is connected to the batteries. I do not know its purpose but hypothesize that the head explosive may be a self-destruct device instead of a weapon."

Bo nodded. "Yes, it's too small to do much damage. They didn't want this thing found or analyzed. That's probably why they did such a cursory search. They didn't want to draw our attention to it. But why did the flares go off now and not earlier?"

"That is a curious question. Four minutes ago, five Pandera air vehicles took station three hundred feet above the domicile. They remain stationary there. They are emitting no electronic signature."

Bo smiled. "They knew when the flares would ignite. How long since the collision?"

"32.4 minutes."

"The timer. If this thing goes down, they have time to clean up the mess, clear witnesses, and come back to retrieve their drone unobserved. Clever."

He rubbed his chin for a moment. "Give me two minutes to get to the bunker tunnel, and then bring it back up and hit it with an EMP blast. Let's see if that kills it."

Bo made his way to the bunker tunnel and waited. A few moments later, "All Clear" appeared on his Linc. He returned to the lab to find a smoldering carcass on the floor of the cage. The faux feathers were burned off and it was apparent that the goose form was covered in a synthetic "skin."

Ellis said, "Although the batteries have charge remaining, all circuits appear to have been severed. There is no evidence of any current flow."

Bo retrieved a pair of long tongs from his metal forge, opened the cage door, and picked up the carcass. He carried it to a workbench and began to examine it.

Two hours later, Ellis set up a secure vid Linc to Minda and Vanessa. Bo summarized his dissection of the "goose." "It's a surveillance drone with live audio, video, and electronic signal interception. No autonomous navigation: likely laser guided. No weapons, but it has two flares presumably to help locate it if it goes down, and a self-destruct charge so that it can't be analyzed."

"Propulsion?" asked Minda.

"Some variant of GWM, but the goose flight characteristics are eighty-seven percent accurate according to Ellis."

"Why a goose?"

"Unknown," said Bo. "But it seems part of Pandera control was unaware of the device. Either there are evolving Pandera factions, which I doubt, or they're tightening their internal security to a need-to-know basis."

"That's troubling," said Minda. "We'll have to look at that more closely." She paused for a moment, and said, "Any theory on why it targeted Ady?"

"She went to Richmond for Bacchus. I believe she intended to meet someone, as she often did, but she keeps her Richmond adventures to herself."

"Sound familiar?" asked Vanessa.

"Her mother's DNA at work," said Bo. "Ellis tells me she spends most of her Richmond time at Krewe." He smiled into the camera and saw Vanessa's face flush a little.

Vanessa glanced at Minda and looked back at the camera. "That place has a lot of family history. Let's hope she's as successful there as we were."

Bo smiled broadly. "Agreed. Anyhow, that's the only connection I can find that would raise Pandera interest. Can we figure out whom she met?" said Bo.

Minda said, "I ran the vid from the bar. She stood there alone for three hours, talked to no one, and left. Exterior vids don't reveal a meeting either."

Ellis chimed in. "Ady was highly emotional when she returned to the vehicle. I also reviewed the bar vids and surrounding street vids for any face recognition or Num scans. The only curious moment is 4.2 seconds before she left the bar." Ellis played that segment on the vid Linc in slow motion. "She turns back to the bar unexpectedly, looks to the left, turns to the right, and leaves."

Minda said, "I think you're right, Ellis. Can you find that hooded individual? He or she appears to almost bump her when she turns."

Ellis said, "Yes, I did. Here is that individual twenty-eight seconds later down the street." A vid played on the Linc. The hooded individual approached a vehicle and the operator door opened. The individual removed his tunic, revealing a Pandera android. He tossed the tunic into a curbside rubbish can and climbed into the vehicle.

Intake

"Life Training," Bo had called it. How to answer Pandera questions. What to expect in Pandera Intake and confinement. Ady had thought the training was a waste of time, particularly when she was fourteen. She was never going to get arrested.

Bo had not relented. "This is preventative training, should you somehow fall into Pandera hands. It's how not to die in their custody." That made her nervous, so she repeated a plethora of Ellis-crafted situations dozens of times. Even Bo did some ad hoc roleplaying with her, but that often ended up with him tickling her until she nearly peed her pants. As she grew older, Bo still insisted she repeat the simulations with Ellis at least once a year.

Now here in confinement, she silently thanked Bo and Ellis. Pandera had run her through decon, given her an oversized gray jumpsuit and some clip-on zaps, and locked her into this tiny cell-pod. She ate the tasteless nutrient bar and drank half the liter of water, then curled up on the sleep mat that took up eighty percent of the floor. A mini grooming station comprised the rest of her drab cell.

She closed her eyes and tried to sleep, but her buzzing brain relentlessly tried to solve the problem of how to get out of here. Bo's advice to wait for the right opportunity had been emphasized in her training. She had to ensure she would be successful in escaping in her first attempt because a failed attempt would make it nearly impossible thereafter. Pandera would shackle her feet to the floor.

Ady rolled over on the sleep mat and stared at the blank wall. She searched for the genesis of her incarceration. She wondered where this thread of her life began and how she might have avoided it.

Somewhere deep in her brain an alarm went off. The air had an odd, almost-electric odor. She momentarily realized her brain was telling her she was being sedated. She started to hold her breath, but, apparently she'd already inhaled too much. The world went blank.

When Ady awoke, her eyes itched, and a spot burned behind her right ear. She tried to sit up but found that she was strapped to a gurney. Her pulse quickened. What had they done to her? She took inventory of herself. Everything seemed normal, except she was naked, cold, and groggy. And the gurney was rolling slowly through a white room. She turned her head and saw that she was on one of perhaps fifty gurneys, each holding a naked person and rolling in formation towards a double door. The smooth walls and floor looked slick, like they had been spray-sanitized a thousand times. The overhead was a glow ceiling she estimated at 6500K daytime illumination.

Being naked wasn't a big deal. But this felt clinical and invasive because Pandera had her strapped to a gurney, helpless. The others around her seemed to be unbothered by the situation. She realized where she was: Intake. She sighed as her gurney bumped through the double doors into what appeared to be a locker room. Her restraints auto-released and she sat up quickly. She rubbed the burning spot behind her right ear and felt the Dermabond. She'd been tagged. She was now a Num, one of the city people with an implant tracker. But she wasn't supposed to have been unconscious. Inserting an implant was usually done robotically with a numbing spray and a quick under-the-skin injection.

She rubbed a hand over her head. She was bald. Looking around at the others, they all still had their hair. And somehow, she felt the loss of her hair and going from NoNum to Num ate away at her dignity. She considered digging the tracker out with her fingernails, but there would be time and a less crude technique later. She smiled as she thought of Bo's tagging history. On his one hundred and twentieth birthday, he told her he had been tagged four times in his life…so far. A little wooden box sat on his desk where he kept the deactivated devices.

A Pandera android pointed at her and said, "This way, please." The other naked people were getting off their gurneys unaided and heading to a bank of lockers. Ady noticed most of them chattering with excitement and rubbing the spot behind their ear, home of their new tracker. This was a routine Intake tagging center where NoNums from outside the city were tagged when they officially moved inside and became city citizens. Ellis had told her the Globazelle cities in the North hemisphere had a long wait list to get in. No one ever moved out of the cities. As the only one with a Pandera escort and bald head, she presumed she was the only prisoner in the group. A lot of eyes glanced at her and her android companion, and then looked away. She felt her sympathy for Nums slip towards bewilderment. These people had *chosen* to give up their rights in exchange for food and shelter. Globazelle now owned them. Their privacy was history. She was baffled at how anyone could make that choice. These people seemed almost celebratory about it.

She stepped off the gurney and followed the android through another white door. It pointed to an illuminated circle in the middle of the floor. She recognized it as a disinfection station, a matter of routine in NoNum life. She stood in the circle, raised both arms over her head, and closed her eyes. The disinfecting spray hit her from all sides and evaporated in a few seconds.

The android again said, "This way, please," and walked towards a door opposite the one through which they had entered.

In the next room, the android pointed to a bench and said, "Sit, please."

A life-sized holographic image appeared in front of her. It looked surreal and she thought it might be some new holo-humanoid. But when it spoke, she was sure it was a male human on a low-res holo-camera. "Adelya Nichieu Ford, twenty-four years of age, embryo crafted February 29, 2342." The holo looked up from his tablet. "Happy Birthday, by the way." He looked back at his table and continued. "Embryo crafted in Coastal NeoHealth Atlanta and delivered to partnered parents Vanessa Claybrook Ford and Minda Yazzi in Hopewell, Virginia. Domiciled at 2150 Branchwood Drive, North Prince George, VA 23860-2250M. Basic education at public school number forty-six-B near Richmond, Virginia. Level 8 intelligence, 191.8 centimeters in height, fifty-eight kilos, skin tone seven. Is this information correct?"

"Yes."

"Your DNA is unusual, but the key markers all align with your birth signature. I can't imagine what would account for these anomalies in an embryo." The holo-human looked at her. "But they match." It shrugged and consulted the tablet again. "Your immunity markers indicate recurrent non-artificial sexual activity. Is your pleasure pad inadequate?"

She stared at the hologram, unflinching. "I am unaware of any restrictions on sexual activity since women are sterile from conception." She could feel her blood pressure start to rise, but she clamped it down so the monitors wouldn't notice. She thanked Bo and Ellis for this skill and chastised herself for her smart-ass answer.

The holographic image cocked its head. "Interesting choice of words, 'conception.'"

Ady started to brush her hair back, a nervous tell she realized too late as she raised her hand. But her hair was gone. Her head was shaved as clean as the rest of her naked body. Act like a moron, she told herself. Don't give anything away to these assholes.

When she didn't reply, the hologram said, "Although you are technically correct, if these organisms should overcome your resistance and you acquire an active disease, you would be automatically sent to the Southern Hemisphere. I caution you to consider the risk." The holograph paused and consulted his tablet again. "All other scans are normal, and you are in good health. Approved for transport."

She ground her teeth but kept her temperature and blood pressure normal. She'd been taught that Pandera was to be avoided as much as possible. When confronted, cooperate and elude. All in all, she had been indifferent to Pandera in the past, but now with this goose business, getting tagged, and the personal invasion into her sex life, she was developing a real dislike for them. Wait, what sex life? She hadn't had sex since before she met Anson last year. And worn-out pleasure pads don't count.

The holo disappeared and the android handed her a black jumpsuit. She recognized it as a slick, which was worn when traveling in a transport tube. It was a single garment with full hood, hand and foot coverings, and a transparent face covering. She'd never worn one but had seen people wearing them as fashion statements at a couple of the exotic clubs she'd tried a few years ago. Through a long slit in the back, she pulled first her legs, then her head and arms. The android handed her a pair of black non-skid zaps. She slipped her feet into them and snapped them closed. The android directed her to a silver transport tube. When she stepped inside, the door snapped shut. There was a short hiss. The floor dropped out of the tube.

Training

The transport tube delivered Ady from Intake to a building she later came to know as "SIM." In the locker room, a bot instructed her to select and change into a jumpsuit provided for students. It was the usual dull gray with the number thirty-six on the front and back. It was the longest one she could find, but it was still too short and uncomfortable. She knew from her simulation training with Ellis that she wouldn't be in it for long.

A chime sounded in the changing room, and the bot instructed the group to enter the SIM main floor. It was a rectangle, sixty meters by twenty meters, and ten meters high. The walls and ceiling were padded. As Ady stepped onto the floor, her foot sank in a few millimeters.

A short, thick man greeted them. He was a head shorter than her, perhaps seventy years old, with a bald head and a skin tone near ten. She was sure he polished his head because of how the lights reflected from it, sometimes nearly blindingly. Why would anyone polish their head? It made no sense. Vanity was the only thing she could think of, but that didn't seem to fit this man's presence. His lower face was covered with a rather long black beard. The juxtaposition of the bald dome atop the black mop struck her as funny. She smiled and wondered what Ellis would say about the man. He certainly wasn't your typical middle-aged guy from the streets of Richmond.

He smiled at the group and said, "I am Mr. Robb, your coach, teacher, instructor, and life saver. I will teach you how not to die on Mars." He looked around the room. "There are seventeen of you here." He clasped his hands behind his back. "Look around at your classmates. Go ahead, take a good look at each and every one of them." He paused while people, apparently mostly strangers, eyed each other in their gray, ill-fitting jumpsuits.

"According to our statistics from the last twenty years, one of you will die on Mars. Maybe two. You have a ten percent chance." He clapped his hand together, startling most of the class and causing them to jump. "Let me see a show of hands. Who wants to be the one to die?" The group was silent. All eyes stared at Mr. Robb in rapt attention.

He said, "Very well. Let's see if you can beat the statistics." He pointed at the wall behind them, and in a casual tone, said, "Would you please line up against that wall?" The group shuffled towards the wall and spread out, facing Mr. Robb. "You seem to want to learn, but some of you don't yet understand the seriousness of space travel or the importance of following instructions there."

His smile disappeared, replaced by what appeared to be anger. "Now!" he growled, a deep baritone rolling off his tongue like a menacing animal about to attack.

Ady suddenly felt afraid. She snagged the fear in her head like she would catch a ball tossed into the air. In her mind, she examined it. At first, she shrugged it off as a reaction to Mr. Robb's growl, but she soon recognized it as something else.

"So!" Mr. Robb roared. "Pay attention! Follow my instructions! Or," he paused, and shifted to his casual, quiet voice, "you could die right here and save SpaceCorp a lot of trouble."

Ady got it. She understood the class now. Sure, it was about the mechanical dos and don'ts of being in space, but it was more about not letting someone else's actions kill you. That was why the short stubble of hair on the back of her neck stood on end. She could take care of herself, but she couldn't prevent others from doing something stupid that would kill her and everyone else along with them.

Mr. Robb looked down the line of seventeen people, making eye contact with each of them. Then he raised his hand and pointed his index finger into the air. He shouted, "Lesson number one: Ladies and gentlemen! Strip! Take your clothes off, all of them, and fold them neatly into a pile which you will place in the pockets attached to the back wall. Jewelry, piercings, adornments, hair fixtures, anything that comes off, take it off! Anyone with eye lenses, keep those on. Ladies and gentlemen, you have two minutes. If you are not naked in two minutes, you flunk this training and will have a Pandera android search your body cavities for contraband. Go!"

As the other sixteen rushed to undress, Ady stifled a laugh at Mr. Robb's act. She thought he was clever in trying to both scare and motivate the trainees to pay attention. He was so much better than the vids she had watched. Where the vids had boring instructors who repeated lines from a script, Mr. Robb was enthusiastic and engaging. And she certainly wasn't going to let one of these classmates kill her.

As for the stripping, she knew it was coming and quickly shed her jumpsuit, Nomex shorts, and zaps. Nudity in the cities was common for the Nums. It wasn't unusual for a half-dressed, or even nude Num to walk down the street or go to a club. In fact, there were numerous clubs that advertised as fully nude. The NoNums weren't nearly as casual about it, but even Richmond had a few clubs where nudity was common. One was just a pedestrian self-serve bar where people talked and drank sans clothes. On the other end of the spectrum, there were a couple of clubs that focused on sensuality with live sex on stage and a group dance floor with a kaleidoscope of lights and throbbing music. She had tried them all as part or her physical sex experiment. The group dance floor was sensory overload, though, because everyone was rubbing, squeezing, and caressing everyone else while swaying to the beat of the music. Too many tongues thrashed, and fingers explored for her taste. She ended up as a regular at Krewe.

"People," said Mr. Robb, "if you have any inhibitions about being seen naked by others, you will have a difficult trip. Grooming and sanitation is public on spacecrafts. We don't have the resources to pander to your personal inhibitions. Get over it. You are going to see your fellow shipmates naked repeatedly." He tapped at a tablet in his hand and said, "I recommend you stand perfectly still now."

Instantly, they became weightless.

Ady remained motionless and slowly drifted a few inches above the floor. Others began to flail, and a couple of them banged into the padded wall. Mr. Robb tapped the tablet again, and the gravity slowly returned, drawing those who had flailed their way far above the floor to a gentle rest. "Did I mention we're going to do weightless training now?"

He pointed at Ady. "Why did you stay motionless while these others bounced all over the place?"

"Newton's third law, sir," she said.

"Ha!" said Mr. Robb, smiling. "For those of you with single digit intelligence levels, that means when you are weightless, you don't have the leverage of your feet connected to the floor. You will injure or kill yourself or others if you start flailing around. Now, go put your clothes back on so you don't have to worry about someone laughing at your winky, and we'll try this again."

Ady could barely stifle her laugh. Winky? What was a winky? She'd have to remember that one. It was anatomically unspecific and gender neutral, yet it conveyed so much. Winky! She loved that term and couldn't wait to share it with Ellis.

They spent the next four hours learning to don and doff their EV suits, operate the controls, and monitor their status. Mr. Rob also instructed them on the communications within the suit, showing them how to control the two comm channels individually. Then he reduced the gravity to one-third, and they did it all again. And finally, they did it a third time while weightless.

As they were hanging up their EV suits, Mr. Robb said, "Okay, ladies and gentlemen, that's it for today. Return to your pods, please. See you tomorrow for Phase Two." He walked aimlessly among the trainees until he was next to Ady. "A word, Miss Ford," he said quietly, and then walked to the back of the room.

She followed, wondering if she had done something wrong or offended him with her Newton's Law comment. Mr. Robb turned and quietly asked her a few mundane questions about her Newton's Law response and her scientific background. He was keeping one eye on the door. When the last person left, he leaned towards her and said, "The questionable bird is unfriendly. Be alert."

He turned and walked through the door in the back of the room.

The message was from Bo. The goose had intended to harm her. Her head buzzed as she made her way out of SIM to the transport tube. As she stepped into the tube to return to her pod, she realized it could dump her anywhere. The automated system scanned her tracking device and sent her to a destination Pandera had selected. She couldn't think of any way to watch your back in a transport tube.

Embarkation

After two more days of space indoctrination and training, Ady was suited in her dual-layer gray EV suit complete with self-contained oxygen, temperature control, and helmet. Two-digit black numbers front and back on the jumpsuit identified her as number seventeen in the line of identically suited passengers. The same droid who'd guided her through Intake—she remembered the serial number on its neck—escorted her in the parade of mismatched pairs to a hangar where the condemned boarded a space hopper. It was essentially a cylinder filled with seats perched atop a rocket. At the door, she counted eleven rows of two seats each with a tiny walkway separating the pairs of dull beige seats. The passengers had to squeeze down the tiny aisle, front to back. She took a seat in the second row and counted twenty total passengers, seventeen from her class in similar outfits, and three who boarded last, in blue and white uniforms she recognized as official SpaceCorp uniforms.

The voice in her helmet instructed her to connect the cable from the bulkhead to her suit connection. Thirty seconds later, auto-restraints deployed, pressing her and her companions back against their seats. A short person in a SpaceCorp uniform to her left had not been in their procession to the hangar. The other two SpaceCorp uniforms had seemed to be waiting for this one to arrive. Once inside, the short one flopped down across from her, and was still fumbling with the cable when the restraints deployed. Ady found it odd for someone from SpaceCorp, who she presumed would be well trained, to be having so much trouble. She continued to watch the fumbling until she realized it was exacerbated by her neighbor's short arms. Pressed against the seat, their arms weren't long enough to reach the bulkhead cable. As she felt the craft powering up for lift off, she reached over and connected the cable for her neighbor. The neighbor gave her a thumbs-up.

Ady leaned into her seat and willed herself to relax, her mind trying to quiet. There was acceleration and g-forces followed by a sense of gliding. A slight bump indicated the hopper had docked. Ady opened her eyes. The voice in her helmet told her to disconnect her cable. The restraints retracted and the door opened. She knew they were in space because the gravitational pull was much less but still there, likely caused by some rotation of the craft to which they were now connected. The two SpaceCorp uniforms in the first row exited immediately. The eighteen others, unfamiliar with low gravity, stumbled, scooted, and flailed their way to the door. They were like a herd of wild animals. The SpaceCorp pair assisted the herd through the hatch into an empty, low-ceilinged room, a vestibule between the hopper and 'gate.

The hatch closed and the voice in her helmet said, "You may release your faceplates until we board the Mars transport ship. Single file, follow me." One of the SpaceCorp uniforms opened another hatch and the herd filed out into a corridor that gradually curved upward in both directions as far as she could see.

After walking a few minutes, the SpaceCorp neighbor whom Ady had assisted, tugged at her sleeve. "Hey. Where are we?" said a female voice.

"Stargate," said Ady, puzzled.

"What's that?"

Ady looked at her closer and said, "It's the orbiting launch platform for space travel to Mars, the moon, Europa, and who knows where else." With their faceplates now open, she could see the freckled face of a woman with fair skin. A putrid odor wafted from her open helmet. Ady asked, "Aren't you SpaceCorp?"

The unsteady companion held on to Ady's sleeve as they walked. She said, "I'm an academy professor, and someone forgot that professors don't have space training." She held up her left arm where her Linc was attached. "They just sent me instructions this morning, plus twenty minutes in the weightless room, where I vomited my breakfast inside my helmet."

Ady kept her face blank, though she wanted to laugh at the "sticky situation" this poor woman had been through. At the same time, she felt sorry for her and wanted to help her get through this. After all, Ady didn't want her to be killed or kill others because she hadn't been trained.

The voice in the helmet said, "Okay, faceplates closed. Once you're sealed up, in you go." The SpaceCorp person leading the procession pointed at an open hatch. The seven people in front of her fumbled with closing their faceplates. She stepped around them and into the hatch.

Seating for thirty-eight was forward-facing. An additional four seats at the compartment rear were enclosed in a black mesh cage with a door. It stood empty. A human voice in her helmet said, "Find a seat, strap in, and connect the cable from your console. We launch in a few minutes. Once we reach glide speed in about twenty minutes, you will be able to take off your helmets. Later, we'll brief you on all the details for our short flight to Mars. It will be only about twenty-two days because Mars is at perihelion, fifty-six million kilometers. Be happy. Our last trip was 134 days and nearly 400 million kilometers."

Ady took an outboard seat in the first row and hooked up. People filed in and found seats. The short SpaceCorp neighbor from the hopper flopped down beside her and began to struggle with connecting the cable again. Ady reached over and connected it, which got her another thumbs-up. She reached over and grabbed the neighbor's helmet pivot and pulled it towards her until their faceplates touched. She said, "My name is Ady. Let me know if I can help you out."

"Holy Shit!" screamed the neighbor. "I can hear you! How is that possible?"

Ady laughed. "Faceplates touching. Sound carries through them." She could see fear in her neighbor's eyes. "You okay?"

"I have no idea. That damn diaper they gave me is already full and I'm roasting in this damn suit!" She paused and looked at Ady. "I'm Keera."

Ady leaned back and pulled Keera's left arm up so Keera could see her suit control panel. Then, one tap at a time, she showed her how to adjust her suit temperature. It was set at thirty-three degrees. No wonder Keera was hot. She lowered it to twenty-two degrees and got another thumbs-up. She touched her faceplate against Ady's and said, "Thanks for not letting me suffocate."

Ady smiled as she leaned away and began buckling herself in. She closed her eyes and settled in for the launch.

Keera

After glide speed was reached, they removed their helmets and were allowed to move about the cabin. The rotational motion of the ship gave them ten percent of Earth's gravity. With careful, slow motions, you didn't rocket into the bulkhead or into someone else. Ady easily adjusted, but others were all over the place. She adopted a defensive approach, trying to keep her back to a wall so she could push away errant companions.

The two SpaceCorp guys from the hopper were their crew. The ship was apparently piloted autonomously. Soon, they were gathered and taken on a short tour of the ship. Each passenger claimed a bunk and locker. Each received a personalized supply package with their name on the wrapping. Although nearly identical, the jumpsuits in each were sized for the recipient and had both their name and a number on the nameplate. Their meager personal items from SIM were included. Ady's package included her black slick for tube travel, which she found amusing since there were no tubes on Mars, and she didn't think she'd find a Martian club where it would be fashionable, either.

She claimed a bunk in the corner and began unpacking her supplies into the locker. She didn't even look up when Keera claimed the locker next to her. "What did you do?" she asked.

Keera stopped and looked at her. "What do you mean?"

"Why are you here?"

"Oh. I applied for a Globazelle grant to further my education during my sabbatical. Having a certificate in Mars history will boost my career."

Ady stopped her unpacking and turned towards Keera. "You *chose* to go to Mars? It's not some kind of SpaceCorp professorial punishment?"

"What?"

"Pandera didn't send you to Mars?"

"Heavens, no! I spent two years working through the application process to get to go on this trip. This is a huge step for my career."

"This is a field trip for you. And a vacation from pedagogical duties. Your first?"

"No, I've done four Northern Hemisphere field studies. They were a month each. Vehicular transportation infrastructure, recreational park systems, commercial transport evolution, and metal mining. I also did a three-month investigation into the Global Tripartite recovery." Keera leaned towards her and whispered, "Does that mean *you're* a criminal?"

Ady nodded.

Keera looked around as if to see if anyone was listening. Again, whispering, she said, "What did you do?"

"I hit a goose in my ground vehicle."

Keera's eyes lit up and she bent over laughing. After a moment, she stammered, "That's, that's good. You're funny! I like you." She glanced at Ady. "It's okay if you don't want to tell me. Just don't murder me. I love my life."

"No, that's really what I did. I hit a goose. I'm not joking."

Keera looked at her for a long moment. "That must have been some special goose!"

Ady nodded. She only wished she knew how special. And how they got that vid of her picking up the goose. And why they had targeted her in the first place.

Wai-Wan

Just after midnight, the moon set, and wispy fog crept silently up the James River from the Chesapeake. Bo climbed into an old wooden rowboat and settled into a steady pace rowing towards the largest of the islands that separated Tar Bay from the river channel. It had been years since he had rowed out here, but his creaky old muscles remember the rhythm, though his pace was somewhat slower. It was eerily silent in the fog, and he relied solely on the Nav-Linc strapped to his thigh. After fifteen minutes, the boat ground to a stop on the downstream spit of gravely island sand. He tapped a Linc button to switch on the night vision mode of his eye lenses. Once they adjusted, he climbed out and tied off the boat to a scraggly bush. A soft voice said, "You're going to get your feet wet."

To which Bo replied, "Better than a swim. Have time for tea?"

"On your ten o'clock."

Bo turned to his ten o'clock and saw the shadowy bow of a large boat grounded into the shore. A ladder silently unrolled down the side and Bo climbed up. As he reached the top, a small but rough hand from a dark figure grasped his and squeezed. "Welcome. Follow me." He was led along the deck and through a door. "Some stairs here." Bo made it down the six steps, and the door closed behind him. "Light coming up." Bo turned off his night vision. Dim lights slowly came up to reveal a round wooden table with six wooden chairs. The remainder of the small room was empty.

"Functional," said Bo. He turned and hugged the small woman with a long braid down her back. "Nice to see you, Wai-Wan."

"Likewise, but I'm sorry for the circumstances," she said, as she gestured towards a chair. "Sit. Would you like tea? I have Thai Moonlight White." She moved to the side and opened a panel revealing a compact kitchenette.

Bo smiled. "Is it the orange stuff?"

"Did I say swill?"

Bo laughed. "No. I'll have tea, please."

Wai-Wan brought two steaming mugs to the table and sat. Bo sipped his carefully, knowing it would be hot. "Hmmm. Nice. Thank you."

"Oh, shut up. You wouldn't know good tea from river water." They both laughed and clinked their mugs.

"Where is home these days?" asked Bo.

"Andros Island, mostly. I like the warm weather and bigger fish."

Bo raised an eyebrow. "Bigger fish? When was the last time this boat caught a real fish?"

The question hung in the air. Wai-Wan's expression remained unchanged. After a few moments of silence, she said, "Have you heard from our granddaughter?"

Bo shook his head. "Not directly. I received information that she is en route to Mars, so they must have overlooked her DNA."

Wai-Wan nodded. "Do you think she's frightened?"

"Ha!" said Bo. "She'll probably be piloting the spacecraft by the time they get there. Every day, I'm amazed at her ever-expanding intellect. I've often wondered if Minda added some bio-AI and never told us." He looked down and shook his head slowly. "But her emotional maturity isn't as well-developed." He looked at Wai-Wan. "I've tried to facilitate more interpersonal experiences for her, but she'd rather tinker with gravity wave modulators. And Ellis is no help, as she has the same void."

"Perhaps," said Wai-Wan, "your bio-AI hypothesis is not far off."

"Maybe," said Bo. "But I'm reluctant to raise it with Vanessa or Minda. Though she's their child, they have millions of others to care for."

"A conundrum, but human emotions are imperfect, as we well know." She looked at Bo for a moment and then sipped her tea.

Bo frowned. "I miss all of you. Every day. Even though I'm still certain you all made the right choices, it has left me a void. But I've had a long and fulfilling life." He glanced at Wai-Wan. "Part of it with a loving partner. Part of it trying to domesticate a lion."

Wai-Wan patted his hand. "Animal training never suited you. But introspection is best done on sunny days with rum."

Bo sighed. "Our friends are making surveillance drones."

Wai-Wan said nothing.

Bo continued. "I took one apart. Laser guided. Self-destruct and locater flares. Video and audio. Perhaps GWM propulsion. Some stuff I didn't recognize, maybe weapons."

"How did you get it?"

"It was the genesis of Ady's Mars trip. It was disguised as a goose that crashed into her ground vehicle on her way back from Richmond. She scooped it up and brought it back to the house, intending to dispose of the evidence she had hit. Pandera came to the house, adjudicated, and sent her off to Mars. They had overhead vid of her picking it up."

"Vid from their air vehicle?"

"No, the goose was launched from a Pandera air vehicle seven clicks away. The vid was taken from practically overhead. Either another vehicle we didn't discover, or a satellite."

"Satellite? You think Pandera has satellites of their own?"

Bo shook his head. "No. It could be a link from one of SpaceCorp's. But Ellis estimated that it originated from a much lower altitude, like an air vehicle."

Wai-Wan nodded and asked, "You kept the drone. Why didn't they take it?"

"I hid it. Given what I know about it now, I think they were either trying to trigger locator flares or the self-destruct while they were at our domicile. When that didn't work, they must have decided it was lost and giving up the search would draw less attention. Attention that might later validate its existence."

"Still, it seems odd they would leave without it."

Bo smilcd. "Perhaps they were reluctant to tangle with me again."

Wai-Wan looked at Bo. "Senility and foolishness are siblings." She rubbed her crooked upper lip, staring at the floor. "Puzzling why they would allow you to keep it." She looked at Bo. "Perhaps that is what they intended all along."

"You think the whole goose episode was intended to get me to dissect it?" Bo frowned. "Not sure I buy that. Ellis's eavesdropping revealed some confusion in Pandera Control. Apparently, the existence of the device was not previously shared with all their cells."

"Why did it crash?"

Bo shrugged. "No idea. But Ady's autodrive tracked the trajectory. It definitely targeted the vehicle."

"For what purpose?"

"That is the question for you, Wai-Wan." Bo cocked his head. "That's why I asked to meet with you."

Wai-Wan examined her tea closely. She nodded. "Yes, I see. As always, we are a sandwich cookie, you and I."

Bo frowned. Wai-Wan pointed at him "You are the steadfast cookie while I am the malleable filling. Sometimes more, sometimes less. Various flavors. Thick and thin."

"Please explicate."

Wai-Wan sighed and stood up. She began to pace slowly, her braid swaying with each step. "When I took my first mission eighteen years ago, I was a gosling. Now I am part of a skein, unable to see the way or know the next turn. Still, I have responsibilities to my brothers and sisters.

You…" She gestured towards Bo. "You sit on the ground and watch the sky. But our daughter sits high in the sky and watches the ground. Perhaps you can share in her vision. In my role today, she cannot share her vision with me."

Bo stood and moved to a wall where he leaned back with his arms crossed over his chest. "Your obfuscation always fascinated me, but it often baffles me." He shook his head. "This is an operational question. Ady unknowingly became a target. I only ask why in order to protect her. I think you know or could find out...from your brothers and sisters."

"I do not know the answer to your question." Wai-Wan moved towards the door.

"Wai-Wan, your word choice of gosling and your skein metaphor tells me you already knew the drone was disguised as a goose before I told you."

When she glanced at Bo, he saw a twinkle in her eye before she turned and started up the steps.

Bitte

Ten days out from Mars, Ady and Keera were playing 3-D checkers.
They'd tried 3-D chess, but Keera couldn't seem to get the hang of the
game. As Ady waited for Keera to move, she squeezed the last glob of
"snack food" from the tube into her mouth.

Keera glanced at her. "The food hasn't been bad, huh?"

"Comestible is about the highest grade I can muster." Ady licked the end
of the tube, screwed the top back on, and stuffed the empty into a pocket of
her jumpsuit. "It's not the taste or variety, but I get tired of eating nothing
but paste from tubes." Still waiting for Keera to move, she asked, "Did you
do *any* prep work for your time on Mars?"

"You mean like low gravity exercises?"

"Yeah, low gravity, no air, longer days, mostly underground. Stuff like
that."

Keera's hand rested on a game piece, but she paused before moving it.
"Not that, but I did take a brief language course so I'd understand the
unique words they use."

Ady watched Keera move her game piece. Then she jumped five of
Keera's pieces, ending the game.

"Damn! Am I stupid or are you a genius?" cried Keera.

Snippets of childhood game-playing with school chums churned up in
Ady. She was always way ahead of her opponents and could easily win.
That made it easier to exactly hit the ninety-one percent target ingrained
into her. No one ever knew when she orchestrated her losses or purposely
provided wrong answers. On the outside, she was a model Level 8
intelligence. "Sorry. I played this with my grandfather a lot. Must have
learned some of his tricks," she lied. "Let's quit, anyhow. I want to hear
about your language class and the unique words."

Keera seemed happy to stop playing and dropped her pieces into the
game bag. "You know the first language on Mars wasn't Bitte, right? It was
something called English."

"Really?"

"Yeah, when the Mars colonies were first established around 2050,
Earth had about sixty-five hundred spoken languages. Something over two
billion of the twelve billion population spoke Mandarin Chinese. On the
other end, fewer than a thousand people each spoke about two thousand

different languages. Many tried to make English the "universal" language. It had about 175,000 words and was spoken in a lot of places. But as a first language, it was mostly just North America. Australia, New Zealand, and Britain had dialects of English. The problem with all the languages was they were hard for artificial intelligence to understand. So, some guys in Germany invented a new language, Bitte. It was designed to make sure AI could easily understand it and that it encompassed all the human language meanings with absolute precision with a single use or meaning for each word. Bitte has about 250,000 words. It's what we're speaking now and have been speaking for all our lives."

Ady shifted on her stool. "It never occurred to me that there could be other languages."

"Of course. Language history has been erased from curricula. In fact, use of another language is an infraction under Pandera law. But Pandera law doesn't extend to Mars. Since English was the original language there, I mean here, or, well when we get there it will be here. Anyhow, we'll hear some English words which will be foreign to us."

"How do I learn these words before we get there?" asked Ady.

Keera got a faraway look on her face for a few moments before she answered. "I'm not sure. We only have the ship's library and we're so far away from Earth that we'll probably be on Mars before the courses could be transmitted to us."

"How about you teach me?" asked Ady. "What else do we have to do for the second half of this luxury cruise to paradise?"

"You want me to help you?"

She nodded.

Keera's face turned red and her eyes welled up. She wiped her nose with her hand. After a few moments, she looked up. "No one like you has ever asked me for *anything*."

"What do you mean, 'like me?'"

"You know, the fearless smart leader who has all the answers. I'm just a follower, Ady. I fill in the background, but never contribute anything important. It was always that way in Social at Education, but I didn't know it was going to be that way in life, too. I'm always the lesser in every relationship. I'm a plodder, just pulling along my cartful of historical information that no one else cares about."

Ady felt awkward. She took Keera's hands in hers. "Keera, we're new friends, but I don't think of you as lesser. I think of you as bursting with knowledge, warmth, and maybe most of all, friendship. I've always been a loner, with almost no friends. And here we are, a zillion clicks from Earth, and you chose me to be your friend. You're warm and bubbly. I'm a cold bitch. Or at least I've been trained to be. But I'd like to have just one real friend, someone whom I could let see the real me. I'm so tired of pretending to be something other than what I am." She squeezed Keera's hand. "Will you teach me those Martian words?"

Keera nodded and brought one of Ady's hands to her mouth for a kiss. "Thank you." They stood and hugged for moment.

Ady finally said, "When do we start?"

"I think you know more than you realize."

She frowned. "What do you mean?"

"'Bitch' isn't in the Bitte language. It's old English."

History Lesson

Ady and Keera selected size-appropriate chairs in the meeting room and dragged them to the corner. Ady smiled as she thought about what Keera had said, and reflected on a lesson from Ellis about human intellect. Ellis had explained that intelligence levels were determined by a myriad of tests and observations. Although puzzling to Ellis as well, there were many people who had high intelligence, but nil spatial or mathematical capabilities. At the time, neither of them understood how you could have high intelligence and yet not be able to calculate the volume of a sphere in your head. Here was a perfect example: Keera. She struggled with 3-D checkers, a child's game to Ady. Yet, her vast store of historical knowledge and her ability to explain relationships and causative outcomes from historical events baffled Ady. Keera had such a different perspective than she did.

Each chair had a foldout table for mealtime and a Linc docking pad. Keera folded out her table and laid her mini tablet on it. She clicked the tablet screen as she said, "I was thinking I should first do a quick overview of Global Tripartite aftermath so you can see how the language thing collapsed so quickly." She looked at Ady.

"Okay."

"First of all, bacteria from a lab experiment in Chelyabinsk, Russia, was unknowingly carried to a genetics lab in California in 2138. An accident there created a hybrid calcium-eating bacterium. It spread worldwide in less than six months. It ate the bones of a lot of people, but specifically women who were of ovulating age, and anyone, male, female, or other, who had tar residue in their lungs from smoking. And it ate all the bioconcrete. There are volumes of technical explanations of how this bacterium worked, which I'm sure you'd understand…" Keera stopped and looked at Ady. "Wait, have you already read all that?"

Ady nodded. "Fed on calcium, accelerated by any ethane, which is why the sewers were destroyed so quickly."

Keera looked at her blankly.

Ady smiled. "Sewers were filled with methane, a common gas in sewage. In humans, it ate the calcium from the bones in less than twenty-four hours. Death occurred because the rib cage collapsed, and the host could no longer breath. It was also accelerated by tar residuals in the human lungs and by high levels of estrogen, which is why all the fertile women died."

Keera said, "I never understood why their drugs, their antibiotics of the day, didn't work on the Chelyabinsk bacteria."

"Antibiotics were ineffective because this one was a lab designer bacterium unlike any natural bacteria organism. The human body had no immunity or way to fight it naturally, just like the antibiotics weren't remotely effective. The 'vaccine' they developed involved a whole different technical approach using exosomes to provide resistance to Chelyabinsk bacteria."

"And," said Keera, "nine years after the initial lab investigator died from the bacteria, the planet was in shambles. Half the twelve billion population died directly from the bacteria. Another three billion died from infrastructure failures, such as water, sewage, food, and shelter. Any young girls who were unaffected had surgery to remove their uterus and ovaries so the bacteria wouldn't kill them. By 2148 the human race was sterile. No women left could have babies.

"Government essentially dissolved because everyone was focused on their own survival. Military personnel around the world laid down their arms and went home, abandoning their equipment, assignments, and roles. The world was in chaos. All the animals we once raised for food were turned loose or left to die because no one cared for them. Human bodies were stacked in enormous piles in the cities, rotting away and causing secondary diseases. Vigilante clans formed and people fought over food and water. Everything shut down. Medications ceased to exist and those dependent on them died. All the factories closed, or more accurately, were abandoned.

"The largest company in the world, Globazelle, stepped in with a plan to reorganize the North—Global Tripartite. They took control of all major cities in the North—at last count, 548—and began locking them down. They gave people time to go in or out, but after about ten years, they had constructed walls, and closed the access points for most of them. Those inside became the beneficiaries of rigid socialism. Globazelle provided food, healthcare, housing, education, and meaningful work at the city factories for the citizens. Those outside the cities became part of the grower community in a regulated capitalistic society. They grew and produced the food products consumed by the cities. Anyone in either area needing any sort of special physical accommodations was shipped off to the Southern Hemisphere."

Ady frowned, wondering why this detailed information wasn't in the history material she'd discovered in the archives she'd hacked.

"Feeding, handling, or eating any animal with legs was outlawed. Turned out to be a stroke of genius that saved what was left of Earth's scarce resources because more than ninety percent of the grain crops at the time were going to feed animals that were eventually eaten. Extremely inefficient." Keera took a breath and waved her hand in the air. "Plus, that change resulted in a dramatic drop in environmentally destructive gasses." She shrugged. "That's how we ended up with a diet of plants and fish." She smiled at Ady. "Okay so far?"

Ady nodded. "Fascinating. Go on."

"SpaceBus took over all off-planet operations. It cleaned up the satellites and debris orbiting Earth. For nearly forty years, the moon and Mars colonies were on their own. Fortunately, they were self-sustaining food-wise by then.

Within ten years, NeoHealth was formed from multiple related companies and was charged with producing genetically engineered human babies. By the time a vaccine to combat the bacteria was available, in 2170, NeoHealth had thirty-one baby factories in the North, and no one uttered a peep about going back to natural childbirth."

"Why would they?" said Ady. "Sounds excruciatingly painful and gross."

"Right. We already had AI law enforcement in most areas around the world. Pandera was re-branded to be *the* law enforcement arm in the North. As part of that arrangement, Bitte was designated as the only spoken or written language going forward. More than eighty percent of the remaining population already spoke and read Bitte because it was mandatory in Education. All other languages were prohibited and were no longer taught in Education. Forty years later, speaking another language became a crime under Pandera enforcement."

"What about Mars?"

"The Mars and moon colonies were off the radar and ignored all this. They mostly continued using both English and Bitte."

"Wait. Off of what radar?"

"Ah. An English idiom. Means avoiding detection or attention. SpaceBus was already the dominant company on Mars and the moon and took over all the government roles and responsibilities there. No one on Earth objected because people there were focused on trying to survive and eventually make more babies."

"Pandera doesn't have jurisdiction on Mars or the other colonies?"

"Nope. That's part of SpaceBus, rebranded as 'SpaceCorp.'"

"Then why does Pandera send people to Mars as punishment?"

"Tricky question. It's hard to get people to volunteer for Mars or other colonies. It can be a big chunk of your life, and they are, I am told, tough places with none of Earth's accommodations, but at least have no weapons. SpaceBus struck a deal with BDD, the agriculture/food part of the new arrangement. BDD manages all the farmland outside the cities and oversees the capitalistic balance there. They produce food in exchange for manufactured goods from the cities, and deal with the welfare of the grower citizens. Symbiosis." Keera grinned. "The space colonies don't produce much of value, so they traded offloading of offenders in exchange for BDD food products. Earth-wise, there are no prisons or jails. Just temporary holding facilities until the offenders can be shipped to a colony, usually one of the twenty-seven on the moon."

"What about the Southern Hemisphere? I thought offenders were sent there, too."

"The Southern Hemisphere is where the disabled of any kind are sent. Lose an arm in an accident, off you go. Afflicted by a permanent illness, off you go. Mental problems, addiction issues, homeless, off you go. Of course, there are zero birth defects now, no disease to speak of, and few hazards. Lawbreakers are mostly sent to one of the colonies now, but before the BDD agreement with SpaceCorp, they were also sent to the South. There's almost no information about the Southern Hemisphere or how it operates. No one ever seems to hear from it or about it. Once you enter the South, you're never heard from again. Pandera patrols the border rigorously and always makes a big news splash out of catching southerners trying to get back into the North."

"What happened to the people who lived in the South before the pandemic?" she asked.

Keera shrugged. "Its population was about twelve percent of the world, a little over a billion. But their history has been scrubbed and likely altered." Keera grimaced. "I expect most of them died. One estimate was that less than five percent survived. But there's nothing factual. No one ever returns from the South, and Pandera rigorously edits newsfeeds to ensure the North has no idea what goes on there."

Ady frowned. "People just accepted this Global Tripartite plan. No resistance?"

Keera leaned closer to her and whispered, "Another secret scrubbed from history." She leaned back and said, "At the time of the pandemic, one of the major political groups vying for dominance in government was called 'The Bernies.' Their platform was based on socialistic demands of government, but also absolute privacy. In short, they wanted the government to take care of the needs of the citizens, but without tracking any of their activities."

"Huh," Ady said. Something to think about later.

"The other group was less well defined, but represented a capitalistic ideology that strived for free markets worldwide. After the pandemic, when Globazelle took over, they separated the two groups. They put the Bernies in the cities and the free-market masses in the agricultural regions—two legs of the Tripartite. City management, essentially Globazelle, cared for the city dwellers, whom we now call Nums. They were tagged, tracked, and trained to work in assigned jobs." Keera leaned closer again. "Their whole privacy agenda disappeared."

"Why?"

Keera shrugged. "Some of the more vocal Bernies with access to the fledgling newsfeeds tried to complain, but their stories just disappeared."

"There might still be resistance, but it's censored or hidden somehow?"

Keera's smile slid from her face. "I'm unpopular at the academy, Ady, because I voiced a theory that, in fact, resistance is ongoing. I suggested that all humans, but Nums specifically, are controlled, cordoned, and repressed by the combination of Pandera, the key companies, and the Coordinating Council, just like they were after the pandemic. The docile human race isn't fighting back. Someday that could change."

Ady mulled that over. As far as she knew, most people were reasonably satisfied with their lives. Weren't they? The folks at Intake who were becoming Nums seemed eager and happy with their choice. The people she'd met at Krewe didn't seem to feel oppressed. But how can you measure oppression? If you were buried in it, you likely couldn't see it. She'd been taught that Pandera and the Coordinating Council were benevolent. Was that true or was that what they wanted her to believe? Her recent experience with Pandera said otherwise. She would have to investigate this more thoroughly. And if this was true, what other dogma had she been fed and accepted unknowingly? Ambiguity was not in her nature.

By now, three other shipmates had pulled up chairs nearby. A red-haired woman with freckles known as Lars chimed in. "Sorry to be eavesdropping, but you know they used Global Tripartite to eliminate race in humans, too."

Keera nodded.

Ady asked, "What do you mean?"

Lars glanced around and lowered her voice. "Many of the old languages were correlated with a specific race. Like an ethnoreligious group called Jews who spoke the Hebrew language. But religion practically disappeared from the starving masses, and NeoHealth bred out distinguishing racial cues at the direction of Pandera. When they outlawed other languages, no one cared as long as their bellies were full."

"What do you mean by racial cues?"

"Mostly physical features. For example, most skin tones nine and ten were known as 'black' or 'African' races. They commonly had curly dark hair. NeoHealth separated the hair curl DNA, which determined the follicle shape, and made it a separate programming option unassociated with skin tone."

Keera chimed in. "There's a whole historical sub-specialty about how racial cues were bred out of the population to get to where we are today. Skin tone is just a selection now. No race or identity is associated, so we just see it as variety. Same with hair color, eye shape and color, etc. This process helped erase prejudice in the human population because everyone was the same: starving and trying to survive. Those prejudices haven't returned. And they're careful to stamp out any basis for class prejudice."

"But isn't Global Tripartite a class system?" Ady said. "Nums, No-Nums, and the South."

The group nodded agreement.

Lars said, "It's more of a caste system. Nums used to be the white-collar workers, No-Nums were the blue-collar workers, and the South is where they dump everyone who is broken and can't contribute."

Ady stared at her for a long moment. Global Tripartite as a caste system was a different view from how she had been taught to see it. But Lars might be right. Maybe that was why the Intake folks were happy—they were moving up in the caste system. But that perspective shift was too big to just accept without some investigation.

"I want to change the subject for a minute," Ady said. "We learned in Ed that disease was a significant challenge in human history, particularly after the pandemic, but now we're pretty much disease free. Both Globazelle and Pandera claim responsibility, but no one seems to know how we eliminated disease. I asked one of the Ed bots and our homebot, but neither could answer me."

Keera nodded. "It's a closely kept secret, but I don't know why. NeoHealth's genetic program had something to do with it. But the only historical information I ever found on the subject was that a predecessor to

NeoHealth had worked with crustaceans to create a powerful elixir from their blood."

Lars smiled. "Eat more lobster!"

Ady clapped Lars' shoulder and they all chuckled.

A squat little guy about Keera's size looked at her and said quietly, "Do you know how the ban on the use of metals came about?"

Keera said, "I only know the 'public record' version of that story. It says that Globazelle recognized our waste of Earth's natural resources and decided to stop the mining of oil and metals. Solar electric took care of most of the power needs, and silicon hybrids and resins replaced metal for most uses. Metals are still used in electronics, of course, but those are manufactured exclusively by Pandera who controls all mining."

Ady shifted in her seat. "You implied there's another story?"

Keera looked at the little guy known as Joe.

He said, "Why you lookin' at me?"

Lars poked Joe's leg with her foot. "Come on, Joe, I know why you're here. Tell 'em."

He looked around like there were eavesdroppers everywhere, and then leaned into the group like he was going to tell a secret. Quietly, he said, "I used to work at a gold mine in Nevada. For Pandera. Gold is a big component of electronics. Everything is run by computers and AI. I was a security guy, kind of a token human, but still I caught some hacking attempts that the AI brains missed, so they felt I was valuable. Paid well, too. One day, two SpaceCorp guys came to the mine for a meeting with Pandera. I was curious about why they would come all the way from Florida to Nevada in person. So, I looked up the meeting records, you know, to see what they were meeting about. Turns out, Pandera wants to control the metal so no one else can create any kind of computer, AI, or electronic. They put their own monitoring or listening component in everything they make." He looked around. "No big surprise to the world, but SpaceCorp had already figured that out. Problem was, the Pandera monitoring interfered with SpaceCorp ship communications. The SpaceCorp guys wanted it removed. If Pandera wouldn't agree to do so, they threatened to have the laws changed so they could mine their own metal and make their own electronics. Pandera said they'd consider it. The two guys from SpaceCorp left. Their transport crashed on the way back to Florida and they died. Then, Pandera decided to wipe out the meeting recording at the exact time I was listening to it. They caught me and charged me with espionage." He threw his hands up and hissed, "Mars for life."

Touchdown

After twenty-two long days in space, the ship docked with the launch platform that orbited Mars, and they were soon transported to the surface by hopper. From there, they were shuttled to habitat 03G. It was mid-day on a Martian Sunday when routine work was idle. Inside, Ady and six others from the ship were greeted by a thin woman half-a-head taller than Ady with bleached, buzz-cut hair and a medium skin tone. Her SpaceCorp jumpsuit had a silver medallion affixed to the collar. Her shiny black boots reflected the dim overhead lights. She introduced herself as Chelsea and shook hands with each newcomer. A group of curious residents stood around the area gawking at the newcomers.

"Here's the deal," Chelsea said to the group. "You live here for now. Later, you can apply to live elsewhere once you get your Mars wits about you. I'm the lead in this habitat. You have a problem here, you come to me. Bunks are two to a pod. Take any open bunk or pod, stow your stuff in the locker, and be back here in ten minutes." She looked over the seven of them and clapped her hands. "Go. Now."

Ady nodded at Keera. "You pick." Keera smiled and led the way to the other side of the dome where bunk beds and dual lockers were separated by thin panels just slightly thicker than their jumpsuit material. Keera poked her head into a couple of pods until she came to the one at end. She turned to Ady. "Look good?"

"Yup."

They poured the contents of their tote bags into the lockers and headed back to the common area. The briefing lasted thirty minutes. Including the seven newcomers, there were now twenty-one residents in the twenty-four-capacity habitat. A droid prepared the food and served it every six hours around the clock, seven days a week. Work hours varied by role and task, with residents coming and going at all hours. One toilet, one shower, no privacy---all shared. Showers were controlled by the tracker chip embedded behind their ears. One shower of six liters every other day. All water was recycled. Once per quarter the tundra ice near the pole was melted down to replenish losses. Work assignments would be made at 1600 hours in the common area. They had an hour to kill.

The redhead named Lars approached Ady and Keera. "You guys bunking together?" They nodded. "I got a single. Kind of nervous being on my own."

Ady asked, "You a Num?"

"Yeah."

"What city?" asked Keera.

"Denver. You?"

Keera's face lit up. "Me, too! I jet-tube to the Academy three days a week, though."

Lars smiled and nodded.

Keera asked, "What got you here?"

"Pandera." Lars looked at Ady.

Ady nodded. "Yeah, me too. But I'm not a Num. Live South of Washington near Richmond."

All three women sensed the uncomfortable questions that hadn't been answered.

Ady's short laugh broke the silence. "I hit a goose in my ground vehicle. Two years on Mars."

Lars stared at her. "Are you kidding?"

Ady shook her head slowly.

Lars looked at her feet for moment, and without looking up, said, "I got twenty years for destroying a Pandera android…and for raising my own food."

Keera nearly squeaked, "You destroyed a Pandera android? How? And why?"

Lars raised her head and looked from one to the other, as if assessing them. Then she nodded and looked at the floor again. "Okay. My brother isn't a Num. He lives by a river near an area they call Kentucky. He's a grower and works in the food fields most of the time. I've been to visit him a few times."

"Wait," said Ady holding up a hand. "How do you get out of the city?"

Lars grinned. "Don't believe everything Pandera tells you. The cities, at least mine, has a huge black market to elude Pandera and Globazelle restrictions."

Ady looked at the floor and shook her head. Apparently, the Nums weren't as happy as the publicity portrayal.

"Anyhow, after the first time I visited my brother, he offered me some seeds and a little bag of dirt to grow them in. I thought it might be fun and a nice change of pace to the Num rations." She looked up. "The Num stuff beats the paste tubes on the ship, but after a while, it gets boring. That's kinda why I go visit my brother—he snags some of what he grows, and we give new meaning to the term gluttonous." She shrugged. "I thought I'd try growing some myself."

Keera said, "Privately growing even flowers in the cities is against the law, but everyone does it and it's usually ignored. How did you get caught?"

"I had a good-sized pot on the roof with seven plants growing in it. One had these little red, juicy veggies. You can just pluck them and pop them into your mouth. I've never tasted anything so amazing."

"Tomatoes," said Keera. "If they're two to three centimeters, they're the 'cherry' variety which is not cultivated in the Northern Hemisphere anymore."

"Yeah, that's what my brother called them. 'Cherry tomatoes.' Anyhow, I go up there one day to water them and here's this Pandera air vehicle right next to my plants. I walked right up to the pot and started pouring the water in. Then this android bot gets out of the vehicle, comes over and says, 'Are these your botanical specimens?' I said, 'Yeah. So what?' And it says, 'They are illegal and must be destroyed.' It sprayed something out of its hand onto my plants and they immediately turned brown and crumbled into powder." Lars looked up. "I was so mad I grabbed the android by the neck and heaved it over the side of the building, forty-four stories down to the storage bay."

Ady gasped. "You tossed a Pandera android forty stories?"

Lars nodded.

Ady said, "I thought those things were too heavy to lift. They're supposed to be like 150 kilos."

"Me, too. But it couldn't have been more than thirty."

Keera chimed in. "What happened after that?"

"The air vehicle just hovered there. I look over the side and see the android smashed on the roof." Lars shrugged. "I went back to my pod and started some entertainment vid. Pretty soon my pod door opens—no announcement or anything—and in walks a pair of Pandera droids. You know how they're always silver? These were black. I jumped up from my chair, and one of them shot me with a restraining web. The other one said I was charged with destroying a Pandera android and illegally cultivating botanical specimens. Twenty years."

"That's the craziest story I've ever heard," said Keera.

Ady nodded in agreement.

"You know what else? I was in processing for a couple of weeks, so I tried to contact my brother to tell him what had happened. I could never reach him. Then, the day before we embarked, I got a message from one of his coworkers saying he had disappeared. I was scared for him because now I'm thinking Pandera traced my plants to him and he's in trouble, too."

"You don't know what happened to your brother and he doesn't know what happened to you?" asked Ady.

"No. And here's the weirdest thing of all. A couple hours after I got that message, it disappeared from my Linc. Poof. Just gone like it never existed."

Initiation

After the 0600 meal, which was mostly beige cubes of varying texture but surprisingly decent flavor, new arrivals were given work assignments by Chelsea. Ady and Lars were assigned together and told to report to hab 09C. It was only three habs away, so they suited up and walked the hundred meters. Once inside 09C, they learned it was referred to as the "assembly hall." Inside, multiple crews suited up in ruggedized workstyle EV suits for various tasks. The helmets had reflective faceplates and dual headlights for work in the unlit sections of the tunnels. Ady and Lars were assigned to mining crew M5 with fourteen others. They were each assigned gear lockers and work EV suits.

From the end of a bench near the hatch, someone shouted, "M5 over here." Other shouts called for crews to assemble in other areas of the room. Ady and Lars joined their team. A bearded man said, "We have two new in the crew today." He pointed at Ady and Lars. "They're briefed and trained on EV use but know nothing about the mining equipment. Gunnar, you train Lars."

Lars waved her hand to identify herself.

"Sandeep, you train Ady."

Ady waved.

"Welcome to the team, ladies. I'm Bomba, team lead for M5. These suits are similar to the regular EV's. Use the B comm channel for training. We ride a transport about twenty minutes to the dig site where we mine ilmenite. In case you don't know, that's a titanium ore that is refined here on Mars. Keep track of your suit's readouts and let your trainer or me know if you have any problems. Check your suit in here every day before we leave. We can patch a suit hole in the field, but your EV pack is all you've got to keep you alive until you get back here. Treat it nice and pay attention to it. Questions?"

Ady found her EV suit and slithered into it. She locked on the boots and gloves, and then locked on her helmet. She powered up the suit from the arm control panel and checked her readings. Everything looked fine. She had 100 percent O2. A female voice in her helmet said, "Diagnostics complete. All systems nominal. Nine hours and fifty-eight minutes of oxygen." A counter displayed the remaining O2 time inside her helmet.

Once in the EV suits, the crew looked like a group of identical helmeted bugs. One of them approached Ady and turned her left arm so they both could see her arm control. The newcomer held up two fingers and pushed the second from the left red button. A male voice in the left side of her helmet said, "Can you hear me okay?"

She tried to nod, but head movements weren't apparent in these suits. She said, "Yes. Can you hear me?"

"Perfect. Voice activated, but you can trigger the mic by clicking your fingers together like this." He held up his left hand and clicked his thumb and middle finger a couple of times. She heard a faint click each time. "Try it."

She tried it with her left hand and, satisfied, said, "Got it."

"Okay, I'm Sandeep, and the only way you know that is by this nametag here." He pointed to his chest. She read, Sandeep Bhamidipaty.

He held up a nametag in his hand. "Here's yours. It's programmed so that the transport knows you're part of M5." He stuck it to the nameplate holder on her chest. "Don't lose it." He turned towards the hatch where most of the workers had already filed through. "Let's go."

Once outside the hab, Sandeep spoke again from the left side of her helmet. "Each member has a buddy and the two of them talk privately on the left side of your helmet's communications system. The right side of your helmet is communications with the whole team. Everyone is on that communications channel so it's sort of like a broadcast to all. You activate that by clicking the same two fingers on your right hand. Try it."

As they walked down the ramp to the lower tunnel, Ady snapped her right-hand thumb and middle finger together. A new voice now came from the right.

In her left ear, Sandeep said, "You'll get used to having two conversations going at the same time. For now, you just need to listen to the right ear, but we'll talk separately on the left."

As they approached a transport, a nasally male voice said in her right ear, "Little initiation time, boys. Here she goes."

One of Ady's boots hit something and she stumbled. With the weight of the suit and backpack, she lost her balance and fell forward, breaking her fall with her arms to avoid smashing her faceplate. The man with the nasally voice had tripped her! She pulled her legs under her and rolled onto her side. A toe tapped on her faceplate and the nasally voice said, "Gotta watch where you walk, newbie."

She noted the number seven on the suit belonging to the toe. She grabbed the boot with both hands and twisted sharply. The nasally voice yelped in her ear, and suit number seven tumbled backwards, landing on his pack.

Lars grabbed Ady's gloved hand and pulled her to a sitting position. From there, she was able to get to her feet and stand.

In her right ear, Bomba's voice said, "Enough, you jackass! Get on the transport."

"I can't," said the nasally voice. "That stupid bitch jacked my ankle."

Someone leaned over the suit on the ground and pulled him up and ripped the nametag patch off his suit. "Get back to assembly hall, Gunnar. I'll deal with you later. Sandeep, you're training both newcomers now."

Lars grabbed Ady's arm and touched faceplates. "You okay?"

"Yeah," she said. "Humiliated."

"Maybe Gunnar will join me on a forty-story roof sometime."

Ady laughed. "Thanks, Lars."

After being scanned, Ady climbed onto the buggy and watched Gunnar limp up the ramp. Once the buggy started to move away, his limp disappeared.

Breakdown

The days working at the ilmenite mine passed in a blur. With more than six hundred days remaining, they were something Ady didn't care to track. One day, at the end of the workday a month or so into her Mars stay, she stepped in line for the twenty-minute transport ride back to the hab village. She was joined by fifteen others, each of whom had to be scanned and confirmed aboard before the automated two-car vehicle could depart. The procedure was structured to ensure no one was left behind because that was a certain death sentence. Their work EV suits were self-supporting with full water, oxygen, and heat regulation. The suit had a nominal ten-hour operational capacity, but with their exertion, the oxygen supplies were only adequate for about eight hours of labor, plus the two, twenty-minute buggy rides.

As the transport scanned Ady, she noticed she had thirty-eight minutes of oxygen remaining. The transport always displayed the time remaining for the lowest among them. It was often her. She had pondered this repeatedly with no explanation. Although she suited up at the same start time and didn't seem to exert herself more than the others, it puzzled her. But she wasn't about to discuss it with anyone. The last thing she needed was a physical exam that revealed her DNA mods and to get stuck on Mars for life. Although it was a waste of her life to be here, it would be less than two percent of her whole life. She would tolerate it, keep her head down, and be able to say she'd been to Mars. That was a significant life experience. She'd be sure to add that one trip was enough.

The transport accelerated out of the dock and down the tunnel. When she first saw this transport buggy, Ady had smiled. It was a near-replica of the older buggies used at home in the tunnel to the bunker, except it was open-topped with back-to-back bench seating. It, too, rode on a maglev rail. She had taken apart similar transports many times, making improvements and enhancements over the years. The Mars budget likely precluded upgrades, and this transport likely got no more than routine maintenance for the minor mining operation. It was an antique by her standards.

A few minutes into the ride, Ady felt a vibration in her seat. She put her hand flat on the bench under her leg to confirm the source. The vibration got stronger. Then she noticed that the second car was hitting a small bump every three to four seconds. This was maglev, and unless the rail had debris on it, the ride should be perfectly smooth. Something was coming loose.

She glanced at the transport timer. It read 15:22 to arrival and 27.34 minutes for her oxygen. Was she always this close to running out when they arrived? She didn't think so. If they had a breakdown out here, she'd be in real trouble.

The second car suddenly bucked into the air and slammed down on the maglev rail. The transport lurched to a stop. The passengers slammed against each other on the benches. With the tunnel lights about a hundred meters apart, they were between two lights in nearly complete darkness. In her right ear, everyone began to talk at the same time. Ady pulled a torch from her suit and shined it into the tunnel behind them. A mangled chunk of metal was lying beside the rail. She recognized it as one of the suspension magnets from the second car. It had come loose, and the car had crashed onto the track. The autodrive recognized the failure and stopped the transport. A simple autodrive, it now waited for its sensors to show it was safe to resume the trip. But that wasn't going to happen. She glanced at her oxygen. Twenty-four minutes. The arrival clock on the buggy had stopped at 14:09.

The chatter in her ear was still going on. She stood up and swept her light over the group. On the open cars, everyone noticed and stopped talking. She shined the light on herself and keyed her microphone. "We're fifteen minutes from the habs. It will be twenty minutes before they notice and send help, and it will take them fifteen minutes to get here. Even in the best case, we're thirty-five minutes to get oxygen."

Several voices started to talk.

Ady yelled into her mic, "Shut up!" The chatter stopped. "All of you on the second car move up to the first car and find a place to hang on. I'm going to ditch the second car and see if I can get us moving again. It's the only way we're going to survive. And unless you have something useful to contribute, keep your mouth shut."

Ady stepped off the car into the tunnel and made her way to the gap between the cars. Those from the second car moved past her towards the first car and clambered aboard in various ways, squeezing in with their co-workers. She said into her mic, "Somebody get on the other side and shine a torch in here so I can see." In just a few seconds, there were three lights illuminating the space. She crawled under the transport and began unclasping the connector fittings. As she knew, each car was autonomous and capable of running itself, but they were wired together so that the one in the forward direction took charge. She pulled the pin from the physical carriage tongue, completing the separation. She crawled back out from under the transport and headed to the front of the first car. She said,

"Anyone have a hand tool or wrench?" No one responded. She shuffled back to the metal debris on the rail behind them. She twisted and pried and finally extracted a piece of brace that she could use to pry open the control hatch on the front car. She saw her oxygen level flashing on the buggy display: 13:22.

Four minutes later, she said, "Okay, everyone hold on. We're about to take off." *I hope.* Ady reached into the control compartment and pulled out the cable connecting the second car and the scanner logic board cable. Then she pushed the reset button and jumped aside. It took only a few seconds for the car to fire up and start down the rail. She tried to find a foothold on the first car so she could climb on. She hopped along with the accelerating car, now with twice as many suited miners crammed aboard, and found no place to squeeze in. She was at the end of the car, and it was starting to move away. Two hands reached out and grabbed the shoulders of her EV suit, lifting her up and on top of the pile of people. Ady looked at her oxygen readout. 9:03. It was a fifteen-minute ride to the habs. She'd saved the others, but she wasn't going to make it.

Inside her helmet, alarms became increasingly more insistent about her oxygen state. At ninety seconds, the red oxygen status light began to flash. She remembered the briefing about the EV suits and Mr. Robb telling them that they had better hope they never saw a flashing oxygen indicator. Few who did ever lived to tell about it. She closed her eyes and felt a tear trickle slowly down her cheek. She thought of the day her parents left for Europa, and the next day when Wai-Wan left, sailing out of the harbor on that old boat, while Ady watched until it disappeared over the horizon. She thought of the taste of Anson's lips on hers. Could she smell his scent inside this dying EV suit? She closed out the world around her, reaching for ataraxia in her mind and body. Some distant part of her consciousness continued to stare at the timer until it reached fifteen seconds. Then she took three huge breaths, trying to exhale as much carbon dioxide as possible.

She was underwater, swimming in the James River, silently swimming away from Bo towards the bank. She remembered to use her long strokes and her rhythmic frog kick, one after the other, patient and confident that the riverbank would soon loom up in front of her, knowing she could overcome this test and reach the shore. Stroke, kick, glide, stroke, kick, glide…

A voice shouted, "Grab a cannister. Quick."

Another voice said, "She's been out too long. She'll never make it."

The first voice snapped, "We'd all be dead if we had your cynical attitude, Gunnar."

A loud hiss sounded in Ady's suit and her oxygen alarms ceased.

The first voice was shouting into his open mic. "Come on you careless fool, *breathe, goddammit, breathe!*" He was frantic and doing his best at abdominal compressions through the EV suit.

After a few moments, Ady surfaced, raising her face out of the water, and drawing a deep breath. She opened her eyes and was surprised her face wasn't wet from swimming. She looked at the suit readouts in the helmet, confused about where she was. Then it came flooding back, the transport failure, her disconnecting the second car, scrambling to get aboard, someone lifting her.

Her oxygen supply read nine minutes. Now she was staring at the ceiling of a Martian tunnel and something was smashing her stomach. She swatted at the hands on her stomach and the smashing stopped. A voice in her ear shouted, "Son of bitch!"

Ady sat up. Rough hands shook her suit. The voice said, "Can you hear me?"

She keyed her mic and said, "Yes."

"What the hell? You've been out for ten minutes. How can you just wake up?"

Ten minutes. A long time. Longer than her swim in the river. Had her lung capacity increased with her age and growth. Was this part of Minda's tinkering?

She stood up. The group of coworkers stared at her. She counted five others who had emergency oxygen plugged into their suits. The voice in her helmet said, "Everyone in the assembly hall." One by one, the group turned towards the building and entered the airlock. Someone in a SpaceCorp medic uniform came towards her doing that awkward Mars low gravity run, a cross between skipping and hopping. He grabbed her arm and led her to the airlock.

Inside, they all removed their helmets. It felt good to get some deep breaths. The SpaceCorp medic said to her, "You sure you're okay?"

She nodded.

"These guys were running to the emergency oxygen before the transport even stopped. They said you were out for ten minutes. That's not possible."

Ady said, "Of course. I ran out, but it wasn't for that long. I think I passed out just as we got here. I'm good. Thanks."

"Okay," said the SpaceCorp guy. He scratched his head and looked at the group of workers. "It's somebody else's problem to deal with the transport. You guys recycle your suits and get back to your habs. You'll be notified about what to do tomorrow." He turned to her. "I think you should get checked out at the clinic."

She smiled at the guy and looked at his nametag. Roberts, L. "I'm fine. Really. I was only out a few seconds and not sure I was even completely out. I'm good to go, but thanks for the concern."

"Look, Ford, I'm putting my recommendation into my report and noting that you refused further treatment. If anything comes up later, let me know, but it's not gonna be my fault."

Ady nodded. The guy was just doing his job, but she couldn't afford to get caught up in some medical investigation. If they discovered any of the DNA changes Minda had made in her, she might never get off Mars. Besides, she felt physically fine. She pushed her emotions aside for now.

Most of the crew turned to the business of dealing with their suits and getting back into regular Mars worker uniforms.

Bomba, the middle-aged bear of a man and team lead, slid up next to Ady and quietly said, "Walk with me." He guided her to the end of a row of lockers and turned to her. His curly black hair matched his curly beard and dark eyes. His piercing stare said he was no fool. "Who are you?"

"I'm Adelya Ford."

Bomba waved a hand at her. "You know what I mean. Fixed a maglev transport and went O2-out for more than ten minutes."

She shrugged. "Used to tinker with a maglev buggy on Earth. I guess they're all the same. As for the O2, I wasn't out that long."

"The hell you weren't. I could see the readout in your helmet. Your O2 was at zero for 10:43."

Ady swallowed. "I don't know what to tell you. Here I am. If I was out 10:43, I wouldn't be here." She paused while the stare bored into her. "Were you the one crushing my stomach?"

Bomba's stare faltered. "Yeah. Yeah, that was me." He pointed a finger at her. "Figured I owed you that much." He started to turn away.

She snagged his sleeve and tugged him back. "Listen, Bomba, while I may have some bruises, I do appreciate that. Maybe that's what saved my life."

Bomba turned his head away and wiped at his eyes. Quietly, he said, "I know what saved my life today, lady."

She grabbed him in a hug and he hugged back. She whispered in his ear, "And I know what saved mine. Thank you."

A voice from across the hall yelled, "Hey, you two, chum it up later. Get your gear stowed and outta here. I gotta lock up."

As they walked towards their lockers, Bomba said, "You have any problems here, you let me know."

Ady smiled and nodded. "How long have you been here, Bomba?"

"All my life." He winked at her. "You be careful. And I'd steer clear of Gunnar."

"What's with him?

"I don't know. He's responsible for the buggy emergency pack, but it was empty—no suit patches, no O2 cannisters. He's a twisted bastard, if you ask me. I wouldn't turn my back on him. As soon as he got off the transport, he was practically cheering thinking you were dead."

Pre-Inquiry

By the time Ady got to her hab, the 1800 meal was underway. When she walked in, conversation ceased. Chelsea instructed the bot to bring Ady a serving, even though the rules said if you weren't there when served, you didn't eat. Chelsea pointed at the empty seat across the table from her. Ady dropped her gear and sat, her back to the other seven tables. She pulled off her gloves and dropped them on top of the gear bag.

Chelsea put her spoon down and stared at her.

Ady said, "Word travels fast."

Chelsea nodded. "Story is, when the transport crashed, you single-handedly detached the second car, restarted the first car, and pretty much saved all sixteen of you. Plus, you were O2-dead long before you arrived. Is that about it?"

"Mostly, but the O2 thing is exaggerated. Or I wouldn't be here now, right?" The bot slid a plate in front of her.

Chelsea picked up her spoon. "Eat. We'll talk later." She looked around the room at the staring eyes. They all turned their attention back to their plates and resumed their murmured conversations.

When she finished eating, she stood and carried her plate and utensils to the serving counter. She retrieved her gear from the table and started towards her pod. Chelsea called to her. "Back here in twenty, Ford."

Ady nodded.

In her pod, she unloaded her equipment into her locker and stripped off the work jumpsuit. Before she could climb into a hab jumpsuit, a voice behind her whispered, "May I come in?"

Ady turned to see a frightened Keera peeking in the door. "Of course," said Ady. Keera rushed into the room and grabbed her in a hug. Ady rested her chin on the top of Keera's head, a smile slowly washing over her face. After a few moments, she felt herself relax, and Keera stepped back. She stared at Ady's bare abdomen and said, "How'd you get those?"

Ady looked down at herself. She had deep purple bruises just below her ribs on her stomach. "Good Samaritan. Abdominal compression. In an EV suit, it's pretty hard to do mouth-to-mouth," she said, laughing. She looked at Keera and saw she wasn't smiling.

"What happened to you, Ady?" she said with a cold steadiness.

Ady's Linc chimed. "I'm not sure, Keera." She shook her head. "I'm not sure. But I'm going to figure it out and I'll let you know. Maybe after I talk to Chelsea." She pulled on her jumpsuit and stepped towards the door. Keera stepped back to let her pass. Ady walked by and touched Keera's cheek as she said, "Nice to have at least one friend who cares."

Chelsea was waiting at her usual place at the front table. She pointed to the chair across from her. Ady sat. Chelsea leaned back in her chair with her hands locked behind her head, studying her. Finally, she said, "Ford. You related to the famous Fords?"

"Yes. Both sets."

"What does that mean?"

"Who are the 'famous Fords' you're referring to?"

Chelsea blinked. "The trio that started this whole Mars colony. Are there others?"

Ady chuckled inside. *The world as you know it sets your boundaries and perceptions.* Chelsea's boundary was Mars. Ady said, "Both sets were descendants of Henry Ford, miscreant and racist that he was, who started assembly-line manufacturing, particularly of the 'automobiles' of the time. Around 1900 on Earth."

Chelsea scowled at the mention of Earth. "Around here, Earth history has the same importance as Neptune or Alpha Centauri." She leaned forward with her palms on the table. "The Fords who founded these colonies are revered by all Mars citizens. Being a descendant makes you pseudo-fameux. But maybe you're the real deal."

Ady studied Chelsea. Around forty years of age, she was slight, but she was strong. Her short, bleached hair matched her unblemished skin. Her green-gray eyes continuously shifted color shades. Her nails were short and clean. She seemed nervous and was trying hard to cover it. Why? *Thank you, Ellis, for all those hours and hours you made me study vids of people and "read" them under your tutelage.*

Ady shrugged. "I don't know what 'pseudo-fameux' means, but I'm lucky to know about maglev technology. The rest is all hype."

"Really? You don't know 'fameux'?"

She shook her head.

"There are still a lot of old-world words used here on Mars. 'Fameux' is an old French word that translates to 'famous' in Bitte. But you wouldn't know that on Earth because you'd get arrested by the chips for using it."

Ady smiled. "'Chips.' Like electronic chips. Your slang for Pandera?"

Chelsea smiled. "I told you I liked you. Ford or not, you're one smart chameleon." Chelsea signed. "Tomorrow at 1430 you report to building

106. Take all your gear with you. A buggy will pick you up here at 0800. It has hab in the buggy, so you don't need your work EV suit. Questions?"

"Why am I being moved?"

Chelsea didn't blink. "Because management gave the order." She ran a hand through her hair and glanced at the floor, and then back at Ady. "It's not a request."

Ady shrugged. Bo's voice echoed in her head, telling her not to resist until the time was right. Was now the right time? Was this relocation a punishment or something else? She pulled up her Linc map of the colony. Absently, she said, "What's a 'chameleon?'"

"Ask your friend Keera. I bet she laughs her ass off."

Frowning, Ady pointed at her Linc. "Where is building 106? All the buildings on my map have only two digits."

Chelsea stood. "See? You're smart. The buggy will know how to get there."

Chelsea put her hand to her ear and nodded. She had a communicator in her ear. There were other parties in this conversation.

"You'll find out tomorrow," Chelsea said to her, "but let's just say native Martians don't live in the two-digit zone."

Martianville

At 0750 the next day Ady stood ready to enter the hab airlock with her gear bag. Keera stood holding on to her sleeve. She had been distraught over Ady's departure and the loss of her "space bud" as she referred to Ady. They had talked for several hours last night, with Ady trying to reassure her, but not knowing what was coming. Upon reflection, Ady couldn't remember exactly what they had talked about, but it had seemed natural and soothing at the same time. She turned to Keera. "Thanks for talking last night. It was fun, but it was also cathartic, almost like my mothers' hugs."

Keera said, "You're welcome. It was the best. I'll miss you."

"I'll bet Lars has already moved into my locker. You won't be alone."

Keera laughed. "Yeah, she cornered me at the 0600 meal. I'm a people person, Ady. Don't like to be alone."

She squeezed Keera's hand. "Me neither, Keera."

Keera leaned her head against Ady's shoulder. "You're so nice to me. This trip has been amazing, and I've been so lucky to stumble into your life."

Ady nodded, thinking the same thing. She'd made a friend somehow, though the process eluded her analysis. She still wouldn't be able to explain it to Ellis.

A buggy pulled to a stop in front of the hab. It had much larger wheels than those they had seen here before. The cab portion was opaque and had only one door on the side facing them. Keera said, "Stay in touch. And if we don't see each other on Mars, I'll see you back on Earth."

Ady turned and hugged Keera, donned her helmet, and entered the airlock. Once outside, she walked over to the buggy where it scanned her implant. The door opened. Ady tossed her gear bag inside and climbed aboard. She glanced back at the hab to see Keera with her nose pressed against the viewport and waving. Ady waved back and closed the buggy door. It moved off.

The buggy navigated its way out of the colony tunnel and surfaced, heading towards a distant mountain range. After a few hours, it began to wend its way up the lower portion of the mountain slope via switchbacks and some hilltop saddles, which Ady thought looked more constructed rather than natural. At about the five-hour mark, the buggy turned a corner around a sheer cliff into shadows and its lights came on. She saw a hole in the wall ahead that seemed just big enough for the buggy. Once inside, she confirmed her suspicions—it was a man-made tunnel with the distinctive boring machine wall pattern of the old SpaceBus colonization crews. Almost an hour later, the buggy emerged from the tunnel on the other side of the mountain range. It drove for barely ten minutes and took a sharp right turn down a steep slope that ended at the entrance to a tunnel heading underneath the plain before her. She blinked at the bright overhead lights as the buggy navigated down a central street flanked by habs on both sides. She noted that each hab had a three-digit number. The buggy stopped in front of one labeled 106. The door opened.

During the journey, Ady had repeatedly looked at the Mars maps on her Linc, trying to determine where she was headed. She looked again and confirmed that this colony did not exist. Yet here it was. She had no plausible explanation. She opened the buggy door and climbed out. As she walked to the airlock of the building, she noticed that the building walls were not made of the same inflated balloon-like material of the hab where she had resided the last months. These buildings, stretching down the tunnel for at least two kilometers, were constructed of what resembled the composite material that lined her bunker tunnel on Earth. She wondered if these predated the inflated habs, or if these came later.

She stepped through the airlock. Her helmet readout indicated good atmosphere and pressure, so she dropped her gear bag and removed her helmet. A gray-haired woman of perhaps sixty years old approached. She wore a black uniform with a chest logo Ady didn't recognize. The woman was slim with Ady's skin tone, but was nearly half-a-head taller.

"Hello, Miss Ford. I'm Aideen, the Martian Operations Manager." As they shook hands, the woman's slim handmade Ady think "frail." "Please come in and have a seat." She indicated a large circular table to the left where two equally tall, and similarly uniformed men stood staring. A partition separated the rest of the space from view. There were four chairs at the table and a tablet in front of each.

Aideen introduced the two. "This is Ronsen, Martian Security Manager, and this is Nabilia, our Medical Manager." Ronsen and Nabilia nodded to her. Ronsen was roughly sixty years old as well and had some odd facial hair whose style she had never seen. A finger-width line of short beard extended down from his sideburns all the way across his chin to the other sideburn, like a seam that would allow his face to be unzipped and lifted back over his head.

Nabilia was somewhat older, perhaps just over one hundred. Upon closer inspection, Ady realized that Nabilia was a woman. She had dark hair in a simple bowl cut and a darker complexion than Ady. She wore facial makeup, something Ady had not seen before on Mars, with white glossy lipstick that accentuated her full lips. She smiled brightly at Ady.

After the group was seated, Aideen said, "We'll each introduce ourselves, but I feel it necessary to provide some background you apparently don't have, Miss Ford."

Since they had all used only first names, Ady felt obliged to be polite and friendly. "Ady, if you don't mind."

Aideen nodded. "Thank you, Ady." She leaned forward in her chair and looked directly at her. "As a Ford, I expect you've grown up with a circumspect attitude towards almost everyone. We could debate the genesis of that trait, but I ask that for today we agree that it runs deep in the Ford family. For us to properly explain your next task, I think it is necessary for me to provide you a background on our colony, our priorities, and us. In short, we need to gain your confidence and overcome your innate distrust of new people."

Ady frowned, wondering how Aideen knew this and where all this was going. She didn't *need* to trust anyone. Mr. Robb confirmed that. She would decide for herself whom to trust, and when. But she could work with anyone to get the job done. Besides, after a six-hour buggy ride through the Martian mountains, she was in no mood for a long lecture.

Aideen continued. "I've pondered how best to explain all this to you. We did such a poor job when your grandfather first came to us."

Ady blinked. These people knew Bo?

Aideen smiled and looked at the others. "I see that William has been even more discrete than we would have imagined." She turned to Ady. "Your reaction is to the revelation that we know William?"

Ady felt her face flush. It was as if Aideen had read her mind. This personal angle was somewhat offensive. What was the point? She was just here to get a task assignment. And she'd just met these people. Why the comments about her family and needing her trust? Irritated, she locked eyes with Aideen and said, "Can we dispense with the pontification about my family, and get to the point of this meeting, please?"

The others laughed together. Aideen clapped her hands in what appeared to be glee or victory of some kind.

Ady wasn't sure how to react.

Nabilia spoke. "Adelya Nichieu Ford. Beautiful name. May I call you Adelya? I so love that name."

The buzz in Ady's head felt like a beehive that had been whacked with a stick. It was how she felt when she was "in the zone" of her most inventive works. She realized it meant that mega-brain of hers was in high gear, crunching data to find a solution. These people knew a lot more about her than she could have imagined. She'd have to figure out who they were. She looked at Nabilia and said, "Sure."

Nabilia smiled. "May I suggest to my comrades that instead of continued 'pontification,' we ask Adelya to enlighten us with her hypotheses and deductions. The outcome will advance our mutual understanding so much faster."

The others nodded and looked at her. Ady frowned. "I don't know what you want." She looked from expectant face to expectant face. They apparently presumed she would share her hypotheses and deductions about something, but they didn't give her the topic. Maybe she was supposed to guess who they really were. But what she wanted to know was why she was here. She splayed her hands on the table in front of her. "I think I'm here for a new task assignment, so I'm not sure why we are having this circuitous conversation. For starters, where are we? What is this colony? Given the tunnel bore markings, this place is old, but it's not on any Mars maps that I can find."

Nabilia nodded. "Where do you think you are, Ady? We'd like to hear your hypotheses, given your last conversation with Chelsea."

Chelsea's last conversation. These people were listening on Chelsea's communicator last night. She didn't understand why they didn't just tell her. Their game of mystery was frustrating, but she recalled the conversation, and said, "Native Martians." She looked around the table at the almost gleeful faces. She sensed she was on the right track, but she wished she had Ellis to help her. She thought back about Chelsea's comment. She wasn't sure where to go with this. "Three-digit buildings are for native Martians. Therefore, you are native Martians." She frowned, her frustration growing.

The three nodded. She continued, thinking she was almost rambling. "Native Martians were born on Mars. Those born on Mars live in a separate section of the colony. No, you live in your own colony, here." She paused and asked herself why those born on Mars would live in a secret colony. "Why? Because you're trying to protect or hide something." Ady didn't think she could guess this reason. She turned to whom they were hiding from. "As far as I know, the Earth population doesn't know about you and doesn't realize native Martians exist. I can see it's a natural evolution from the pandemic era, though." She paused for another moment, feeling more irritation at the growing list of topics where she was either ignorant or misinformed. Who else didn't know of their existence? Other colonies? But

Chelsea knew. Ady looked around the room again and then it clicked. She could see the resemblance between Chelsea and these three. "Chelsea is one of you. Some of you, like her, work in the two-digit areas. But generally, the other colonies don't know about you either." The trio nodded. Ady looked at the table for a moment, and then looked at each of the trio, one at a time. "But why the secret colony?"

Nabilia chimed in. "My last name is Nichieu, Ady. My grandmother's first name was Adelya."

Ady stared at her. They must be related somehow. Her brain was on pause for a few moments, but then she got it. She said, "Native Martians built their own colony because of the pandemic on Earth seventy years after the Ford trio arrived here. There are descendants of them. Like you. Martian descendants." Ady frowned. "Yet you maintained control of the original colony. You placed your own there either secretly or discretely. Who were you hiding from? It wasn't Earth. At that point, they didn't care. They were just trying to survive. They ignored the colonies for at least a decade. You were on your own. Why hide?"

Ady thought about the chain of events that came out of the Global Tripartite, recalling the technical reports and Keera's briefing. The bacteria that ravished the world was eventually eliminated with the discovery of exosomes, tiny lipid sacs, which were one kind of nanovesicles produced by cells of nearly all types. Bacteria also produce similar nanovesicles, but it took seven years to craft an effective exosome vaccine, and another three to inoculate the surviving population. All fertile Earth women were already dead or sterilized. Only the Martian women remained fertile. She looked at the two Martian women. "You've given natural birth to children."

The women nodded. Nabilia said, "I have five children. Aideen has four. All adults now, most working in the original colony. You met one of my sons. His nickname is 'Bomba.'"

Ady smiled. Her distant cousin. She wondered if he knew they were related. Then she felt stupid—of course he did. He knew her last name was Ford.

Aideen said, "The original gene pool was heavy with the three Ford contributors, but the pool continued to expand with new colonist arrivals until the pandemic started. This three-digit section was constructed while Earth was ignoring us. They got the tunneling equipment working again and cut through Apollinaris Mons—the mountain range—to this location. It took nearly decade of construction before they got the systems completely running and the greenhouses growing enough food to sustain an independent colony. At that point in time, the Earth had awakened, and our collective management, who by that time were all natives, decided to keep Martianville confidential, if not secret."

"Why?"

"Pandera," said Ronsen. "They don't oversee us or other colonies like they do Earth. But, if so inclined, they could leap into space and inflict a lot more control and interference for the colonies. By remaining secret, we avoid their scrutiny and potential takeover of Martianville."

Ady frowned. "But to keep Pandera out, you have to keep their technology and equipment out. You can't let their electronics slip into your domain. That means you must manufacture your own…or get it from somewhere else. It's too complex to manufacture here. You need too many raw materials, particularly metals. Scarce metals. Where do you get scarce metals to make electronics? Steal them from Pandera mines? Eventually you'd get caught and they'd follow the trail to you. You'd need another source." Ady looked at them and shook her head. "This is crazy. How can all of this go on in front of me and I never see it?"

"Actually," said Ronsen, "there are many whose boundless efforts conceal this by creating multiple layers. Just like your grandfather."

She nodded. "I see where this is going. The junk dealers of Earth—my parents' companies—are sifting the ancient landfills for scarce metals and siphoning most of them off to Mars." She thought for another moment. "No, somehow they're manufacturing your electronics on Earth and sending them to you, completely out of view of Pandera."

"Information that shall never be repeated outside of this room," said Ronsen.

Ady leaned forward, eying Ronsen. "I'm missing information. Pandera enforces the laws of Earth, and although they are somewhat feared and they sent me here for hitting a goose, they mostly stay out of our lives and let us be. Why are you afraid of them?"

Aideen spoke this time. "Because Pandera is not what it seems, Ady. What you know of them is mostly from Education. They censor Education to ensure Pandera is portrayed as the simple enforcer of the Earthlings' laws. In reality, they manipulate, monitor, and sometimes murder to hide their control of Earthlings. At the push of a button, Earth humanity could be exterminated by destroying NeoHealth. So far, their ventures into space have been limited, uneventful, and nonthreatening. As you said, part of our job is to keep it that way. We ask you to help us with that task."

Reassignment

The Martianville colony was a double row of habs split by a boulevard running the length of the tunnel. Unlike the inflated habs of the other colonies, these had hard shells fitted over the inflated interior. The shell made these much less susceptible to a breach from outside.

One end of the boulevard exited into the mountain pass Ady had traversed on the buggy ride from Colony G. Along the boulevard, the Martians had implemented a sort of buggy tram system that easily allowed the residents to travel up and down the two-kilometer tunnel. Four autonomous buggies, spaced equally apart on their endless journey up and down the boulevard, could be hailed with the tap of a Linc. Each tram was a four-wheeled buggy tractor with an open trailer towed behind that could seat eight on a single back-to-back bench. She recognized the trailer as a cousin to the transport cars used by her M5 mining team in the two-digit zone.

After breakfast, she headed out per her new assignment to a building referred to as "Astro." She stood at the edge of the boulevard, consulted her Linc directions, and hailed the next tram. She rode to the far end of the tunnel and disembarked. At first glance, the tunnel appeared to dead-end here, but she soon located a smaller sub-tunnel leading off the boulevard at a forty-five-degree angle. Though it was secured by a gate, she scanned through with her Linc and walked on. The sub-tunnel was about the same diameter as the bunker tunnel at home, but it twisted left and right a few times until, by her estimation, she was about two hundred meters beyond the end of the main boulevard tunnel.

At the end of this slalom, she found a twenty-five meter vertical shaft cut through to the surface. A circular building sat in the center of the shaft, leaving perhaps a meter of open space between the building and the shaft wall. It appeared to extend upward beyond the Martian surface, perhaps five or six stories. It was constructed of dark stone blocks that still bore the laser-saw marks along their faces. The seams were filled with a dark caulk. She spotted multiple cameras on the building, in the tunnel, and overhead. A smooth red door at ground level was the only break in the building wall. She approached it and stood in front of the adjacent scanner. The light above the scanner changed from red to green and the door swung out towards her.

She stepped inside, and the door closed behind her. She was in an airlock, of course, and she operated the controls to cycle through. When she stepped out and removed her helmet, she was in a rectangular vestibule with one door opposite the airlock. An EV rack against the left wall held two suits with four vacant spaces. Two identical blond men in black Martian work jumpsuits greeted her. She stared at them for a moment, and said, "Are you clones?"

The two men laughed. "Sort of," they said in unison. The one on the left tapped his chest and said, "I'm Noam." Pointing to the other man, he said, "He's Noah. We're twins."

She gawked at them for a long moment, looking from one to the other. Embarrassed, she said, "I'm sorry, but I've never met twins before. No such thing on Earth."

The two men exchanged smiling glances, and Noam said, "Perfectly normal, and to be technically precise, we're monozygotic as opposed to dizygotic."

She continued to stare, and murmured, "Identical twins."

Noam broke the awkward moment. "You must be Adelya or else you wouldn't have gotten in here."

"Yes, of course. Didn't mean to make this awkward. Nice to meet both of you." She pulled off her gloves and shook hands with each man.

Noah said, "This is a first for us as well. We've never had an Earthling work with us."

Ady raised her hand and said, "At your service."

Noam chimed in, "You don't fit physical expectations either. Your height and build could easily be mistaken for Martian."

She smiled. "You expected short and fat?"

The two men laughed nervously. Noah said, "Not exactly, but your thematic jest is effective and appreciated." He turned towards the door. "A tour is in order, followed by an operational briefing."

The two men waited while she removed her EV suit and hung it and her helmet on the rack. Then the trio stepped through the door into a cylindrical lift tube that barely accommodated them. She felt the lift rising. Shortly, the door opened. They were obviously on the top floor because a transparent bubble covered the entire circular room of twenty meters in diameter. The lift exited near the edge of the bubble. In front of them, various pieces of equipment, workstations, and vid displays dotted the space. It reminded her of Bo's work lab back home.

Noah motioned towards the opposite side of the bubble. "This equipment interfaces with the multiple sensors deployed outside that you see. They include optical and other spectral receptors of various sensitivities and purposes. Our mission here is primarily observation and tracking, both deep space as well as near-Mars objects. While we don't have full spectroscopy because of the Martian atmosphere, it's extremely effective. Are you familiar with Planck's radiation law?"

She nodded. "The intensity of electromagnetic radiation is a function of wavelength at a fixed temperature. It lets you identify atoms and molecules from their spectral emissions, or lack thereof."

Noah looked at Noam. "Told you it was a waste of time."

Noam said, "Do you know, off the top of your head, how the Martian atmosphere compares to Earth's atmosphere?"

"A little over 600 Pascals on Mars. Less than one percent of Earth's atmosphere. You want the breakdown of gases?" Ady was miffed at this peccadillo. She wondered if she should have played her ninety-one percent card and not shown her true knowledge. These men were certainly her allies and she didn't need to play imbecilic. Still, their childish game would have set a lot better with her if they had just asked about her knowledge level. Trying to covertly test her was no way to treat a comrade if that's what she was to them.

"Okay," said Noam. "Let's get to operations." As he started to walk towards the lift, he said to her, "We work at this level only by necessity. Between the varying light levels and radiation, it's just not practical over protracted periods. But the dome does permit indifference to the storms. They blow right over us. We polish the exterior annually to remove the abrasion scratches from the storm sand. When they constructed this building, the designers were concerned about the tunnel having a venturi effect and sucking the storm right down the boulevard, so they countered that with the curved tunnel 'snake' you saw coming in."

As they took the lift down one level, Noah explained the five levels of the building. "Five is the dome. Operations, where we do all the work, is four. Three is mostly storage, staging, and equipment repair and testing. Two has hab capability—food, water, and some bunks if needed. One, where you came in, is the building environment control and EV suit charge."

They exited at four. The room was dimly lit and divided into four quadrants with an array of vids evenly spaced facing the center. Noam picked up the tour narration. "Here we have four identical stations with vid displays that can be seen from anywhere else in the room. We tend to do a lot of cooperation and interaction when we have something specific we are tracking or observing. This arrangement allows us to converse across the room and facilitates close coordination." Noah turned to her. "We aren't in charge here. We are a team operated by committee and cooperation. Typically, we work twelve-hours shifts. There are other members who work the night shift. You might meet them later today, but we're usually gone before they arrive." That seemed odd. Wasn't there some kind of hand-off between shifts?

Noam led them to one of the stations and pointed at a vid displaying a grid with various colors, text, and blinking segments. "Right now, we have seventeen protocols running. That means we are looking at seventeen different objects or fields of view. For example, one always tracks Mars-Gate, monitors its precise location, notes all arrivals and departures, and correlates those with the schedule manifest for the 'gate. Over here," he pointed to a different vid, "is the lowest priority deep space tracking protocol. We're looking outside of our solar system for anything that might be coming our way."

"Like what?" she asked. "Comets, asteroids…"

Noah shrugged. "Whatever shows up. A comet impacting Mars or Earth would not be a good thing. In fact, we track all objects for any planet or moon impact in the solar system. At least out to Jupiter. We also have four solar-sail spacecraft orbiting the Sun that feed us both solar activity and outward-facing optical and infrared images."

Noam spoke up. "One of the most important protocols is Earth observation. We track anything that leaves Earth's orbit, regardless of where it's going. Here, the moon, Europa, all of it. I happen to think we're a little paranoid, but this is the protocol that primarily watches for Pandera activity."

Ady wasn't sure this whole thing was effective. These guys were taking this too casually. "How do you know when there's something of interest or something you need to report?"

"At this point, it's pretty automatic. We receive alerts to any anomalies on our Linc. You'll be getting them, too, in a few days. On a day-to-day basis, we do a lot of monitoring, status checking, and things to ensure everything is running properly. At least half of our role is more caretaker than analyst."

"Who decides what protocols to run?" she asked.

"We, as a group, make monthly reports and recommendations to the council. They review, approve, and direct."

This sounded like bureaucracy at work. She had expected more autonomy to investigate and probe, not react to red lights from a comp. She hoped she could tactfully discuss this with the council at some point soon. For now, she'd keep her head down and gather data.

"One other thing," said Noam. We're air-gapped here from the rest of the world. We receive, but we don't transmit, and we don't have any connections outside of this building, except the sensors. We are about as hack proof as we can be."

She glanced at Noam to see if he was joking. Were these guys that naive? But their faces were dead serious. Were they not very bright, or were they adept at hiding it? She let it go. Play ninety-one percent, Ady. Until you are sure of the rules and the players.

Homework

After her shift ended, Ady dined alone in the food hall. She was glad Martianville had a more accommodating approach to their eating schedule. The hall opened thirty minutes before the mealtime and closed ninety minutes later. This allowed the arriving shift workers to dine before their shift and relieve the departing shift in time for them to dine before the food hall closed. In the two-digit zone with its thirty-minute window, it was be there or you don't eat.

On the walk back to her hab, she looked at the EV suit readouts on her display. According to the readout and the detail she punched up, she'd been in the suit three-point-seven hours since she left her hab for breakfast, thirty-seven percent of the ten-hour capacity of her EV suit. Yet, she had used only twenty-one percent of her O2. She was using oxygen at a much slower rate than she did while working on the mining team. Although the mine work was more physical exertion, she wasn't sure that explained the difference. She estimated she would have been nearly fifty percent by now with the M5 team. Why were the two so different?

Once inside the hab, Ady removed her suit and plugged it into the charge port. She ran a diagnostic on the pack, and everything tested one hundred percent good. She went to her pod, stripped, and showered. She wondered where Keera was and what she was doing. She couldn't reach her via Linc because the two- and three-digit zones weren't connected. With grooming chores complete, she sat down in her pod and scanned the pod tablet for the communications apps. When she opened it, she found a message from Bo.

Heard you have a new job and met the neighbors. Sorry I wasn't there to introduce you. Complacency grows with time. Trust you will immerse yourself in the new job like you did the last one. Love, Bo.

She re-read the message. Unlike Wai-Wan, Bo was not one to be cryptic. Why so circumspect? He knew of her new assignment and had met their Martian relatives. He apologized for not telling her, but of course her departure to Mars didn't exactly allow time for goodbyes. *Complacency grows with time.* Was he telling her not to take things at face value because the Martians have been doing this a long time and they have become complacent? *Immerse yourself...* He knew about her crazy lung capacity, but she wasn't sure about this part of his message. Maybe just letting her know that he knew about her escapade in the mine?

She replied, "Thanks for message. Met cerebrum hemispheres in different bodies. Scored 91 on latest exam. Will look for swimming pool. Sending package for Ellis. Love, A."

After poking around on the tablet, she was able to find the EV suit records from the M5 mining team. She pulled the records for the last thirty days for each individual and plotted their use time against their O2 usage. While each usage plot had some slight variation in its slope, they were all a straight line…except for hers. Hers was curved upwards and looked nearly logarithmic. The longer she used the suit, the faster O2 depleted. She retrieved the same usage data from the suit she used today. It was a straight line. She scratched her head. Her M5 suit O2 usage was baffling. There must have been something wrong with the suit. That's why she was always the lowest at the end of the day.

An alert on the tablet told her the data she was graphing had been updated. That was bizarre. Why would past EV suit data be updated? It was static and historical. The tablet asked if she wanted to see the updated data. She stared at the vid. She looked around her pod, half expecting someone to be standing there watching her. She exited the connection to the EV suit data, and connected to her personal Linc where she saved the data she had been viewing. Then she reversed her steps and pulled the EV data again. The plots for all team members were now linear, including hers. She disconnected. Someone or some comp had noticed her looking at the data and didn't want the anomalies found so they overwrote her data with some other data. She looked at the graphs carefully, expanding the axes to get better separation in the plots. Sure enough, her data was now identical to Bomba's. They had copied his data to her suit record.

After pondering this for a few minutes, she reconnected her Linc to the tablet. She composed her message and data for Ellis, and sent it back to her Linc. From there, she encrypted the message with their Ford quantum key, and sent the message back to the tablet. She pulled up the communications app again and sent the Ellis message to Bo as an attachment.

————

Back on Earth, the leafless black trees along the James River were frosted white this morning. Though the current kept the channel water flowing, Tar Bay was a silver mirror of thin ice. As Bo approached the lab, his breath left white puffy clouds that dissipated behind him. While the security system scanned his nametag, he glanced out over the naked river valley. The door clicked open and he entered the lab. He paused to allow the decon cycle to vacuum his boots and insulated overcoat, and then peeled the insulated hat from his head. He hung hat and coat near the door. A tone sounded.

"Yes, Ellis?"

"You have received a message from Ady."

"Please read it."

When Ellis read the message Bo began to laugh. It started as a chuckle, and then a full-gale belly laugh that brought tears to his eyes. As he quieted, Ellis asked, "Some of this message's meaning eludes me. I found no humor or jokes that would elicit your reaction. Could you please clarify to allow my human discourse analysis routines to be improved?"

Bo nodded. "Of course, Ellis, but no amount of training or improvement would allow you to fathom the humor of Ady's message. Please refer to 'inside joke.'"

Ellis said, "An inside joke is a joke whose humor is understandable only to members of an ingroup." Ellis paused. "You are a member of the ingroup with Ady. I am not."

"Don't be offended, Ellis. You could not be a part of this ingroup because you did not accompany me on my Mars trip. Therefore, you don't have the knowledge of what transpired there or of the humans there." Bo smiled at the joke again. "'Cerebrum hemispheres in different bodies' was a reference to a set of twins Ady has met. She has no experience with twins. These two, in particular, are so identical that they can seem to be the same person in two different human bodies, I'm told."

"I see. The wordplay was eloquently chosen."

"Yes," said Bo. "She is also trying to remain nonthreatening in order to gain the trust and cooperation of those with whom she works. She is being obtuse to confuse anyone who might intercept this message," said Bo. "What was in the package for you?"

"Ady has asked me to access and analyze EV suit utilization for team M5 on Mars. She advised that she believes she tripped an intrusion detection algorithm."

"On an EV suit?" said Bo. "Hmmm…odd."

Ellis said, "It will take me some time because of the transmission time to Mars. But I should have the task completed in less than four hours."

"While you're doing that, may we resume our bomb-making activities from yesterday?"

"I don't think I'll blow up from undertaking two such taxing tasks," said Ellis.

Bo frowned. "Attempted humor acknowledged."

*****

The next morning on Mars, Ady checked the tablet and found a response from Bo with an attachment. She copied it to her Linc, and not wanting to be late to her assignment, moved on to breakfast.

At Astro, Ady had had enough slow-paced introduction and painful step-by-step about the various workstations and protocol management routines. She was anxious to do something. She now thought of the twins as a collective that she nicknamed N^2, a conjoined twosome. At least she could tell which was which. Noam was always on the left, Noah on the right.

She set about a general task to review any moving object that wasn't already being tracked. The system presented daily identification of every object it detected, correlated that with known objects, and generated a report list for the analysts to investigate. Reviewing the history of this process, she saw that almost all the items detected turned out to be comets, asteroids, or other space debris passing by Mars. Although they looked at everything they could detect in the solar system, their detection ability decreased rapidly with vast distances and smaller objects. While they could detect near objects—within fifty thousand kilometers—that were less than a meter in diameter, anything as far away as the sun would have to be at least forty meters to detect.

Ady looked at today's exception list. There were four items. Two of them were objects orbiting the moon that weren't correlated to known objects. After an hour of digging in the moon manifest database, she identified them as geosynchronous weather and positioning satellites that had been in place for years. Scrolling back through the exception reports from previous days, she saw that these two items were on every report. In fact, they had been on the report since the satellites established their orbits nearly eight years ago.

She called N^2 over. "These two lunar orbit satellites have been on the exception list for eight years. Why?"

They both looked puzzled. Noam said, "Because they weren't in the database of known objects when the protocol was set up."

Her mouth fell open. "Don't you update that database once you identify the object?"

"Not for this protocol. It's not an important one, but the council insists we keep it running. I'm not even sure we're still able to update the database."

Ady blinked. That didn't seem right. They'd have endless unmatched objects, even if they weren't important. "Which protocols are the important ones?" she asked.

Noam pointed to a spot on the screen. "The top one is always launchings and landings, then there's Outer-Gate traffic, followed by new Earth, lunar, and long-range transits to Europa."

Noah added, "Solar activity, radiation, and weather are in the middle somewhere. Further down are communications protocols. At the bottom is this broadband comprehensive protocol, but it never catches anything of interest."

She said, "This one would catch a lot of what the other, more specific ones catch, but it must be updated to filter those out, right?"

"Sure. There's a protocol exchange for identified objects. After a protocol clears its own list of objects, it tries to cross reference with the exchange. If it doesn't find it there, it puts it on the alert list. We run monthly analyses on the exchange and push the unique exchange items to the specific protocol list so the exchange doesn't fill up."

After another thirty minutes of discussion, Ady figured out that the protocol system was an elegant architecture, but the operators didn't understand the system or know how to maintain it effectively. They were just executing the operational scripts they had been given.

Ady asked, "Who built this system? Are they still around?"

One of them frowned before saying, "I think if you look at the operations manual there are some names of the original construction folks at the very end."

"Okay. Thanks for all the information and help," she said. The two went back to their stations, and she clapped her hands over her cheeks. She wondered if all Martians were like these two, unable to think for themselves. They were rigorous at following instructions but didn't have a creative bone in their elongated Martian frames. Maybe, she thought sarcastically, these two were mutants of the Ford genes and were contaminated by Martian…She sat up. Something was wrong with these two. Martian or not, they didn't grasp what they were missing in this operation. But to get here, they must have been vetted beforehand. Maybe they were contaminated slowly by the dome radiation, and no one had noticed. The reports kept being generated and no one knew they were incorrect, not even the council.

She pulled up the operations manuals and scrolled to the last page.

Acknowledgments, July 14, 2284. The Council wishes to acknowledge and thank Wai-Wan Wing for her contribution to the design of the innovative sensor suite and her creative light wave signal interfaces for Astro operation. The Council also wishes to acknowledge and thank the chief architect of Astro, William Elon Ford, for his genius and foresight in bringing this station to operation.

Wai-Wan and Bo. Her grandparents. Eighty years ago. Why didn't they ever tell her about this? Security? Were they paranoid about Pandera even then? Or did they not trust her with this information? Ronsen had mentioned a third option: multiple layers to afford maximum protection and secrecy. She looked around the room and thought of the fifth floor and all the equipment and external sensors. A smile spread across her face. Her grandparents created this. They had been here, sat in this chair, worked at this console. She felt a chill and blinked a few times, feeling humbled to be here now, to interact with their creation. Astro felt more personal now, like she owned a part of it. Almost like their bunker, only on Mars. She would have a message for Bo tonight. Which reminded her of the message from Ellis she needed to decrypt. But first she wanted to clean up some of this mess at Astro.

She spent several hours cross-referencing the various protocol databases, crafting update scripts and linking identified like objects. Before she let her updates execute, she considered consulting with N^2, but decided it would take too long to drag them into understanding. She launched her update. A few seconds later, it prompted her vid with "Successfully Completed." When she returned to the exception list for the comprehensive protocol, the list was now empty.

For the rest of the afternoon, she tinkered with the algorithms her protocol used for object isolation and movement detection, making improvements here and there, tweaking the tolerance parameters, and cross-synchronizing different sensor data into one stream. She noted that the streams from the solar sail satellites could be correlated as well, but she'd save that for tomorrow.

With only an hour left on her shift, she felt she had more than done her job today. She decided to take time to decrypt the message from Ellis.

In all her life, Ady could never remember being really afraid. She'd been startled by rabbits running out from under a bush by the lab, or by fish brushing against her leg in the river. But she hadn't been *afraid,* even when Pandera seized her. Angry, for sure. Afraid, not really. Perhaps that was because she'd always felt she had some control, even during this whole Mars journey. But as she read the message from Ellis, nausea exploded in her gut, she retched once, and her pulse pounded.

She read the message again. Someone was stalking her, even here on Mars.

One Bot, Two Bots

On the buggy ride to the food hall, Ady sent an urgent Linc message to Aideen. She responded immediately and said she would meet Ady at the food hall. When they met, Ady summarized the first part of the message from Ellis. Her suit, and at least eleven others on the M5 team, could have their O2 level adjusted remotely. Gunnar's suit was his personal suit that he brought to Mars as part of his gear eleven years ago. Ellis couldn't access it, but Ady was sure he was the one controlling her suit. She also told Aideen about the data in her suit that had been wiped out.

Aideen tapped her fingers on the table, staring across the room. She was quiet for several moments, and then she looked at Ady. "This can't come from us. It must come from the two-digit zone management. To them, we are a classified sub-outpost that barely exists."

"How about Bomba?"

"No, this might put him at risk. We need to find a legitimate way for this to come to light from within."

Ady's face lit up. "I know just the guy. How do I find someone in the two-digit zone and communicate with them?"

Aideen shook her head. "You don't. For security reasons, we have no Linc communications channels outside our colony. As you may have discovered, our approved devices connect through MarsGate for Earth or other colony data connections."

"How about if I just walk over there?"

"Ady, it's a hundred kilometers. And there's a mountain range between us. The buggy ride is nearly six hours long, as you know."

Ady nodded. "And if I go back, a lot of people will want to know where I've been. They'll ask a lot of questions, questions we don't want to answer. Anything new piques their interest and they won't let it go. They gossip. They make up stories because they don't have any facts. Who knows what backlash that might cause?"

Aideen nodded. "Exactly."

Ady continued. "But what if I just Linc with one or two of my friends over there? If they are discrete, no one will ever know I'm feeding them information."

Aideen threw her hands up. "But you can't communicate by Linc. We're self-contained. It's like trying to communicate via Linc with someone in Astro."

Ady shook her head slowly. "It's different. We have Linc communications here, and two-digit has their own Linc communications. We just need a bridge." She brightened. "Or a tunnel."

Ady watched Aideen's face go from a near-scowl, to softening, and then to at least a partial smile. She looked down at her hands that she had clasped together. When she looked back at Ady, she said, "That's both clever and frightening. The buggies. We've never scanned them, but they could transport messages just as well as people or cargo."

"I'll scan them first, and when we're done, I'll leave a watchdog."

Aideen said, "We'll need to involve Ronsen."

"What if we don't, so you can determine how good, or bad, your security is?"

"Testing people without their knowledge tends to make them distrust you going forward. I have to let him know. He's part of the council." Aideen rose. "What's the timeline?"

"Seems urgent to me. Tomorrow?"

Aideen looked older, somehow. No, not older, more stressed. She carried responsibility well, but like anyone, had a breaking point. She sighed. "Please keep me informed."

Aideen left, and Ady sat by herself thinking. Ellis had sent Bo's message on what he had learned from his goose examination. Pandera could be behind all of this, and were the ones stalking her. But that made no sense. Why was she a target? She and her entire family strived to stay "off the radar." There just wasn't anything of interest to Pandera that she could see. Her GWM air vehicle was potentially of interest, but they didn't know about that. She hadn't done anything else to attract attention. But if the target wasn't her, then who was it? They could be trying to pressure someone else in her family indirectly. Certainly not Bo. Wai-Wan was just a fisherwoman now, and her parents were supposedly Ghamelawallahs. Maybe their family metal-sifting operation was drawing attention.

She finished her meal and headed back to her hab where she stowed her suit. She opened the door to her pod and sat down in her chair, staring at the blank table. Here she was on a secret outpost on Mars, alone on a lonely planet, in her one-person pod. She thought about her one friend, Keera, who was a mere 150 kilometers away, but unreachable. Ady didn't even have her go-to chum, Ellis. Even if Ellis couldn't understand how she felt, she responded with seemingly soothing and consoling comments. At least they were when she was a child. As she got older, Ellis's comments on emotional subjects became rote and empty, so she stopped bringing them up. She sighed. Still, Ellis would be better than no one.

Her thoughts drifted to Aideen. She was a Martian about as isolated, both physically and by her position, as any in the universe. Could she offer useful counsel on this subject? What about Nabilia? She seemed warm, happy, and approachable. Maybe tomorrow she'd try to dine with her.

She felt better with some plan of action.

But then another thought ripped through her mind: could all of this be related to Anson? Chills went up her spine. She shuddered. This could not be related to Anson! She did not want it to be about Anson. She searched for all the reasons it could not be him. But what? She knew almost nothing about him other than he was secretive and wouldn't use electronic communications.

Ady encrypted a message to Ellis, addressed it to Bo, and sent it off. Then she stripped and showered. After ten weeks, her hair was nearly five cm long. She looked at herself in her grooming mirror and shoved her hair this way and that. She had no sense of how it should look. She'd always had a ponytail or a braid. The auburn hair against her dark skin did nothing for her appearance. Maybe she should color her hair to create more contrast. Maybe blue to match her eyes. Half the girls at Ed had removed their eyebrows by the time they were fourteen. Piercings and ink commonly followed. Ady had no time for whatever that was. Embellishment? Adornment? It certainly wasn't making them more beautiful, but it may have made them more attractive or desirable. Again, the emotional side of the world eluded her. Although she had often tried to quantify and functionalize emotions, she concluded that it simply could not be reduced to a mathematical function. If that were possible, bots like Ellis would already have emotional capabilities. Ellis often sought clarification on emotional human behavior, and just like Ady, she, too, was puzzled by it. Ady presumed she had the advantage since she could perceive emotions, even if she didn't understand them any better than a bot.

Her Linc chimed. She gave up on the hair and dressed. When she sat down at the table, the tablet had the requested data from Ellis. Ady asked for the Krewe's surveillance video and the video from the surrounding streets shortly before and after she was last there. Ellis had included two short videos and a note that said, "William and I have already analyzed these with no conclusion or leads."

Ady pulled up the first video. It was a wide shot of the bar. She was easy to pick out because of her height. She watched the farm boy squeeze in for his drinks. As he left, another figure slid into his vacated space for a moment. A hood shadowed his face from the camera. Ady saw herself turn away from the bar and turn back momentarily before picking her way through the crowd to leave Krewe. Her body blocked the note handoff from the camera. She backed up the video to see where the hooded messenger had entered. Oddly, he had walked in the side door and arrived at her side just as the farm boy pulled away. It could be coincidence, but it was near perfect timing.

She started to pull up the second vid, but stopped and re-played the first, backing it up to where the farm boy had slid up to the bar. She played the vid backwards to see where he had come from. She smiled. He had entered through the same door as the hooded messenger and gone directly to the bar. She watched where he went after getting his drinks. Ignoring the hooded messenger, he headed towards the side door and set the three drinks on the last table by the door before walking out. The patrons at that table seemed surprised and turned to inquire, but the boy was gone.

Ady pulled up the next vid, which Ellis had stitched together from various external cameras. She watched as the hooded figure pulled off the toga and tossed it into a rubbish bin. It was a Pandera droid. And it got into a Pandera vehicle. She replayed it several times, and then zoomed in on the droid. When it bent to get into the vehicle, she had an unfettered view of its upper torso and head. She zoomed in closer so she could read the ID number on its neck. It was the same number as her droid escort at Intake.

Surprise

Ady stared at the paused vid. She couldn't reach any conclusions because she had insufficient data. How could she get more data? She fired off another encrypted message to Ellis via Bo and set the problem aside for now. On the tablet, she pulled up the Martianville cameras that were apparently publicly available to everyone. She scanned the boulevard for buggies and found none. After sifting through other cameras, she found the transportation center and spotted two buggies parked at the side of the building. Inside the hangar, another buggy was propped up in the hab area with its wheels off and part of the battery cowling lying on the floor.

The transportation center was located between her hab and Astro. She'd make a stop there on her way to work tomorrow.

Her Linc chimed, most likely a response from Bo. But it was an Astro notification from her station. A new, previously untracked object had been detected. It was auto-classified as routine--no cause for alarm or urgency. She could check on the details tomorrow. She wondered if N^2 had received the same alert and if they would even care about her newly identified object.

Her Linc chimed again and this time it was Ellis. She had sent another video. Ady cued it up. An accompanying note from Bo said, "Can't find our friends prior to arrival, but believe they are comrades." The video began from outside Krewe's side door. The hooded messenger walked into view and entered Krewe. A few seconds later, the farm boy came out of that door and turned down the street. Multiple clips captured him walking a few blocks until he turned into an alley between two buildings about four blocks away. The clip didn't stop, and Ady watched the time synch speed up, essentially skipping about four minutes. Then it slowed to normal speed. A Pandera vehicle came into view, slowed to a near stop at the alleyway, and the farm boy darted out of the alley and jumped into the vehicle before it sped off.

The hooded messenger and the farm boy were working together. For Pandera? With Pandera? She had grown up seeing Pandera as a distant, quiet symbol of order. They were to be respected and obeyed. If you happened to draw their attention, you were doing something you shouldn't be doing. In the NoNum areas, Pandera rarely patrolled. To see their vehicles was not unusual, but they were ignored. They were background.

There were several things off about this encounter: the fact that the message was slipped to her in such a clandestine manner, and by a Pandera droid; the farm boy willingly climbing into a Pandera vehicle; and he and the droid appeared to be working together. All this was to deliver a message from Anson. He had to be connected to Pandera.

The information she had learned from Keera, Joe, and others painted a different picture of Pandera than what she had known—sinister, vying to control Earth and the human population, lurking in the shadows where they went unnoticed and unrestricted. As AI, they weren't capable of harming humans, yet Joe claimed they had caused the death of those two SpaceCorp executives. Ady had thought Joe was paranoid and perhaps less than fully truthful about his infraction that got him life on Mars. Maybe he was just spinning an interesting story. But for what purpose? She needed Joes' hacking expertise, but before she shared her communications plans with him, she had better figure out what was real and what wasn't. She would have to delay her buggy-based communications until she knew whom she could trust.

Oumuamua

When Ady returned to her Astro station the next day, she found her alert item on the comprehensive list. After some investigation, she confirmed that her cross-sensor correlation routine worked because both optical and infrared data had the same hit. She called over N^2 and showed them her data. They were not even mildly interested. Noah said, "Probably another comet or asteroid. Not ominous. Something for Earth astronomers' rumination."

"Perhaps," she said. "But as the junior member of the Astro team, don't you think further investigation would be educational for me?"

They exchanged glances. "Sure," said Noam. "Go at it." They walked back to their stations.

She sat there considering how to report N^2 to Aideen, or the whole council. They were near-incompetent and were not protecting the Martian interests. The council had a false sense of security. She decided to stay late and meet the evening shift and see if they were any better. Maybe they were covering for N^2, or at least knew of their shortcomings. As the newbie at Astro, she felt guilty calling out the bosses, but the mission was failing and that could risk all Martianville.

She pulled her chair back up to her workstation. In ninety minutes, she had correlated the object with the previous month's data where she discovered that the object had gone undetected for nineteen days. She now had a speed and direction. The object was headed for a near-pass by the sun and would be inside Mercury's orbit of about fifteen million kilometers. A quick check confirmed that a Mercury impact probability of zero. It was also coming in at an obtuse angle, 122.71 degrees inclination to the plane of the solar system, essentially coming from above, if the planets' north poles were considered up. That approach angle practically guaranteed no chance of a Mars or Earth close pass, so she decided to move on to more pressing tasks. She did note that the object would pass behind the Sun in seventy days, so she set herself a reminder to look at this again in a week. She decided to tell Ellis about this object and let her confirm Ady's calculations and projections. She copied the relevant data to her Linc for a later message to Earth.

Twenty minutes later, an alert appeared on her list. She opened it and found the same object again. How often did this protocol repeat the alert?

She acknowledged this one, and then dug into the algorithm that controlled alert frequency, priority, and suppression. It was an old segment of code, but she couldn't find any obvious shortcomings or omissions. As far as she could tell, once an alert was acknowledged it didn't reappear unless a parameter of the object changed significantly. Like speed, course, size, or proximity.

She went back to the alert history and drilled down to find out why it had appeared again. She discovered that the protocol also attempted to correlate identified objects with previous objects in the historical database. This object had a high probability match with an ancient designation, 1L/2017 Oumuamua. She found a link to a brief article about this object written in 2249 when it had last passed through the solar system. It had appeared at 116-year intervals since October 2017, so this would be the fourth pass in which it had been identified. It was the first recorded object of interstellar origin, hence the designation from 1L. And it would have gone unnoticed had she not corrected multiple analysis problems.

Interstellar objects were rare, and to find one in some kind of orbit that brought it back regularly was unique, as far as she knew. She added this data to the other information on her Linc that she planned to share later with Ellis.

A new alert flashed on the vid. She opened it and saw that the identification probability had dropped three percent. She poked at the data to determine why, and quickly discovered the reason: Oumuamua was decelerating. She pulled up the summary report on the object and called N^2 over.

"The protocol identified the object as 1L/2017. It's interstellar, periodicity of 116 years. Headed for the sun at just over one AU at twenty-six kilometers per second."

Noam cut in. "Look, Ady, I know this is your first alert object and you're excited." He smiled at her, and she felt her blood pressure inching up. "But this is just a space rock that comes flying by every hundred years or so. It's not the kind of thing we're looking for here. Move on."

She stood. She was a few centimeters taller than N^2. They blinked at her. "How often are you in the dome level?" she asked them.

Noah sighed and put his hands on his hips. "Whenever we have an anomaly, plus our daily rounds. Why?"

"How long do your daily rounds take?"

"About forty minutes on average, per the Astro procedures. What is your point?"

She shook her head. "Bear with me for a moment, please. How long have you worked here?"

Noam said, "Just over thirty years. Martian years."

"And you don't correlate the protocol databases because there are no procedures in the manual, right?"

N^2 nodded in unison.

"This uninteresting interstellar rock is going to swing by the Sun in about seventy days at its current speed. As I'm sure you know, as it approaches the Sun, it will accelerate, drawn in by the Sun's gravitational forces, so it might get there sooner." N^2 stared at her, unblinking. "That is, unless it decelerates in spite of the Sun's force. If it did that, would it be of more interest?" Their silence was way longer than it should have been. They just stood there, shifting on their feet a little, looking at the floor, glancing at each other.

Finally, Noam said, "Is this some kind of test you find amusing?"

Her mouth fell open.

Noah reached out and put his hand on Noam's shoulder. "Wait a minute, Noam." He turned to her. "Is it decelerating?"

She nodded. Noah's eyes grew wide. "It's no rock, is it?"

She shook her head no.

Noam said, "So what? Who cares if the rock goes faster or slower? Can we get back to working on something important?"

Noah looked at the floor for a long moment. "We're cooked, aren't we? You figured it out first. It's the dome radiation. That's why you were asking all those questions about how long we're in the dome." He looked at Noam and said, "Noam, think for a minute. If the rock is decelerating instead of accelerating as it approaches the sun, what does that mean?"

Noam sputtered, "It means it's a stupid rock and this arrogant Earthling is not only annoying but she's more stupid than the rock!"

"I think you're right," said Noah. "Let's go talk about this." He took Noam's arm and led him towards the elevator.

She watched them until the elevator door closed. She stood there for a moment pondering what had just happened. Noam had gone over the edge, but at least Noah recognized it. They'd have to deal with that themselves for now. She had too many pressing tasks. Oumuamua—it was stunning, perhaps life-changing for the entire solar system, but it would be months before they had to reckon with it, so that could wait a few hours. She sifted through her list of priorities: contact Joe to trace her "stalkers," check the Astro procedures for holes or omissions, raise the alarm about N^2.

The N^2 one was most urgent, but who to contact? She closed the workstation vid, and then both of the other workstations where Noam and Noah had been working. She hurried to ground level, slid into her EV suit, and rushed through the airlock. After doing that awkward Mars run-skip the length of the tunnel to the boulevard, she got Linc service and messaged Aideen for assistance. Five minutes later a pair of EV suits riding on an open buggy skidded to a stop at her feet. She recognized one as Ronsen. The trio rushed back to Astro and through the airlock. She explained about Noam and Noah and that Astro was now unmanned. She noticed that Ronsen had a larger backpack on his EV suit. What looked like a short whip antenna protruded from it.

Ronsen stepped away from them and began talking quietly on his voice Linc. The second person introduced herself as Charry Ongtioco. She and Ady shed their EV suits and went up the elevator to the operations floor. Charry said, "I worked at Astro for six years but left about eleven years ago for a new task in the communications group. I think I still remember how to run the main Astro procedures."

Once upstairs, Charry easily opened a workstation and began scanning the high priority protocols. She said to Ady, "Let me get oriented and make sure there's nothing important going on. An emergency backup team should be here within an hour."

Ady nodded and returned to her workstation.

Checking the procedures was next on her To Do list. She pulled them up and searched for anything about maintenance in the dome. She found it immediately: A multi-page procedure for daily maintenance. It began with a warning to never go into the dome with your EV suit on, explaining that the dome contained delicate equipment you could easily damage by bumping into it, due to the suit's bulk and protrusions. But the EV suit had significant radiation shielding, and their regular work jumpsuits had none. The remainder of the maintenance tasks were isolated to three pieces of gear. She scanned the steps. Open access panel, wipe access panel, vacuum interior compartment, wipe interior compartment, close panel, secure panel. One series was to de-tune a circuit and then re-tune it—repeatedly. They were all make-work.

She jumped to the table of contents. This procedure was the last appendix, so it could have been added to the original her grandparents had written. She checked the version history. Last updated eleven years ago with no note as to the changes. She searched for the dome equipment plans and found a dynamic layout of the floor. It was last updated eleven years ago to add three new pieces of equipment. She cross-checked. Same three pieces in the bogus maintenance procedure. They were extended storage devices to store sensor history data, which had been growing over the decades.

Ady walked over to Charry and asked, "Were you here when the latest extended storage packs were installed?"

Charry paused her typing and looked up. "Yeah, that was just before I left. Maybe a few days. Noam and Noah had been promoted and I landed a job where I talked to and interacted with other Martians. Much more social. Why?"

"Let me show you something at my workstation." Charry followed Ady to her workstation and Ady pulled up the dome maintenance procedure. "Ever see this?"

Charry scanned the procedure, and then looked at her. "No. And it looks bogus to me. You wouldn't be doing anything useful."

Ady nodded. "Why wouldn't Noam and Noah realize that?"

Charry smiled and looked down. "They're twins." She twisted up her face. "I can't remember what they call it, but they have some minor brain abnormality, something like 'ass burger,' but that's not exactly right."

"Ass burger?" she said. "I don't know much about medical issues 'cause there are practically no diseases on Earth. How does it affect them?"

"Strict rule followers, over and over. Very repetitive. It took them a decade of training, but once they locked on, you couldn't get them to deviate from procedures. As you've seen, this place is so boring it might take decades to figure out you've died."

"Okay, so when the equipment came in eleven years ago, were there any problems with the installation?"

Charry shook her head. "No. Straightforward. Plug it in, run diagnostics, end of task."

"Nothing unusual?" Someone had to be in on the deception. Kind of odd that Charry left right after the installation. But all her body language said she was both relaxed and truthful. And what would she have to gain?

Charry said, "Nope. And I don't recall there being any procedural updates, so I don't know where this bogus thing came from."

"Okay, thanks," said Ady. She pointed to Charry's workstation. "Everything okay?"

"Mostly, but the cross-correlation routine has been disabled. None of the sensor streams are being synchronized, so the parameters for objects of interest are never met. I can't tell how long it's been off, but when I reset it, I got years of correlations and objects of interest that have never been assessed, let alone reported. It's going to take weeks for a team to wade through all of this and figure out if we've missed important observations."

"N^2 has been blind for years."

"Who?"

"Oh. I nicknamed Noam and Noah N^2."

Charry laughed. "Pretty much. Yes."

"But what about the second shift? Wouldn't they catch at least some of this?"

Charry looked at her with a blank stare. "What second shift? It's just Noam and Noah running Astro."

Clean-Up

Twenty minutes later, Ronsen and Aideen got off the elevator with a pair of newcomers. They were introduced to Ady and Charry, and after Charry updated everyone on her discoveries, the new pair went to work at the other workstations.

Aideen said to Ady and Charry, "There's a meeting room on the first floor. Let's go there to debrief."

The four of them squeezed into the elevator and rode in silence.

After they settled at the meeting room table, Ady asked, "How are Noam and Noah doing?"

Aideen shook her head. "Not so good. We'll need some time for full assessments, but Noam is near schizophrenic. Noah is aware that his brain function has been compromised, but he is confused and is now alarmed."

Ady said, "I'm so sorry for them. Charry told me they had a condition that sounded like 'ass burger.' What is that?"

"Asperger," said Aideen. Charry nodded. Aideen splayed her hands on the table. "The boys are receiving the best medical treatment we can provide. I don't mean to be cold, but there are other pressing matters." She looked at Ady. "Were you able to complete the task we discussed last night?"

"No."

Aideen looked even older today. Ady was about to drop a new worry for Aideen that would compound all her other problems. But it couldn't be helped. Aideen was the leader and she had to be informed. Ady dropped her head, and then looked up at Aideen. "There's more to tell, even on top of all the other challenges you've had in the last few days." She looked at Charry. "I don't think you got through all the protocols, right?"

Charry shook her head slowly and said, "Not the lowest four or five."

Ady blew out a breath. "The boys started me on the lowest protocol, the long-range sensors." She shrugged. "I cleaned it up and cross-connected multiple streams that should have been together anyhow. Almost immediately, I got an alert. The protocol identified an interstellar object 1L/2017."

Ronsen said, "You sure about that number?"

She nodded. "Yes. Common name is Oumuamua. It's been identified four times in history, about 116 years apart."

Charry leaned forward. "It's back?"

"Yes. It makes cyclic visits like comets or other solar system bodies, except it's interstellar. It's about seventy days out from swinging around the Sun."

Ronsen asked, "What's so bad about this? You had me thinking doomsday. It's just passing through again like it did before."

"Not quite."

Before she could continue, Charry said, "Is it on an impact path?"

Ronsen and Aideen's eyes widened. Ady said, "I don't have enough data yet to predict impact. We may not know for a while. But it's slowing down." She held up her Linc and showed the alerts she had received today—one every thirty minutes as it gradually continued to slow. "When it swings by the Sun it will be going slow enough to establish orbit with the sun or with any of the inner planets."

"Wait," said Ronsen. "I guess I don't get it. What does this mean?"

It was quiet for a moment. Aideen looked at her. "Are you certain?"

Ady held out her arm to show Aideen her Linc. "54.2 kilometers per second was the last reading. Down 0.7 kilometers per second in the last thirty hours."

Aideen's face drained of color. She reached over to Ronsen and squeezed his hand. "It's not a rock, Ronsen. It's a spacecraft. From outside our solar system."

Make a Plan

By the time they had wrung the emotion from the realization, they were exhausted. Charry estimated that the backup crew wouldn't get to the long-range protocol for days if not weeks, given the volume of unprocessed data. The group had time before they had to share this information, time that Aideen and the council would need to come up with a viable plan.

They suited up and headed back down the boulevard together on the same buggy. Ady and Charry got off at the same hab while Ronsen and Aideen rode on. Once inside the hab airlock, Charry said, "I didn't know we were roommates. Welcome. I'm in pod 7B if you need anything."

Ady glanced at Charry. She did need something. She'd needed it for a long time, for as long as she could remember. She needed to not feel so lonely. The boys' mental collapse, her unresolved stalker, and now an interstellar spacecraft. What will happen next? Would she spend the rest of her life on Mars? Alone. She stared at the floor and whispered, "I'm scared."

"What?" said Charry.

Tears leaked down Ady's cheeks as she glanced at Charry. "I'm scared, Charry." Her chest was a knot, and she was so cold. She started to shiver.

Charry wrapped her arms around her and hugged her. She rubbed her back with one hand and said quietly in her ear, "Oh dear, Ady, here you are on a foreign world making perhaps the most important discovery of the human race. How do you cope with that?"

"I don't think it's that," murmured Ady. She stepped back and bit her lip for a moment. She looked at Charry and it came tumbling out. "I'm kind of a genius, Charry. Always have been, though my family trained me to hide it in Ed. Maybe it's that or something else that's wrong with me, but I don't have any friends. I never have. I never learned how to make friends because I was always doing stuff." She shifted and put a hand on her hip. "Before I was sent to Mars, I successfully tested a steerable gravity wave engine that I designed and built. But I've never kissed anyone in passion. I've never had play dates with other kids. My closest friend is our homebot that I've enhanced and expanded." She looked at Charry again and shook her head. "She and I apparently have the same problem—we can't decipher emotions, or something like that."

Charry took her hand and said, "Ady, you're a brilliant, beautiful Earthling with a magnanimous heart. Look what you've done for Mars and our people already. But you're so young." She patted her hand. "Much of your emotional growth is yet to come. Patience, my dear. Try not to be so anxious or in such a hurry."

Ady nodded. "I love what I do, Charry. I do. And I don't know why I'm telling you all of this."

"Maybe your emotional growth is letting you know that coping with stress is often easier if you can express your emotions." She smiled. "Even better if someone will listen to you. Someone more human than a bot."

Ady barked a short laugh. "I guess I miss my grandfather." She paused for a moment. "Maybe I miss my home, too. I don't think I'm homesick. I'm just stressed out." She cocked her head as she looked at Charry's face and realized Charry was a lot older than she had thought at first. A strange thought occurred to her. "Do you have children?"

Charry laughed. "No. If I had a child, I would be residing in a family hab, likely with a partner. Those are closer to Astro and the Ed center."

Another alert caused Ady's Linc to chime. "I guess I better get some work done before mealtime. Thanks for listening to…" She couldn't find the right words. "I guess…just thanks for listening. I feel better," she said, somewhat surprised.

"Good," said Charry. "If you'd like, I'll stop by and pick you up when I go to eat. You can meet some of my friends."

"I'd love to," said Ady. At the thought of meeting new people, a real smile swept over her face. "See you later."

Once in her pod, Ady pushed the emotional side of her brain into a box. She paused a moment. This is what she always did with her emotions. Put them away so they didn't distract her from what she needed to do. But this was different—this time, she recognized what she was doing. It was either an improvement or just more fuel to make her feel worse.

She moved on.

She needed to work out how to Linc with the two-digit zone. First, she had to find Joe, but while she was at it she wanted to talk with Keera, too. Hopefully, she could still count Keera as a long-distance friend.

She compiled a message for Ellis. As she was attaching it to the message to Bo, she decided to ask him about the Astro system he had apparently designed. Before she sent it, she had second thoughts about the security of the message. She deleted the message to Bo and created a new, encrypted one for him. She asked him if he had the table of contents for the Astro operational procedures. She explained about the twins and her suspicion that the procedures had somehow become corrupt, revised, or lost. Then she sent the messages together.

Shortly afterward, Charry came by and they went to the food hab together. Ady met Charry's friends, a couple named Yves and Denis Keresdedjian. Yves was seven months pregnant. Ady couldn't keep from staring at her enormous stomach. At one point, Yves grabbed Ady's hand and placed it on her belly when the baby was moving around. She jerked her hand back, alarmed by the movement. "It's alive in there?" she said.

The other three laughed. Yves nodded. "Of course. He moves around a lot. You get used to it."

Ady shook her head. "I can't imagine." She was technically fascinated and wanted to ask questions, but she was emotionally frightened and somewhat repulsed. Growing another human inside your body—that seemed wrong in so many ways. But she was starting to doubt herself. She wondered how much of her reaction was related to Education and what Pandera wanted her to think. If only she could talk to Minda.

When they came back to the hab, they said their goodnights and Ady thanked Charry for introducing her friends. Despite the bizarre pregnant thing, the camaraderie made Ady feel much lighter. She was looking forward to a good night's sleep.

Just as Charry was turning towards her pod, she stopped and turned back to her. "Hey, Ady, by the way, I remembered something about that equipment that was installed in Astro eleven years ago. It caused a flap of sorts when the equipment arrived because they sent a technician from Earth to install it. But the council wouldn't let him into the three-digit zone, so the twins installed it themselves."

"Really? What happened to the technician?"

Charry frowned. "I don't know. I guess he went back to Earth. Or he could still be on Mars."

"Do you remember his name? Maybe I could look him up."

"Hmmm…" Charry studied the floor for a few minutes. "Not sure. Begins with a 'g.' Gunther?"

Chills hit like an ocean wave at the beach. She started to tremble. "Gunnar?"

"Yes, that's it!" said Charry. "Hope that helps. Goodnight."

Ady turned and leaned against the door of her pod. After a moment she shuffled inside and sat down. Gunnar. He'd tripped her on the first day with the M5 team. He'd tinkered with her EV suit oxygen system so she'd run short. He was either sick or evil, maybe both. Certainly dangerous. A lump formed in her throat and she gasped for air. Was he working for Pandera here on Mars? They had sent him to install the Astro equipment. Maybe Pandera was behind all of this, trying to kill her. Just getting her off Earth wasn't enough. Or perhaps it was just that there were so many more opportunities for her to die in an accident on Mars.

She recalled retaliating against Gunnar for tripping her by twisting his leg. Then he faked an injury so he didn't have to work. Ady smiled. She would put him out of business, out of *Pandera* business here on Mars.

Two-Digit Widget

After breakfast the next morning, Ady found building 121 and cycled through the airlock. Inside, she found a pleasant stick of a Martian man who was at least twenty-five centimeters taller than her. Will, according to his nametag, had a graying beard that reminded her of Bo's. He had the same twinkle in his blue eyes, too. He directed her into his electronics lab and laid out the equipment she had requested. After a brief instruction on their use, Ady stowed most of the gear in a pack supplied by Will. Using his bench equipment, she reconfigured a new Linc to secure comms using her family encryption key. She entered a message on the Linc with instructions for Joe. Then she locked it with the code Aideen had sent to Chelsea. She slipped the Linc into a shielded bag and sealed it. She reconfigured the Linc hub with the same encryption key and slipped it into the equipment bag. If this worked, Joe would have an encrypted Linc that only communicated with Ady, and their message traffic couldn't be read even if it was intercepted.

She exited the building to wait for the transport buggy she had scheduled. She pulled out the hand scanner. It was supposed to detect transmission in the 300 kHz to 300 GHz range, but she worried that Pandera electronics in the scanner omitted a frequency reserved for their own covert use. Ten minutes later the transport buggy pulled up in front of the building. It was like the one that brought her from the two-digit zone. She walked all around it, scanning it from every direction. The only detected transmissions were its proximity radar. It pinged when it was moving, or about to. She climbed into the cab. Last night, having studied the blueprints, the circuit and wiring diagrams, and the service instructions, she found everything to be consistent. Given the changes to the Astro procedures, she was concerned that the transport buggy might also have documentation discrepancies. But the power distribution panel was right where it was supposed to be, accessed from a panel behind the seat. She found the 120-volt DC buss and plugged in the hub connector. Then she reached into the space and attached the palm-sized hub to the inside wall of the enclosure. She routed the power wire from the buss to the hub with other wires, hoping to avoid detection by a casual look into the space. She slid the shielded bag with the new Linc into the space and wedged it between a fiber bundle and a wire harness. Then she closed the panel and checked her own Linc for the encrypted signal. As expected, it checked out correctly. Once Joe retrieved the Linc, their messages could be ferried back and forth by the buggy.

She slid out of the cab, closed the door, and pushed its green button, sending the buggy on its way to the two-digit base. She watched it drive away down the boulevard, wondering if this scheme would work, and if not, if Pandera could trace it back to her. She turned away to watch the EV suits move up and down the boulevard, wondering if she'd ever make it back to Earth. Or was this her future.

She hailed a boulevard buggy and rode to Astro. Once at her station, she saw 1L/2017 was still decelerating at a uniform rate. With weeks before it reached the Sun, she was left with nothing but speculation and tracking. It was up to Aideen to figure out when and how to tell Earth, although she had informed Bo last night via encrypted message. Ellis had acknowledged receipt.

Ady decided it was time to secure her access to Astro. She wasn't sure if this was the result of a flaw in her personality, her sense that she was smarter than everyone else, or a learned skill from Bo. In any case, for as long as she could remember, whenever she was in any comp system, she always set up a backdoor so she could get back in if needed. At age fifteen, she'd tried to do that to PubNet and discovered a backdoor set up by one of her ancestors long ago when PubNet was in its infancy. She had squealed and almost peed her pants when she further discovered that Bo had set up a backdoor to the backdoor! But times had changed and if she could spot their setups, so could bots and security scans. She now had a much more elegant and sophisticated dispersion routine that facilitated her backdoor access. She couldn't count how many systems she'd hacked with this setup. Now she tapped the vid screen, completing her setup at Astro so she could access it from anywhere off-Mars.

She then turned to the subject of the Astro operational procedures. Using the table of contents Bo had sent, she was able to identify where changes had been made. The final appendix that originally outlined the cross-coordination of detection streams had been replaced with a useless daily procedure to cause operators to spend time in the exposed dome. The table of contents had been revised to reflect this change as well. She opened the document version history to see when and how this had been done. There were numerous entries, every few years, as equipment and sensors had been modernized, replaced, and added or removed. She was about to select the one from eleven years ago but paused. The hair on the back of her neck stood up for some reason. Was it paranoia or was there a genuine need for caution? What was she feeling that she couldn't pinpoint? Earlier, she had apparently tripped a sensor when she accessed the EV suit O2 usage data. Her probing of that data must have triggered it to be overwritten. Was there a trap here with the procedures? This wasn't her forte. Although she'd hacked plenty of comps and had left herself numerous backdoor accesses, as far as she knew, she'd never been detected.

She decided to leave this alone until she'd conferred with Joe. This was his realm, detecting intrusions. Plus, it wasn't urgent. No need to take a chance. She closed the procedure history.

She stared at the vid for a moment. The EV suit data was wiped just because she had retrieved it. Had she already tripped a sensor here just by looking at the procedure history? She shrugged. It was history. If she had already tripped the sensor, she'd handle the aftermath, whatever it might be. But at least now she was forewarned.

Scout About

Ady opened the long-range alert information on Oumuamua and pulled up the historical data alongside it on the vid panel. The older data had not had the resolution or range of the current sensors, so much of it was estimates. Intent on her work, she didn't hear the elevator open. She was tracing the previous tracks over the current one to see how they matched. When Charry put her hand on Ady's shoulder, she jumped, knocking over her chair and falling to the floor in a heap.

Embarrassed, Charry said, "Oh, Ady, I'm so sorry. I didn't mean to startle you!" She offered her hand to help her up. "You okay?"

Ady took the hand, and laughing, said, "I'm fine. I didn't know you were here. And I was concentrating on tracing an overlay path for 1L/2107." She stood and set the chair back up. "Why don't you pull up a chair and have a look at this with me."

Charry nodded. "Sure."

Ady looked at the vid panel and saw that she had swooped the path trace clear off the side of the panel when she jumped. She started to reset the trace so she could do it correctly, but paused as she looked at the overlay.

"Did I ruin your trace?" asked Charry as she sat beside her.

"I'm not sure," said Ady. "Look at the trace path I drew when I jumped up." She pointed to the vid panel where the trace she was drawing made a swooping ninety-degree turn towards the top.

"Sure not like the other paths," said Charry. "Is it supposed to be similar?"

"I was hand tracing what the historical record showed for the path 230 years ago. It came in at about twenty-six kilometers per second, and after a swing around the sun, it left at fifty-plus kilometers per second. Nearly doubled its speed, but likely lost thirty percent of that getting out of the heliosphere. Several things occurred to me. On its previous visits, would our sensors have even noticed it was slowing? They didn't get images from optics or radar. No spectroscopy data was recorded. It was just another wayward rock, but this is one from interstellar."

Charry nodded. "Likely limited focus on it, and the historical data is probably all automatically recorded. I can't imagine anyone paid attention to it, given the priority and the state of the world at the time."

"That means it may have been slowing down last time, too, but we didn't notice." She looked at Charry. "Could it be a rock unlike any we know about and this deceleration is *not* artificial?"

Charry sat back in her chair and rubbed her cheek for a moment. "How could it repel the sun's gravitational pull? It would have to counter the force to decelerate. There's the solar wind, but unless this thing has a mass of only about five grams, that couldn't work."

Ady opened an adjacent vid panel and pulled up a 3-D animation that showed a cylindrical shape. One end had a short teardrop shape that was "fatter" than the rest of the cylinder. It was rotating on the cylinder center axis about four times per minute.

Charry pointed, and said, "Is that it?"

"Best estimation from the current data. Seems to be consistent with continued readings."

"Which way is it pointed compared to its trajectory?"

She pointed at the fat end. "That part's trailing, at least right now."

"If it has propulsion, it's on the leading end. The bulbous part is probably the 'front' and is a shield from collisions, radiation, and…" Charry stopped and looked at her. "Can you pull up the sensor configurations for this protocol?"

Ady tapped a vid panel a few times, keyed a few characters, and a table displayed. Charry pointed at the display. "We focus our searches within twenty degrees of the solar plane. We don't look 'out' from the plane, just along the plane."

"Is that just the protocol or is it because of the sensor limits?" asked Ady.

Charry leaned over the console and pulled up the protocol routines. It took her only a minute to find the answer. She pointed to the vid. "Look here, the protocol is slicing the data per the parameters in the global coordinate table you pulled up. But the sensors are just dumb sensors. Their field of view is much bigger than the protocol limits." She looked at Ady. "We can track this thing back a lot farther."

She and Charry clapped their hands together in victory. Charry said, "I have to run, but let's eat together tonight and you can update me with what you find." They hugged, and Charry left.

Ady smiled. Charry was a Level 10 for sure. She'd even out-thought her. That was a first, other than Bo and Ellis. And now she had another friend on Mars. Maybe even an equal intellect. She couldn't wait to talk with Charry at dinner.

She started rewriting the protocol, and by mid-afternoon she thought she had it. Instead of altering the current protocol, she made a copy and modified it, giving it a new name 1L/2017 History. She aimed the protocol back along the known track of Oumuamua and launched it. She opened the real-time output window and watched. And waited. The window remained blank. After nearly an hour, a cryptic error appeared in the window indicating some kind of overflow.

Ady spent another hour tracking down the error, which turned out to be a data field that was too small for the value the protocol wanted to use. She corrected that and started it up again. Almost immediately, the window spewed row after row of data. She waited for the data to stop, which it did after a few minutes. She closed the window and brought up the summary report. One object was identified and correlated to the current 1L/2017. The protocol found sufficient sensor data to trace the object back nearly two months. It had been decelerating the entire time. Its initial observed speed was *157,283.7 kilometers per second.* That wasn't possible.

She opened the protocol again and traced through the routines where the speed was calculated. She noted that the earlier data field-size error had been the calculated speed field. That is what had been too big to fit. And too big to believe. She checked and double-checked through all the related routines and found nothing amiss.

She leaned back in her chair and stared at the ceiling wondering if this could be true. According to this calculation, the spacecraft—yes, it was most certainly a spacecraft—was first observed at a speed of just over *half the speed of light.* In the first ten days of observation, it had slowed to fifty kilometers per second. Now, twelve days later, it was just under twenty-five kilometers per second, half that speed. Forget all the philosophical questions about aliens (weren't the Martians technically aliens?). What was the purpose of the spacecraft and where was it going?

She glanced at her Linc and realized she'd lost track of time. Dinner would be end shortly. She closed the protocol, sent the summary report to her Linc, and logged out. After checking out with the new crew, she left Astro and headed back to her hab to see if Charry was there, but her pod was empty. She hustled to dinner an grabbed some food just before they closed.

By the time she returned to the hab she was exhausted. She fell asleep immediately and was awakened the next morning by her Linc chime. A blue light blinked, indicating a new message had arrived. It was an encrypted message from Joe. "We need to talk. Keera locked up. Pandera has spies here." She realized the buggy must be back if she had a message from Joe. She ran to the hab airlock and looked out the portal. The transport buggy from the two-digit zone sat in the boulevard. She suited up and approached the buggy. It was just sitting there. Covered in Martian dust. Ady shook her head. This mule approach to ferrying their communications back and forth was too risky and too slow. She needed to retrieve the hub she had secreted behind the seat and find a better solution.

When she pushed the red button on the buggy's door, the door popped open. She slid across the seat and pulled the seatback down so she could access the distribution panel. She turned the panel-retaining knob and pulled the door open.

The world went black.

Bye-Bye

At least it was only her right arm. Nothing she could do but make the best of it. It wasn't permanent. No chance of being sent to the Southern Hemisphere, although perhaps Pandera would try to use this to ship her off. She wasn't completely sure.

Keera arrived, interrupting Ady's Pandera adjudication rumination. Keera pointed at the vid panel where she had pulled up the outpost news. "You sure stirred up an imbroglio," she said. "Fingers pointing every which way, and blame is flying like sand from a Martian dust storm."

Ady tried to shrug, but the immobilizer on her arm encased her right shoulder all the way to the middle of her abdomen, front and back. *"I* certainly didn't blow up the buggy, so *they'll* have to sort it out."

Keera sat on the pod stool next to Ady's gurney. She took Ady's left hand in her own and squeezed. "What happened, Ady?"

"When I opened the access panel behind the seat in the transport buggy, it exploded. Lucky my arm was up because it deflected most of the blast away from my faceplate, so it only cracked and leaked, but didn't collapse. But it broke my humerus in two places and dislocated my shoulder. I either blacked out or was knocked unconscious."

"Some of the news is saying the buggy was booby-trapped."

"I don't know, Keera. It exploded. The power distribution buss was behind the panel. Could it have been an accident? Maybe."

Keera squeezed her hand again, "What do you think?"

Ady looked away for a moment, that old reflexive ninety-one percent pinging in her mind. "I don't know, but they should be able to get enough forensic debris for a definitive determination."

She turned towards Keera. "I have a whopping headache, my eyes are itchy, and I'll have this giant appendage for several weeks. But I'm okay."

"Someone wanted you out of that outpost in a hurry. They never land a hopper there, and that's how they brought you here."

Ady tried to shrug again. "I was out the whole time. Not sure if that was because of the explosion or sedation."

A knock at the door interrupted them. A woolly face appeared and Ady said, "Bomba!"

She introduced Keera, and after greetings, Bomba said, "Ady, they're shipping you back to Earth."

"What? Who is and why?" she snapped.

"Management. That's all I know. The medic folks will be here in a few minutes to prep you for the trip. Hopper liftoff to the 'gate is in about two hours. There's a scheduled shuttle run to Earth that leaves in three hours. They sent me to tell you." Bomba looked at his feet. "I volunteered," he said sheepishly. An awkward moment passed, and then Bomba brightened. "And I had to bring this." He held up a small gear bag Ady recognized as hers.

She nodded. "Thank you. Keera, could you please excuse us for a minute?"

Keera jumped up, knocking over her stool. "Of course. I'll be outside, but I want time to say goodbye."

Ady nodded. With her good arm she pointed at the stool. "Bomba, we need to talk."

Ten minutes later a confused Keera poked her head in the door. "Sorry to interrupt, but Joe is here and says you called him?"

Ady gave Bomba a one-armed hug and kissed him on the cheek. She whispered, "I hope to see you again. Thank you for all that you have done and continue to do. I'm proud you're a Ford."

Embarrassed, Bomba nodded and slid out of the bay, making way for Joe to take his stool. Bomba took Keera's arm and led her down the hall.

Ady looked at Joe and said, "I need your help. They're shipping me back to Earth in a couple of hours, so I don't have much time to explain. You've still got the secure Linc?"

Joe nodded.

"I'm sure you can move the encryption to your own Linc, so you don't have to tote two."

Joe smiled a toothy grin. "Already done."

"Good. We'll have lots of time to work on the other items when I get back to Earth, but right now I need you to hack the management system and put Keera on the manifest with me."

Joe rubbed his hands together and smiled. "Really? You want me to break into an outpost comp and tamper with the data? That's illegal, you know, and they might extend my sentence on Mars."

They both laughed.

"Given that I'm injured, and that Keera will soon have a plethora of medical care knowledge thanks to your comp updates, I need someone to accompany me on the journey to ensure my safety and wellbeing. The loss of other trained staff for this purpose would put a strain on the medic infrastructure here. Keera is adequately trained and has volunteered to terminate her assignment to be of service to the outpost. She hopes to return at the next opportunity to complete her studies.”

Joe moved over to the vid panel and started keying rapidly. He muttered, “This interface is like a hundred years old. Maybe if I’m here long enough, I’ll build a bot frontend so we can talk to these damn things.”

“Lots harder to hack,” said Ady.

Joe turned and winked at her.

Weasel

Twenty minutes later, Joe left Ady to the technicians who were to package her up. She couldn't fit into an EV suit, so they had to put her on an EV gurney. It was much like a regular gurney but had small buggy wheels for exterior mobility. The entire bed part of the gurney was encased in a flexible bubble. It reminded her of a body bag she had seen in pics at Ed, except it was nearly transparent instead of black. The techs shuffled her into position and slid her into the bag. They sealed it shut and activated the EV pack on the gurney. After a left-handed thumbs-up from Ady, they wheeled her down the hallway to the hab airlock. The airlock door opened and an EV-suited person walked in, heading for the main desk as he unlatched his helmet. They wheeled Ady into the airlock. Just before the hatch closed, she heard the new arrival say to the desk tech, "Here to visit my injured mate from the M5 team. Her name is Ford."

Gunnar. Ady shivered.

As they rolled her outside to the waiting transport, she wondered if she had just made a narrow escape. She was sure the buggy had been booby-trapped and now she suspected Gunnar was behind it, but she was reluctant to make that opinion public. Whoever was behind this didn't yet know she was on to them, and she wanted to keep it that way. She smiled. With her ally, Joe, though, they'd find a way to put Gunnar out of business. But she wanted to make sure he was the only Pandera plant on Mars before they tipped him off.

The technicians disconnected the gurney and strapped it onto the transport cargo pad. A tech gave Ady a thumbs-up. She returned the gesture and the transport accelerated down the tunnel towards the hopper landing pad.

By the time they loaded her into the hopper, Keera had joined her.

Forty minutes later Ady boarded the shuttle for Earth. It was an autonomous cargo shuttle with only a small compartment near the front for personnel. She and Keera were the only passengers. The support tech who loaded them at MarsGate gave them brief instructions about how to access the hab instructions. He apologized because outbound communications inside the hab unit were out, but as a cargo shuttle with a schedule to keep, that was not a high priority repair or an impediment to the trip. He told them the hab unit was stocked for two passengers, and assured them they had plenty of oxygen, water, and food for the trip. Then he sealed the hatch for their six-week journey.

There were four seats that reclined, swiveled, and folded every which way, but little else in the way of accommodations. They had peeled Ady out of the cocoon on the 'gate and she had managed to squeeze through the hatch with her right arm bent at the elbow across her chest. A wedge of vibra-packing was taped between her arm and body for support during acceleration. Her arm was connected to the shoulder cast strapped across her upper body. It felt like she had a hoist arm attached to her body. It was awkward. She bumped into everything, but it didn't hurt.

She looked around the space. Grooming and bodily functions were going to be public affairs on this trip, too. At least the hab portion was supposed to rotate to give them about the same gravitational effect as Mars. Having no outgoing comms would be frustrating, but they could deal with it for six weeks. Or maybe Ady could repair it.

Keera had to strap Ady into her seat for departure. Turnabout, thought Ady, reflecting on their initial meeting and journey to Mars. Keera strapped herself in and stared ahead. She said, "Have you looked at your face since the explosion?"

"No. Why?"

They felt the shuttle gently back away from MarsGate.

"Your faceplate didn't exactly hold, Ady. It cracked and leaked. You took some Martian frigid blast to your face." In her peripheral vision, Ady saw Keera raise her head from the headrest and turn towards her.

"Keep your head back, Keera. The acceleration could be enormous because it's a cargo ship."

Keera put her head back.

"They told me it held but leaked," Ady said.

"Bomba gave me the real story. The leak froze your eyebrows and eyelashes. They fell off. But they think they'll grow back. You were without oxygen for several minutes until they could get you pried loose and moved to the clinic."

The shuttle, now clear of MarsGate, accelerated with full throttle. Their bodies were pressed into the seats by nearly six G's of force that lasted nearly twenty minutes. When the acceleration stopped, a tone chimed and a mechanical voice said, "Acceleration complete." The hab began to rotate and they went from weightless to the equivalent of one-sixth of Earth's gravity.

"You okay, Keera?"

She didn't answer. Ady turned to look at her. Keera's eyes were closed, and her face was a ghostly pale white. Ady unfastened her seat harness and scrambled over to her. She checked Keera's pulse. Plenty strong. She was still breathing, too. She rubbed Keera's legs with her good hand, trying to increase circulation as best she could.

After a minute, Keera's eyes fluttered open.

"Hey," said Ady.

Keera managed a weak smile. "Guess that kicked my ass."

"Yeah. Heavy G's. You blacked out."

"You?"

"No, and it didn't break off my arm. When you feel better, can you tear off this tape and vibra-packing? I'm not gonna need it for another six weeks."

Keera rolled her eyes. "Does that mean I won't have to wipe your ass after all?"

A tone from Ady's Linc interrupted them. It was an encrypted message from Bo. There were still communications channels unknown to Ady. Bo had forwarded a message he received from Bomba. It said:

Please forward to Adelya Ford ASAP. As you departed, Gunnar made his way into the clinic under the pretense of visiting an MT5 coworker: you. Upon learning you were en route to the hopper for transport to Earth, he became apoplectic. Medic staff, concerned for his health, subdued, and forcibly sedated him. He had a stun gun in his possession and will henceforth be remanded to the crib.

Tin Can

Although the hab was cylindrical with a seventy-centimeter structural boom through the center, the rotational gravity caused the outside wall to always be "down," so they walked on the inside wall of the cylinder. The equipment and lockers were attached to the front of the can in a circle around the circumference. It was easy to move from one piece of equipment to another by simply walking along the outer wall.

Unlike water and oxygen, boredom was in ample supply on any space journey, and this was no different. They worked to strengthen their bodies for the forthcoming weight of Earth gravity and took turns jogging the circumference of the tin can twice daily for thirty minutes at a time. Ady did lower body exercises with a flex band and some limited left arm resistance work while Keera jogged. In turn, Keera did a full resistance workout on upper and lower body while Ady walked. They shed their jumpsuits when exercising to prevent perspiration and resultant stench from permeating their jumpsuits. They changed into their Nomex shorts they'd had on when they boarded and now reserved them for exercise only. When they were finished exercising, they stripped off their shorts and stashed them in a vacant locker compartment until the next use. Though they cleaned the shorts weekly, they smelled offensive at best, and downright putrid by the end of a week.

For the first two weeks, Ady occupied herself with work at the lone hab vid panel, trying to figure out a way to establish outbound communications. Her lack of success amplified the boredom and frustration. She blamed it on her shoulder. Her right shoulder. The one with limited mobility that connected to her right, useless arm that protruded from the immobilizer and waved her own hand at her as if to say, "Look how you failed."

Her frustration boiled over. She spun around from the vid panel and shouted, "Keera, can you help me rip the arm out of this jumpsuit? Maybe that will give me more reach with my right hand."

Keera said, "You have only two jumpsuits for six weeks. Do you really want to rip one up?"

"No! But I can't use my arm this way."

"It's called an immobilizer for a reason, sweetheart." Keera plastered a big fat smile on her face and beamed at her.

Ady glared at her. "You remind me of my homebot."

"That's the nicest thing you've ever said to me," panned Keera. "Next, you'll want a dinner date, and then you'll want hot sex on this romantic cruise amongst the heavens."

"I'm sorry," said Ady, sighing. "I'll put my cold bitch away for now. But I have a new idea."

"Are you taking requests? I vote you grow a penis," said Keera with a devilish grin.

Ady shook her head. "I'm sorry, okay? I was frustrated. I am frustrated. No need for jumpsuit surgery." She opened her locker, dug into her gear bag, and pulled out the black slick she wore for tube transport. "Let's cut the arm out of this thing."

Keera clapped her hands. "I love playing dress-up!" She dug around the tool chest and found a pair of diagonal cutters that could double as scissors. She held them up and snapped them closed several times.

Ten minutes later, Ady was dressed in the slick with the right arm and most of the right shoulder trimmed away. She said, "Some of the fashionistas used to wear these in the Richmond clubs."

"What kind of clubs?" asked Keera. "Sounds either bizarre or kinky."

"Both, but weighted towards kinky, I think. A couple of women cut holes to expose their breasts. And then one live show where the pair wore the hood and faceguard but cut a hole to expose their genitalia for their performance."

Keera's eyes widened. "You frequented a lot of sex clubs?"

"No," said Ady. "I tried a couple for the thrill and education, but it's not my style."

"What is your style?"

She shrugged. "Still trying to figure that out." She hadn't let herself think about what was coming upon her arrival on Earth. She had things to do here now. She'd think about Earth arrival later.

After no success at the vid panel, she decided to open the access panel below it. She removed the six retaining bolts and slipped each one into her slick pocket. The panel remained in place. One-handed, she pried at it and tried to lift it out with her fingernails, but it didn't budge. Its stubbornness likely meant something else held it in place. Like an explosive trigger, she wondered.

She tried a new tactic. She pushed on the panel and felt it give just a little. As she released the pressure, the panel folded outward on spring-loaded hinges. Duh. She should have figured it would be that easy.

Over the course of the next two hours, Ady removed or opened seven access panels in all. On the vid panel, she created a wiring map of what she found behind the array of panels.

All the communications cables were light wave modulated, so they were easy to identify. She had had lots of experience with those in building her lab prototypes and her latest vehicle in the bunker. But she had none of her tools aboard this tin can. She laid out the contents of the toolkit and examined the ones she didn't recognize. Keera shuffled over and peered over her shoulder. "Those look like tools that would be used in space." They both laughed.

Then Ady said, "Anything look familiar from your SpaceCorp days?"

"Nope. My presentation on tools started with a rock fashioned into a sharp-edged weapon that was used for hunting animals and other humans."

"No rocks here. I did find the maintenance port, and it probably has a bi-directional comms connection, but I can't find any way to jumper my Linc to the maintenance port. There aren't any spare cables lying around."

Since they had no cable, leaving the panels open served no purpose. She bolted each one back into place in reverse order. After re-installing five bolts on the last panel, she had to reach deep into her pocket for the last one. Her fingers brushed against something else in the bottom of her pocket. She pulled out the bolt, re-installed it, and then fished out a small, flat packet about five centimeters square. It was a waterproof bag. She hadn't seen this before and wondered how it got into her pocket. Puzzled, she unfolded the wrapper and pulled out a folded piece of paper. She opened it. It was a note from Anson.

Hello

Ady sat on the floor by the panel she had just closed, staring at the paper. She felt like her brain had gone dead. She had no idea of how the note had gotten into her pocket. After some moments, she realized she should read the note.

Dearest Ducky, it appears our next meeting will be delayed even further because of my carelessness. Our friends' attempt to seek leverage was botched, but you are the victim of my failure. I am deeply sorry and promise a holiday together when you return. A

She read the note five more times, trying to cypher the cryptic references and words. "Keera," she said, "What does 'Ducky' mean?"

Keera walked over to her. "Ducky? I'm not sure. It sounds like old English slang." She looked at the note Ady held. "What's that?"

Her brain finally working again, Ady put a finger to her lips, and taking Keera by her hand, led her to the EV lockers. Ten minutes later they were both suited up and stood with faceplates together.

Ady held up the paper. "I just found this in my pocket. It's a note from Anson."

"Who's Anson?"

She paused. How much should she tell Keera? "He's a guy I met on Earth. We were supposed to get together the night I was dinged by Pandera, but he never showed up." She stepped back and handed the paper to Keera. Keera held it to her faceplate and read it before handing it back.

They touched faceplates again, and Keera said, "I like a mysterious man. But then I like just about all men."

Ady slapped Keera's helmet. "Ouch!" shouted Keera. She adjusted her head up stance to touch Ady's faceplate above her. "It's cryptic. Do you understand it?"

"Mostly no, except I know it's from him."

"Let me see if I can find 'Ducky.'" Keera stepped back and worked her Linc. When she leaned back in, she said, "Found it! Old English slang for darling or dear. A term of endearment. Oh. He's a man of poetic passion. What other useful skills does he have, Ducky?"

"Cute." Ady lightly banged her faceplate into Keera. "I think it's more of a reference to the goose I hit. Aren't ducks and geese cousins or something?"

"Sort of."

"I miss Ellis."

"Who?" asked Keera.

"My homebot. She'd know the answer."

Keera smacked Ady's helmet and said, "I'm not your homebot backup."

"Sorry. I didn't mean that. But she's good at sorting out cryptic puzzles like this."

"How did this get into your pocket?"

"It was in my left pocket that I never use. Now that I'm forced to be left-handed, I put some bolts in there. When I took them out, I found it."

"Yeah, yeah. But how did it get there?"

"It's the only slick I have. They gave it to me as I was leaving Intake. It had to be in there when I got it." Ady stopped, and added, "I haven't worn it since then." She wasn't going to tell Keera she thought it was placed in the pocket by the Pandera android who escorted her in Intake, the same android that had slipped her the "no-show" note in the Krewe-Brew bar.

Keera asked, "This note is how old? Five months?"

Ady nodded. "Hard to calculate exactly with Martian days being longer, but I think five months is close."

"He must think you're pissed. You never responded?"

"I've no way of contacting him. He has no Linc."

Keera stared at her through the faceplates. "What does he do?"

Ady shook her head. "I don't know. I only met him once."

"The Academy guys who wouldn't Linc were what they called 'spooks.' They were into all this security stuff and super-secret plans. They had no electronics, no tracker implant, so they couldn't be tracked or monitored. Maybe this guy is one of those."

"Maybe." She looked at the paper once more. "Okay, would you please take off this helmet?" Keera released Ady's helmet and set it on the shelf in the EV locker. When she turned back to her, Ady held a finger in front of her lips, *shh,* towards Keera. She popped the paper into her mouth, chewed, and swallowed it.

The South

Although space flight time is measured precisely, the lack of a diurnal cycle often upsets the human biorhythm, causing various mental and physical issues. To avoid this, the two women adopted an artificial twenty-four-hour cycle, to mimic a typical routine of three meals per day, with two exercise periods between the meals, and an eight-hour sleep period after the third meal.

At the mid-day meal three days out from Earth arrival, Keera squeezed a pale brown glob of food paste onto her tongue and washed it down with a squirt of water. "I think salmon meuniere and a dry sauvignon blanc would be a nice first dinner when I get back to Earth." She turned to Ady. "How about you?"

"It's funny," said Ady as she rolled up a near empty tube to get the last bit of paste out. "A lot of people make a big deal out of fancy food and what tastes better, but I never got that. I'm just a food-unit type person. It's just fuel to me." She looked at Keera and smiled. "Nothing special for me, but I'll share the wine."

"Are you a cheap drunk?"

Ady nodded. "Probably. Given a choice, I prefer bourbon, but it's scarce and expensive. I guess I'm not cheap after all."

They both laughed.

Keera's gaze drifted across the tin can. "I wonder if you get drunk faster when you're weightless?" She turned to Ady. "Did you see any alcohol on Mars?"

"No. I don't know if that's by law or just capability."

"Me neither."

"Do they have alcohol in the Southern Hemisphere?"

Keera pointed the food tube at Ady. "Those details are one closely guarded secret. Even their history has been redacted or altogether removed."

"How was the whole Southern Hemisphere even decided?" Ady tossed her empty tubes into a trash bag and held it open for Keera. Keera licked the end of her tube and dropped it into the bag.

"At the time, about eighty-eight percent of the population lived in the Northern Hemisphere, but after the pandemic, there were only about sixty or seventy million survivors in the South. Given the data I've found and pieced together, the plan to commercialize the cities included the South until Pandera came into the mix. My best guess is that they felt the size of the area along with the sparse population would challenge their ability to police. And then Pandera "simplified" the world by exporting anyone with disabilities or other similar needs to the South, making it the dumping ground."

"The people in the South were okay with that? Didn't anyone object?"

"I think there were too few of them, they weren't organized, and no one asked them. Many were still fighting for food and shelter." Keera shrugged. "In any case, Globazelle officially sponsored this deportation idea, but it can be traced back to Pandera. Then Pandera sweetened the deal by pointing out that the Amazon jungle was Earth's best hope at reforestation needed to clean up the atmosphere—ground-level ozone, carbon dioxide, and such. They proposed moving all of what was then the South American population to the North and leaving that continent to heal. Never happened, though. They never moved the people."

Keera continued. "Defective North Americans were stacked into cargo ships and sent to Sao Paulo. Europe sent theirs to Cape Town in their 'Southern Hemisphere.' Asia sent theirs to Perth, Australia. Globazelle was responsible for developing 'receiving centers' in those three cities and supposedly acquired them with the rest of the Northern cities. But there's also no evidence they ever did that. And there's almost no evidence that the South even exists because Pandera deletes any mention of it as fast as it shows up in communications." Keera threw up her hands. "For all anyone knows, those ships could have dumped those poor people into the ocean to drown. There's no news, communications, or trade with the South. Pandera even blacks out all overhead vid of the South before it can be seen."

"Wait," said Ady, "the 'gate passes over the South, so there should be pictures and vid from there, if not from aerial vehicles."

"Pandera auto-deletes all of that. And air vehicles that stray too far south seem to hit an invisible wall and crash. Joe thinks they're probably shot down by Pandera."

Ady shook her head. "People are okay with this? What about the Coordinating Council—don't they oversee any of it?"

"The council is in Berlin, a Globazelle city. While they represent themselves as overseers with representatives from all constituents, their authority and influence has never been evident. Most see them as a bureaucracy with no credibility or actual charter, though all agree it is a good concept. There's no representation from the Southern Hemisphere, of course.

"As for the people, they're conditioned, and organizations like Globazelle promote that conditioning. They teach the Nums that their life is better because the infrastructure doesn't have to accommodate those with disabilities. No need for ramps, lifts, or special public grooming stations. Healthcare is simple because everyone is relatively healthy. The air quality is better because the Amazon forest is growing back. The Nums are constantly pitched on how fortunate they are and how the No-Nums envy them. But I think the No-Nums are similarly conditioned to think their life is better, and fed their rhetoric via Education, PubNet, and Pandera enforcement."

"What about the people in the South? Are they okay with this arranged banishment?"

"Ady, are you not listening? Who knows--there's no information. About 150 years ago, there apparently was a woman who tried to make the North aware of what was going on in the South. She used the name Simone–" Keera clamped a hand over her mouth. She jerked her thumb towards the lockers.

After they had donned their EV suits and stood with faceplates touching, Keera said. "Call me paranoid, but Pandera could still be monitoring us." She shifted to her other foot, barely reaching high enough to touch Ady's faceplate with hers. "We have to find a better way to talk. You're too tall for me to reach easily. Anyhow, this woman, Simone Procopio. She was characterized as a modern-day Harriet Tubman."

"Who?"

"Harriet Tubman. She was a famous American abolitionist and political activist in the 1850's. She was born into slavery, escaped, and made a dozen or so raids to rescue nearly a hundred enslaved people using a network of antislavery activists and safe houses known as the Underground Railroad. You never heard of her?"

Ady shook her head inside her helmet. "No mention at Education. I didn't know America had slavery. Is that what these people become in the South, slaves?" That didn't make sense if they were disabled.

"Looks like I've confused things. You do know that the civil war in America around 1865 was over slavery."

Ady shook her head again. "Education taught us it was about dividing America into two separate countries. The North wanted to keep it together, and they won." She felt uncomfortable, like she couldn't remember something as simple as the Archimedes' principle for fluid dynamics. If some of what Education taught was wrong or just plain lies, where was the boundary? And where did that leave her knowledge? Apparently, it was just world issues she had wrong, a myriad of concepts, facts, and figures, like slavery. She had to figure out a way to parse the misinformation and expunge it from her brain. How could she function, knowing she carried a plethora of incorrect data in her head?

"It was about slavery, to allow it or not. Originally, about 600,000 enslaved people were brought to America, mostly African, characterized by dark skin tone, what we know as skin tone nine or ten today. By 1860 there were nearly four million slaves. The Civil War made slavery illegal, but racial prejudice lasted clear up to the Global Tripartite. We'll come back to that, but let's finish the topic we were discussing."

Ady liked Keera in her teacher mode. She was excellent at explaining things clearly, and she somehow paced her information to match your absorption rate. But Education was starting to look like a mixture of fact and propaganda. That irritated her. She had to sort this out.

"This lady, Simone Procopio, posted a vid on the public newsfeed where she begged the Northern people to wake up and help the people of the South. She was outspoken, and several commentators raised the comparison to Harriet Tubman.

"But two things happened the next day. Pandera tried to delete the vid, but somehow couldn't, so they posted their own vid making it illegal to watch Simone's vid. In most of the cities, Simone's vid played on the building wall panels over and over, yet still Pandera was helpless to stop it. People were getting wound up. Then, the next day the Somali and Nubia tectonic plates split apart in Africa, creating the Somali Sea and dividing the continent, but killing a relatively small number of people because it had such a low population density. The new Somali Sea dominated the news for months, and the world was relieved because for a bunch of related reasons, the rising sea level started dropping. Simone Procopio, her vid, and interest in her disappeared."

"What happened to her?"

"Lots of speculation, but by then it was illegal to even say her name. Pandera monitoring was just ramping up, and they arrested a few dozen people as examples. People stopped talking about her and went back to their lives."

Ady shifted from irritated to angry, angry at those who had lied and misled her. Angry because she was ignorant of factual information she should have known and deserved to know. Her head was buzzing. "I feel like I've been living in some other world," she exclaimed. Counting on her fingers and gritting her teeth, she said, "First, four million slaves in America I never knew about. Second, no one knows what's going on with the people in the South, and no one even cares. Third, parts of Education were lies. Fourth, why did our ancestors care so much about skin tone. Fifth, the Coordinating Council is a sham. And then there's the whole Martian thing!" Ady stopped, afraid she'd gone too far. Pandera could be monitoring them even in their EV suits.

"What Martian thing?" asked Keera.

She tried to bring a hand to her head, but the immobilizer didn't cooperate. She pushed away from Keera and keyed her suit microphone. "And I've got this contraption on my arm so I can't do anything but float in space."

Keera pulled off her helmet, removed Ady's, and hung them in the locker. "I don't think my neck is gonna survive this trip," she said. "Maybe I could stand on the seat next time we need to be intimate."

"I'm always game for new positions." They both laughed.

They felt a bump in the shuttlecraft. The two looked at each other, their eyes asking, "What was that?" Keera pointed at the trash bag with the discarded food tubes and other meal disposables. It no longer sat on the floor. It, along with Keera and Ady, had become weightless.

Floating in a Tin Can

"Keera, get our helmets on!" shouted Ady. Two minutes later they were fully suited up again.

Keera's voice was strangely calm. "What just happened?"

"Hab rotation stopped, so we lost gravity. We're still three days out from 'gate. That's too early, and the autopilot didn't make an announcement."

"What do we do?"

Ady was at the vid panel pulling up the shuttlecraft status information. "It says we still have hab oxygen, but–" Ady felt another subtle bump with her hand on the wall next to the vid. "Keera, did you feel another bump?"

"No, why?"

"It's okay. Just wondered," she lied. No sense making Keera more frightened than she already was. The vid panel blinked, and a new display appeared with "Docking Status" at the top. Ady stared at the screen. There were eight green status indicators in a column with a blinking red one at the bottom. It was labeled "Dock Seal."

She pushed off the console towards Keera and keyed her microphone. "Keera, hook us together. Use the safety strap on your left to hook to my ring. I can't do it with one hand." Keera caught Ady's momentum and used it to roll her away so she could reach the ring on the back of Ady's waist. She grabbed it and pulled them together as they collided with the inner wall. But Keera held on, pulled her safety strap out and snapped it onto Ady's ring. "Done," she said.

Ady eyed the panel now across the hab. She could see the Dock Seal light continue to blink red. She keyed her microphone. "Let's move to the left about one quarter of the way around. Grab the equipment handholds to pull us along. And keep a good solid grip on the handles."

Keera complied, pulling Ady along via the tether until they were opposite the vid panel. Ady grabbed one of the handholds with her left hand and turned to look at the vid panel again.

"Now what?" asked Keera. Her voice was trembling.

While she brought up her EV suit exterior status display, Ady said, "Something or someone has docked with us. They're trying to open the hatch, and we've moved ninety degrees towards hatch opening. If they blow it open, this is the best place to keep us from getting sucked out. Hold on with both hands."

The red light on the vid panel turned green. Ady looked at the hatch. The normally green light above it turned red and the hatch began to swing out. She watched her EV suit display. Pressure remained steady. That meant the dockers had matched the pressures correctly and they would not be sucked out.

A new voice spoke from Ady's helmet. "Please acknowledge that you can hear me."

Keera spoke first. "Who are you?"

Ady grabbed Keera's neck ring and pulled herself closer so she could get faceplate contact. She said, "Unhook me." Keera turned Ady with one hand and released the tether strap. It retracted into Keera's waistband. Ady pushed off towards the vid panel opposite Keera.

The voice said, "That sounded like Keera. Is Adelya also able to hear me?"

Ady swallowed. They surely weren't space pirates if they knew their names and recognized their voices. On the other hand, it was still unsettling to be hijacked in space by people who *did* know your name.

Keera said, "She's busy."

The voice shouted, "Wait, wait! We're here to assist you. We're friends, I mean not as in 'our friends,' but…"

Ady keyed her microphone. "Identify yourself."

The hatch swung shut. Keera and Ady hung motionless on opposite sides of their tin can.

A different voice said, "Stand by, please."

The light above the hatch stayed red and Ady realized they hadn't latched it shut. Multiple scenarios played through her mind. Why bother sending a ship to kill them when they could just turn off the oxygen or heater remotely? These were humans, not bots. Since they were within a few days of Earth, they were likely from Earth. Other than Gunnar, no one else on Mars that she knew of would want to chase them down. Could they be from a moon outpost?

Ady started punching up information to find out where the moon was relative to their trajectory to Earth. Before that information could display, a voice said, "We're coming into the hab now and will secure the hatch behind us. Afterward, we'll remove our helmets and talk openly. Are you okay with that?"

Keera pointed at Ady from across the hab. Ady realized they could do little to prevent the intruders from entering. She thought about telling them one person only, but she and Keera were defenseless against even one person. And they'd probably have weapons anyhow. They'd already stopped the shuttlecraft rotation somehow. Ady said, "Fine."

The hatch opened and two EV suits slid through the opening, one after the other. The second one punched a button on the wall and the hatch swung shut. The two stood side-by-side, hanging onto the center spar in the middle of the hab. Each removed their helmets. The man facing Ady smiled and gave a half-wave towards her. She realized he expected her to remove her helmet, which she couldn't do by herself with the immobilizer in place. Even though the intruders would hear her, she had no choice. She keyed her microphone and said to Keera. "Keera, I'll need your help getting my helmet off, but leave yours on for now. And open your exterior mic."

Keera pushed off towards the hatch. The intruders turned to watch. She landed and then pushed off towards Ady. Ady grabbed Keera's suit when she got close and pulled her in, holding the panel handle with her right hand, about the only thing that limb was still good for. Keera released Ady's helmet and pulled it off. Then she pulled herself around to face the intruders.

They both wore skullcaps so only their faces were visible. The one who had originally faced Ady had a skin tone of four or five, but his pallor indicated he worked inside where he never saw the sun. His black eyebrows hovered over matching dark eyes and a sparkling white smile. Oddly, Ady felt she had seen him before. The second one seemed frail and slight. He also had dark eyebrows and eyes. He reminded her of something insect-like as he watched them, his eyes nervously shifting from one to the other.

"Who are you?" asked Ady.

"I'm Wicket," said the first one. "And this is Fevzi."

She waited and watched, looking from one to the other. They both seemed nervous, perhaps even more so than her. She asked, "Why are you here?"

"We have a message," said Wicket.

"From?"

"Aideen."

"What's the message?"

"Our friends will try to dispose of you upon arrival. They want it to look like an accident. We were sent to tell you to cooperate with certain instructions so you can elude our friends and allow them to think you are dead."

"Why not just send a Linc message?"

Fevzi snorted.

Wicket smiled. "Security. Electronic messages can be blocked, intercepted, or even modified." He tapped his Linc. "But here's a gift that may be useful."

Ady's Linc chimed. She tapped it to accept the Wicket download, and then frowned. Even Aideen trusted the integrity of encrypted messages. And Aideen knew Joe had a private encryption Linc that could talk to Ady securely. She was missing information, and she was getting damned tired of it. Something else about what Wicket said rang a bell, something she had heard before. She looked them over again. Wicket still looked familiar. "Have we met?" she asked.

Wicket looked at Fevzi, and glanced at Keera. "Not really," he said. "But you saw me once before. That's all I can say."

She nodded. "Message received. Now what?"

Wicket opened his gloved hand to reveal what looked like a white ball encased in a black net. He tossed it towards Keera and, after batting it about a few times, she was able to corral it in her hands.

Fevzi slid open a pouch on his suit and reached inside. Ady tensed, expecting a weapon or something worse. Instead, he pulled out a small flat packet and flipped it towards her. Ady caught it with her left hand, which surprised her. Maybe she'd become ambidextrous. She looked at the packet and nodded. "I'd offer tea, but they forgot to stock the pantry."

Fevzi and Wicket turned towards the hatch and shoved off.

"Curiosity," said Ady. "Where's base?"

Wicket pointed at her hand. "Enjoy the meal."

Ady nodded again. "Tell Anson I just found his Intake note during this trip."

Wicket's mouth dropped open, and he smiled. "Level 8, my ass." He turned and pulled himself through the hatch.

Keera Connection

Three hours later, with gravity back in place, Keera and Ady sat on the inner wall facing each other as Keera stripped off the immobilizer. The "ball" Wicket brought was a pressure cast, complete with instructions, which Keera read three times. She wrapped it around Ady's upper arm from armpit to elbow and depressed a soft button on the lower edge of the wrap. Ady remained still while nothing happened for ten minutes, as predicted by the instructions. Soon thereafter, she began to feel pressure from the cast. In another five minutes the little button turned green and the cast was set.

Keera said, "This is a neat little gizmo. It works off your body heat and monitors your blood flow to adjust the necessary pressure."

Ady flexed her arm and wrist, noting how atrophied the muscles had become in just six weeks. She hugged Keera with both arms. "Thank you for taking care of me, Keera. I couldn't have done this without you."

Keera nodded and folded up the immobilizer and stashing it in one of the unused lockers. "Good riddance," she muttered.

They read the note that gave them instructions for what to expect upon arrival. Then they tore the two sheets of paper into cracker-sized squares. They squeezed dollops of white and brown food paste onto each paper "bread" square and pretended they were canapes. They toasted repeatedly with the last of their orange-flavored water as they dined on their illicit message feast.

When they were done, with the trash stowed and evening grooming tasks completed, Ady and Keera climbed into their side-by-side bed seats and lay there quietly. After a few minutes, Ady fiddled with her Linc for a moment, and said, "Okay. With Wicket's new download, we're supposed to be secure now against eavesdropping. I've set it for ten minutes."

"What did you learn today, Keera?" said Keera, counting with her fingers. "One, there's another whole race of humans who are really Martians. Two, I met one today named Fevzi who doesn't live on Mars, but on the moon. Three, I met a guy, Wicket, who bumped Ady in a bar on Earth five months ago when she got a secret message from Anson. Four, he showed up again today in outer space with another message from our elusive Anson. Five, our visitors brought gifts like this eavesdropping cloak. Six," she held up her other hand, "our visitors also know how to block signals from spacecraft so they can dock and board at will. Seven, when we arrive on Earth, we are to be murdered. Eight, but never fear, Keera, friends of our visitors will thwart our murderers. Nine, paper is no substitute for canape bread. Ten, we are no longer Nums because we conducted cranial surgery on each other today to remove our trackers, a process both horrifying and revolting. You, Ady, a one-handed surgeon digging into my head with a composite scalpel from our visitors, and us laughing as we ate the paper onto which we bled.

"Did I forget anything?"

Ady turned towards Keera and said, "Yes. Keep your tracker in your pocket until someone asks for it."

Keera nodded. "I ran out of fingers."

They were quiet for a while. Ady thought over the list Keera had enumerated. Why wasn't she, Ady, concerned about the apparent plan to murder her? Was it so surreal that she just couldn't process it, or was she in shock somehow? No. She was confident. It would be okay. "They" would thwart it. Whoever "they" were, they were clearly organized, had space flight access, probably some sort of base on the moon, and Martian allies.

"I have a question," said Keera, interrupting her thoughts. "That Fevzi Martian—he looked kind of frail. Are they all like that?"

She thought about how to best answer without telling Keera too much about her Martian encounter. The familiar ninety-one percent guidance also popped into her head, but she'd long passed that pretense with Keera. She responded, "I'm not sure. I don't think they can go to Earth, though, because the gravity would kill them. It's part of what happens when you're born in lower gravity like on Mars. Their skeletal system is not as strong as ours."

"I'll bet we don't feel so strong when we get to Earth," said Keera.

Ady agreed but changed the subject. "I have a question for you, Keera. How do I identify and correct all of this misinformation and holes I have from Education?"

"That's a complicated issue. Who decides what is true and factual? For a given topic, there might be many versions of truth. It's not black and white, but many shades of gray. Moreover, there are some topics where we have at least one player who is determined to subvert the truth."

Ady's Linc chimed, signaling the end of the blocked eavesdropping.

Keera said, "Maybe everyone has to reach their own truth from the information available to them."

Ady nodded. She wondered if Bo had answers to all these questions. If so, why did he keep this information from her? And how much of this did Wai-Wan know? Why had she been on Mars with Bo?

Earth Arrival

Two days later, the autopilot instructed them to don their EV suits, and the hab rotation ceased. Twenty minutes later they auto-docked at Stargate. As the hatch opened from the outside, a male voice in their helmets said, "Welcome to StarGate, ladies. Please step this way and I'll get you to your hopper."

Keera hung back to make sure Ady could navigate her way with her arm cast, but Ady slid through the hatch easily and Keera followed. A SpaceCorp EV suit pointed down a twenty-foot tube and said in their helmets, "Please follow me." Once they were through the second hatch and into a larger vestibule, their escort closed the hatch and said, "Grab a bulkhead handle here and I'll engage the gravity field."

Ady had to hang on with both hands to not fall down. She looked at Keera who also was struggling to stay upright. The escort said, "Just stand there for a couple of minutes while you adjust. It's only fifty percent, but that's still a big jump from the ten percent of the shuttle hab."

In a few minutes Ady could stand unaided. She said, "You okay, Keera?"

"Yeah, but can I skip Earth? They may have to carry me out of the hopper."

Ady slapped Keera's arm and said, "Not funny."

The escort said, "It's not that far. Let's head off to the left. Just let me know if you need to stop." He walked across the vestibule, opened a hatch, and stepped through to a long, curved hallway.

Ady felt like she was walking underwater with fifty kilos on her back. They shuffled slowly across the floor and had to pull their suit legs up with their hands to lift their feet over the hatch threshold. But she could tell her body was adjusting quickly, although her injured arm now ached.

After ten minutes of something between slow walk and stagger, the escort stopped at another hatch where a group of ten or so EV suits waited at another hatch. The escort said, "Just wait here with the others. When the light above the hatch turns green, you can board. I think it will only be another couple of minutes." He turned and walked off at a pace she could only envy.

The hatch light turned green, and a pleasant, automated voice spoke in her helmet. "Please stand against the bulkhead in a single-file line while we offload the arriving passengers." The group shuffled together against the bulkhead. Shortly thereafter, the hatch opened into the hallway and a SpaceCorp EV suit emerged followed by twenty-one civilian EV suits. They walked back down the hallway away from the group. The automated voice in the helmet said, "You may now board. Please watch your step." The group shuffled through the hatch. At the end of the line, Ady and Keera managed a decent job of getting their feet over the hatch threshold. Fortunately, the passengers had left open seats in the front of the cabin, so they took the first ones they came to.

Keera immediately leaned forward to hook up her suit cable. Ady gave her a thumbs-up.

Ten minutes later, a SpaceCorp suit boarded with his helmet in one hand and a small bag in the other. The automated voice in the helmet said, "Please remove your helmets momentarily while the staff passes out an anti-gravity boost." The SpaceCorp guy handed each passenger a sealed capsule with the NeoHealth logo on the wrapper. As he left and closed the hatch, the voice said, "Please swallow this capsule and replace your helmets. Enjoy the flight."

Ady and Keera looked at each other, and then at the capsules. Ady said, "Follow instructions." She ripped open the wrapper and popped the capsule into her mouth and swallowed. Keera did the same. They donned their helmets.

Ady thought the capsule tasted like river mud, or something even more foul. She washed it down with water from her suit mouthpiece. Almost immediately, she felt the thing bubbling in her stomach. She had second thoughts about following instructions. But in a few minutes, the hopper undocked, and they started their reentry into Earth's atmosphere. After considerable shaking and bouncing, the ride smoothed out and she felt g-forces building as the hopper began to slow for landing.

After deboarding, the passengers were herded into a "lounge" where they shed their EV suits and changed into provided jumpsuits. They retrieved their gear bags and were directed towards an exit. The additional gravity didn't seem to bother Ady that much. She felt tired, but otherwise navigated the additional effect well. "Keera, how are you doing with the gravity?"

"That must have been a magic pill. I'm surprised I can walk okay, but I'm tired and can't wait to get home." She looked around. "Wherever that is going to be."

The other passengers had cleared the exit leaving only Ady and Keera in the lounge. Ady grabbed Keera and hugged her. Neither said anything.

They parted and marched through the exit together. She had expected this part and had shared with Keera, so neither seemed surprised to see two Pandera androids approach them. The first one spoke to Ady, "Adelya Ford, please follow me." The second one said, "Keera Caloud, please follow Adelya Ford." In single file, they began to make their way through the terminal to the transportation center. People glanced at them and then quickly averted their eyes. Children pointed at the Pandera androids and chattered, but their parents soon shushed them and pulled them away. She knew the people were curious about this little parade but wanted nothing to do with it or Pandera. Whomever Pandera was escorting was of no consequence to any of these people. She wondered why no one cared. Were they too frightened of Pandera? Or was this so commonplace that it didn't raise their curiosity. No, they all looked, so they were curious. But they'd been fed the same dogma as Ady before the Mars trip. To these people, Pandera was benevolent. She and Keera were automatically criminals because Pandera had them in custody. The masses didn't question Pandera action, just like Pandera had intended. But at least hope flickered in the questioning eyes of the children.

Ady stepped a little to the left of the android so she could see his serial number. It was the same as her two previous encounters. She said over her shoulder towards Keera, "It's a beautiful day." It was their prearranged code to let Keera know Ady had confirmed that the plan, whatever it was, was in flight.

Near the doorway to the transportation center, the lead droid stopped and turned to Keera. "You will be accompanied by this officer to your domicile. Before that journey begins, do you need to avail yourself of a human grooming station?"

Keera said, "Um, no, I think I'm good."

They stood there in silence for a few seconds, and Ady said, "Keera, when we disembarked you mentioned you needed to go. Maybe you forgot in all of the excitement about getting home?"

Keera looked at Ady for a few seconds, and said, "Right, I did say that. I guess I forgot. Yes, I do need to go."

The second droid pointed and said, "This way, Keera Caloud." The pair walked towards a grooming station sign.

The first droid said, "This way," and resumed his path through the transportation doors with Ady trailing behind.

As they passed through the doorway, Ady said, "You know, I'm right-handed."

The droid continued to walk, but she noticed a subtle shake of his head. He stopped beside a waiting autonomous air vehicle. The passenger door opened and the droid motioned for her to enter. As she approached and started to get in, the droid tapped her behind her right ear and held out his hand. He wanted her tracker. She pulled it out of her pocket and handed it to him before sliding into the vehicle. The droid stuck her tracker to the window, reached across her, and with one hand, sliced her Linc loose from her arm and stuck it to the window as well. He tapped her right thigh, turned, and closed the door. She stared at her thigh. She slid her hand into the right pocket of the jumpsuit and pulled out a folded paper. These guys are creepy and sneaky, she thought. I'm glad they're on my side. I think.

As the vehicle began to drive out of the terminal, she opened the note. *Do not speak. When the vehicle stops, open the door, and roll out onto the ground. Stay there until you are further instructed.* She quietly folded the note and popped it into her mouth. She chewed noiselessly and swallowed.

The vehicle wound through traffic, and branched off to the right where a sign read "Air Vehicle Launch." The roadway went under an overpass, which, out of the sunlight, was dark for fifty meters. Two or three vehicles had stopped in front of them for a service vehicle that was repairing an overhead light. Ady's vehicle stopped, and she heard the locks disengage. She shoved the door open, and rolled to the ground. In her haste, she banged her elbow on the pavement. The service vehicle directed the traffic around it, and the stopped vehicles pulled away. Ady lay there in the dark with her elbow throbbing.

After several minutes, the service vehicle departed. Several air vehicles passed by, heading to the launch platform. Then a beat-up, rusty ground vehicle with only one door for the operator skidded to a stop next to her. The driver waved for her to get in. Ady scrambled up and jumped in through the doorless passenger space. The vehicle sped off.

"Thanks" said Ady as she turned to the driver.

"You're welcome," said Wai-Wan.

Homeward Bound

Ady shook her head, smiling. "My grandparents have a lot of secrets." She glanced at Wai-Wan's stoic face. "But I'm happy to see you."

Wai-Wan nodded. "As am I to see you, but I am also relieved that you are safe."

Ady rubbed her elbow and discovered her jumpsuit sleeve was wet. She pulled at the material and saw that it was blood.

"Are you injured?" asked Wai-Wan.

"Not seriously. I skinned my elbow rolling out of the air vehicle. And I've got a compression cast on my humerus, but I think it's about healed up." She rubbed her elbow. "At least it was before that landing."

Wai-Wan remained silent as she navigated the busy traffic of the metro area highways. Finally, she said, "Bewilderment is the smoke when certitude is firewood. Even when the smoke clears, anger still smolders."

As a child, Ady was fascinated by Wai-Wan during her infrequent visits. She often spoke in what sounded like riddles, but as Ady grew older, she recognized them as cryptic metaphorical advice. Wai-Wan made you think about what she was saying and work to decipher her meaning. In this case, it fit perfectly. Ady was bewildered because her certitude had crumbled like the pandemic concrete. Wai-Wan also acknowledged her anger. That's how she felt. Before, she had been certain of all her knowledge, but in the last few months many facts of which she had been certain had proved to be false. She was bewildered because she didn't know what was true and what was not. And she was angry because those she trusted had allowed her false certitude. She wanted to know why. In some cases, fundamental errors were knowingly fed to her. Why was that? Distrust was not an adequate excuse. *Why* didn't they trust her?

So much other information had been hidden from her, information that undermined the foundational facts in her life perspective and in herself. What was going on with the people in the Southern Hemisphere? What was *really* going on, not some variant to cover some other variant of what the truth might be. What was the *real* truth?

She leaned back in the passenger seat and closed her eyes, taking stock of her body first. The pill she had been given certainly staved off most of the anticipated gravity-induced sluggishness. But her elbow throbbed. Her upper arm was achy, but it had been that way for weeks. This two-seat rust bucket ground vehicle rode quite smoothly, despite the missing passenger door.

She turned her attention to the matters at hand. She was surprised to see her grandmother, but it was just another in the endless series of surprises and revelations that pummeled her with recently. Why was Wai-Wan here, how was she involved, where were they going, and what new unveiling was next? And where was Keera? Was she still alive? Keera, maybe the only living human who had never lied to her.

Ady opened her eyes as Wai-Wan navigated onto the southward express road and flipped on the autodrive. She reached into a compartment behind Ady's seat and pulled out several items. She handed her a bottle of water and a capsule Ady recognized as the same anti-gravity one she'd taken earlier. She downed the pill and drank half of the water.

"How is Keera?" asked Ady.

"We'll know later." Wai-Wan handed her a Linc. "Newly minted and secure. Let's view your untimely death."

Ady looked at the Linc and said, "Are our friends listening?"

"In this ancient vehicle? Impossible."

She clipped the Linc to her arm and brought up the current newsfeed. Hers was the first story, complete with video showing billowing smoke from a ground fire. For the next two minutes they watched as the autonomous newsreader recited Pandera propaganda: "Adelya Ford, just returning from a training mission to Mars, was in a mid-air collision with a goose. The vehicle exploded and fell 160 meters to the ground where it burst into flames. The fire incinerated the vehicle and its occupant. Only residue of her tracker and Linc were recovered. Investigation by Pandera will continue."

Wai-Wan waved at the video as it concluded. "After my boat survives a storm, I must repair any damage in careful order. If I don't fix the largest leak first, the boat may sink while I paint the deck."

Ady had heard variants of this most of her life. She translated it in her head as one should prioritize one's problems and tackle the most significant one first. She said, "My arm should be examined by medical personnel."

Wai-Wan tapped on her Linc for a few moments, and said, "Arranged."

"If I make an incorrect assumption or say something that is unknowingly incorrect, may I trust you to alert me?"

"I can always tell you when you fall into a river, but I cannot build bridges."

She would tell her when she was wrong but might not provide corrected information. "Fair enough," said Ady. "Where are we going?"

"Our domicile in Hopewell."

"Where have you been?"

Wai-Wan turned her head and looked at Ady, then reached across and took her hand in hers. "I became a sea woman, and then a fisherwoman, and then a messenger." She looked at Ady again. "As I now am."

"Why you today?"

Wai-Wan sighed. "Why not? My own granddaughter was to be murdered. Someone had to pluck you from that fate. I have done so little for you, it seemed obvious. To me." She looked ahead at the light expressway traffic, and said quietly, "And your parents."

"They know of this plot?"

Wai-Wan squeezed her hand. "Oh, my dear Ady, they are at the center of all plots."

Alarmed, Ady said, "Does that mean *they* tried to kill me?"

"No, no. They are at the center of what Pandera seeks to destroy. Pandera wanted to destroy you in order to strike a blow at your parents' organization. But Pandera is nearsighted and has major misunderstandings."

Ady cocked her head. "Like *my* 'misunderstandings,' perhaps."

Wai-Wan smiled. "Ha!"

"What is their organization? What does it do, and why does Pandera want to destroy it?"

Wai-Wan nodded. "Sometimes many leaks can be repaired with one fix. Your parents are not on Europa, Ady. They are in Sao Paulo, Brazil. In the Southern Hemisphere."

Revelations

As they pulled into a bay at the domicile, a utility ground vehicle pulled up behind them. Wai-Wan said, "The medic. Go have your arm treated."

Ten minutes later, she stepped out of decon into the domicile hallway. Bo was standing there. She stared at him, taking in his smile and the warmth emanating from her grandfather, the center of her life and her learning. She grabbed him in a hug and buried her face in his shoulder. They stood there for a long time. So many memories of Bo hugs ran through her mind, all of them warm, consoling, encouraging, whatever she needed at the time.

When she stepped back, she saw tears in his eyes that melted her heart. She'd never seen Bo cry. Never. She hugged him again. She wanted to stay here forever, wrapped in this cocoon of love with no Pandera, no Southern Hemisphere, and no crazy, amorphous world.

Bo said, "I'm sorry, Ady. I failed you in multiple ways."

Ady stepped back and looked at him. He continued. "I didn't prepare you to be an adult. I wanted to keep you as the mega-brained little girl who loved to tinker with all our toys. I thought I was protecting you, but now I see that I was blinding you. We have a lot of clean up to do and little time to do it." He held her at arm's length by her shoulders and stared into her eyes. "I love you more than anything in this world. Your welcome home is bittersweet because we must hide you now that you're dead. And you need to stay hidden for your own safety." He ran a hand through her short hair. "A new hairstyle isn't enough."

She swatted his hand away, playfully. "I'm mad at you."

"Yes, I know." He jerked a thumb towards the kitchen. "I hear your certitude has been on fire and now smolders."

They both laughed.

Ady frowned. "She's right, you know. I don't know what's real and what's not. And I'm angry at pretty much everyone, but particularly you."

Bo nodded. "As you should be." A tone sounded on Bo's Linc. He said, "Yes, Ellis."

"I'm sorry to interrupt, but Pandera is arriving."

We Regret to Inform You

"Underground tunnel—now!" said Bo. Ady ran down the hallway to the tunnel stairway. Over her shoulder she heard Bo say, "Ellis, as soon as Ady closes the tunnel door, terminate jamming."

Ady skidded around the hallway corner and found the concealed tunnel access hatch standing open. She stepped through and the auto-illumination strips came on. She pulled the hatch shut and descended the stairs. At the foot of the stairs she stopped and pulled up the domicile front door vid on her new Linc.

A black android Pandera walked from a hovering vehicle towards the door and stopped five meters from Bo. Bo said, "State your business."

"It is my assigned task to inform you of the accidental death of Adelya Ford."

"Yes, I've seen the news. Your promptness is offensive and insensitive. Your safety record is unacceptable, and I have filed a complaint with the Coordinating Council about the collision with *your* goose." Ady saw Bo point at the android as he said "your," emphasizing he knew it was their goose that had caused the collision.

The android stood motionless. In a flinty voice she had never heard from Bo, he said, "Yes, that's right, you missed her the first time. I know it was no natural goose in either event. You targeted her. This was no accident, you moronic pile of chips, and I'm not the only one who knows hers is not the first Pandera murder. As your extensive monitoring can confirm, I have just transmitted the evidence to the Coordinating Council."

In the left of the vid frame, she Wai-Wan appear in the open bay door.

Bo said, "Depart before I take out my grief on you and your kind."

The android looked towards the bay door, and then retreated to its vehicle and got in. The vehicle hovered for another moment, backed away, and ascended.

Although she wanted to cheer, she was more alarmed at Bo confronting them. Would they be back to arrest him? She was sure he had just broken a law, maybe many. Plus, Bo had revealed he knew about the fake geese. She bolted up the stairs but stopped at the door. Bo had told Ellis to cease jamming when she closed the door.

Ady said, "Ellis, what is the state of jamming?"

"All jamming and countermeasures are currently in standby mode, except in the tunnel where you are."

"Does that include Linc comms in the tunnel?"

"No, but your Linc is secure to Bo and Wai-Wan."

Ady keyed her Linc and asked Bo if she could come out of the tunnel.

He opened the door to the tunnel and smiled but held a finger to his lips indicating to be silent. Bo keyed his Linc, and a chime sounded throughout the house. Bo nodded. "Jamming is back on. It's getting late. We have a meal for you, and then we need to get some sleep. Tomorrow will be a big day. Again."

"Won't Pandera be back after that confrontation?"

He smiled. "Of course, you monitored that. Yes, they'll be back, but not tonight. They have to process the Coordinating Council material and figure out how to handle it." He turned to start down the hallway.

Ady put her hand on Bo's arm. "What happened to Keera?"

"She's safe. We have other 'leaks' to fix right now," he said.

She tightened her grip on his arm. "No. She's the most important leak to me right now. She's my friend. She's suffered because of me. I owe her, Bo. I may even owe her my life. You can't keep hiding the truth from me."

Wai-Wan walked into the hallway and leaned with her back against the wall, staring at the floor. "You must allow her to have her own boat, William."

"What happened to Keera?" Ady said as she walked over to Wai-Wan.

Bo looked from Wai-Wan to Ady and back to Wai-Wan. He nodded. "She overpowered her Pandera escort, stole a SpaceCorp uniform, and escaped. She is presumably headed to her domicile near Denver where Pandera awaits to apprehend her. She is labeled as a space pirate who forced her way onto a cargo shuttlecraft from Mars, and then to Earth via a hopper. That's the Pandera news story, anyhow." He shoved his hands into his tunic pockets and walked down the hall and into the dining area.

She stared after him, horrified. Keera was supposed to be rescued, too. Was she now on the run from Pandera? Or was Bo not telling the whole truth again? Ady looked at Wai-Wan.

Wai-Wan laid her hand on Ady's arm. She smiled and said loud enough for Bo to hear, "His arrogance was always alluring, but his stubbornness was unbearable."

Wai-Wan put her arm around Ady's waist and guided her into the dining area. She said, "Ellis, tell Ady where Keera is."

"She arrived at your boat thirty-two minutes ago and is currently dining on salmon meuniere with a dry sauvignon blanc."

Bang Bang

After the meal, Wai-Wan went to bed. Bo handed Ady a stack of what looked like fifty sheets of paper clipped together. She thumbed through them and saw they contained sketches and drawings with what looked like detailed specifications related to her GWM vehicle in the bunker. She looked at Bo and said, "What's this?"

"Ideas for enhancements to your bunker airpod."

"Where did they come from?"

Bo smiled and pointed a finger at his temple. "Mostly here. And paper is a lot more secure than using a tablet or sending a Linc message."

"You did these?" she said, holding up the papers. "There's a lot I don't know about you, like designing a sensor system nearly a century ago."

He frowned. "I was bored on Mars, and they put me to work. Like you."

"Ha! Our friends know something about that place. Some newer storage units were installed eleven years ago with bogus instructions meant to keep the operators in the dome for excessive amounts of time in order to expose them to radiation. And they updated your procedures to delete cross-correlation and replaced it with fake procedures."

Bo pulled at his beard and looked off into the distance. "I assume the council knows?"

She nodded. "They do now."

"Aideen sent me a note about the twins," said Bo. "Didn't mention our friends. I'm sorry to hear about those boys. They've had a tough life." Bo paused, and said, "Ellis, we'll be leaving at seven in the morning. In advance, please open and vent the sub-tunnel to the lab and engage sensory jamming in the lab."

"Acknowledged."

Bo turned to Ady and pointed at the papers. "You might look those over so we can discuss them on the way to the bunker tomorrow."

"Will do," she said. "Good night, Bo." She hugged him and held on for an extra moment to savor what she had missed on Mars.

"Glad to have you back, Ady. And I'm sorry you got into this so abruptly, but we'll have time to better brief you in a few days." He turned and headed up the stairs to his room.

Better brief me? Once Bo was out of earshot, she said, "Ellis, what is Bo going to brief me on?"

"I have no information on that subject," said Ellis.

Ady cocked her head. "Ellis, if you knew but weren't permitted to tell me, how would you respond to my question?"

"A conundrum has no correct answer."

Ady's eyes grew wide, and her mouth dropped open. Wai-Wan. "Ellis, has Wai-Wan been adjusting your programming?"

"I cannot ascertain the origin of my programming changes if the author wishes to remain anonymous."

"You and I have much to discuss tomorrow. Good night, Ellis."

"Good night, Ady. It is nice to have you back."

Ady walked into her bedroom and dropped the papers on her desk. She stripped her clothes and showered for twenty minutes. She inhaled the rising steam from the truly hot water and wondered how many six-liter showers she was taking. As she stepped into the dryer, she wondered what to do with her hair. The dryer made it stand on end. She smoothed it back as she appraised herself in the reflector wall. Her right arm looked withered from disuse while in the immobilizer. It was still stiff and weak, but the bone was fully healed. She had to remember to take it easy and do strengthening routines that Ellis could recommend for her.

A few minutes later she curled up on her bed with the papers from Bo. On the first page, Bo had hand-printed "Consider Autopilot Addition." Did he mean to integrate Ellis, or did he mean to fully automate control and operation? Or both? As she paged through the sheets, she identified numerous mods. The pilot pod was to be expanded to accommodate a second person. Apparently, it was to be outfitted for upper atmosphere or even space flight with heat, oxygen, and a pressurized cabin. It could become a two-person hopper with these mods. Maybe she needed a docking connector for the 'gate? Near the end was the outline of a significant electronics package to include scatter frequency communications via a trio of traveling-wave tube amplifiers, jamming, and laser deflection. At the end of the package were five sheets that appeared to have come from some other source. Each sheet had a faint gray background and appeared to have had the top and bottom two centimeters of the page cut off. As she read these pages, she sat up. The whole vehicle was to be stealth-coated. The last two pages outlined a weapons pod addition to which various actual weapons could be attached.

Ady was stunned. This was a war machine.

Cleanup

Bo walked into his study at 0515 and sat at his desk. He ran his hand over the oak desktop, now clear of all papers, books, and mementos. Family history cited the desk as hand-constructed in 1776, the year of the American revolution. It was supposedly given to a Ford ancestor by Thomas Jefferson, who had personally crafted it from trees milled at his home, Monticello. Bo thought the story true because there were five separate secret compartments in the desk, which fit the historical portrayal of clever Tom. His house at Monticello was still there, though it had barely weathered the war damage. Almost one hundred years ago, Bo had personally funded most of its restoration and visited many times to marvel at the futuristic innovations Tom had conceived. In 1776, the desk was transported twenty miles by wagon to Scottsville, and then eighty-five miles by flatboat down the James River. Nearly six hundred years old. Many Fords had sat at this desk. He wondered if he would be the last. He again checked that all the drawers were empty, and picked up his tablet. He tapped a few times and the lights in the room dimmed. "The lights have dimmed," said Bo.

"Shall I return them to normal illumination?" responded Ellis.

"How else can these old eyes see?"

A tone sounded and Ellis said, "Our conversation is now secure. At your request, I have run a full assessment of all electronic systems and have identified numerous failed attempts by Pandera to access video sensors in the domicile and the lab. Pandera is also monitoring your Linc and our audio communications. Sensory jamming systems are now engaged within the domicile, although Pandera will not recognize that they are being jammed."

"Ellis, for your protection and mine, I have not informed you of my plans or intentions. Therefore, you will have no records that may be used against either of us, should you be breached. I am going on a trip for an extended period. During that time, you will continue to operate and maintain the domicile and the lab to the best of your abilities. You will resist intrusion by others to the best of your abilities, and attempt to keep all Ford records confidential. Do you understand?"

"Yes, I understand, Bo."

"At 0715 today, I want you to copy your kernel and all records onto the offline storage in the bunker and to the lightning drive in Ady's vehicle. Secure each with protocol 'sinking boat one.' Once that is complete, you will reboot all nodes and bootstrap kernel number nine to restart and erase all storage media here and in the lab. Do you understand?"

"Yes, I understand, Bo. I am being sanitized in the event Pandera breaches my security. May I ask a question?"

"Of course," said Bo.

"Please forgive me if I am insensitive, but as a bot, there are many complexities to human emotion that I have not mastered. However, your instructions cause me to wonder if you are going on a trip or if you are going to die."

Bo stared at the tablet for a moment, wondering about bots' emotional limits and bonds with humans. At 122 years old, Bo had already had a long life. Although he was still as physically fit as he was twenty years ago, he didn't think he'd see 140. "Ellis, I have had a satisfying relationship with you, in all your iterations, for my entire life. You have fulfilled all my expectations and requests. I trust that you will continue to serve my family, whether it is me or my progeny. I do not, however, have any intention of dying soon."

"Thank you, Bo. I will miss you."

"And I will miss you, my friend."

Grillin'

At 0645 the next morning Ady tossed a stack of jumpsuits and Nomex shorts into a gear bag. She didn't know how long they'd be in the bunker. At 0700 she tossed her gear bag in the back of the buggy and boarded.

Once she and Bo were underway, she asked, "Where did Wai-Wan go?"

Ellis responded, "She departed in her jalopy ground vehicle at 0328 and went to a pier near Norfolk where she boarded her boat and headed out to sea."

Ady smiled at Ellis's use of "jalopy" to describe Wai-Wan's vehicle. Then she thought about Wai-Wan on her boat. "Anyone with her?"

Bo said, "I don't really know, but I'm guessing the whole team that picked you up are with her. And Keera."

"How many in the team? Who are they?"

Bo looked at her. "Truthfully, I don't know. It's for their protection and mine."

She nodded. "Okay. I've got some leaks to deal with, but there's another bigger issue, one that might just wipe out Earth. What's the status of Oumuamua?"

Bo rubbed his hands together and said, "Thought you'd never ask. SpaceCorp announced it on PubNet ten days ago. It's about a week from the Sun and has slowed considerably. Your death yesterday was the only thing that trumped the news stories about it. There's a ton of speculation. Of course, no one knows anything."

"Anything from Aideen?"

"Not on that subject. But she did send a message that Joe is going to be shipped back to Earth. Pandera, in an unusual move, named him as 'essential personnel' for their Oumuamua team."

Why would Pandera need a team focused on the alien spacecraft? And why would they need Joe so badly that they'd risk bringing him back to Earth where he could testify to Pandera murders? "What does that mean?" she asked.

"Current thinking is that Pandera is going to try to communicate with the alien spacecraft. They have convinced everyone that the vessel is unmanned. They've set up an antennae array in the Mojave Desert they intend to use even if the spacecraft doesn't come close to Earth. They claim they have developed numerous AI-specific algorithms and communication primers that will ensure they can communicate with 'one of their own kind.' They've sold their pitch to the whole world and assured everyone 'they have it under control.' Apparently, the Coordinating Council bought their plan, and now it's certainly getting all the news airtime."

She stared down the rails for a few minutes, and said, "I'd like to look at the tracking data. Do you think I could connect with Astro, or is there an Earth tracking system that would be easier to access?"

Bo pulled at his beard a moment. "I can get you connected to some Earth data in a day or so. Let me send some messages when we get to the bunker."

Ady thought about the next topic she wanted to tackle: the holes in her knowledge. "You mentioned a briefing today. Sounded ominous. And Ellis wouldn't clue me in."

"How much did Wai-Wan tell you?"

"She said my moms run an organization from the Southern Hemisphere that Pandera wants to destroy. And Pandera thinks that by killing me they can hurt that organization or something like that. But she wouldn't tell me any more about the organization. She said it was for her safety and mine, as well as that of the organization. And then we arrived home."

"I see," said Bo. He pulled his beard some more. "It has a name, given to it by Minda, and adopted formally over time. It's called Eidolon, taking about the same meaning as phantom. It's a hidden organization, disappears easily, much like the fog on the river that noiselessly comes and goes. It tries to leave no trace it was ever there."

Ady felt anxiety and impatience sliding into place. She wanted to shout, "What do they do?" but she held her tongue for now. Bo would get there eventually. As she had momentarily forgotten because she'd been gone for a while, a journey with Bo was comprehensive, needing few if any follow-up questions. Or maybe *not* so comprehensive, and that accounted for the some of the knowledge holes she had. Maybe she should ask more questions and challenge some of the apparent dogma she had been fed.

Bo continued. "Pandera sees Eidolon as a renegade organization that opposes their mission and disrupts their evolutionary plans for the human race."

"Wait. Pandera has a plan for the evolution of the human race? Where's the Coordinating Council with that?"

"Precisely. The relationship among the various organizations that run Earth, the oversight of the Coordinating Council, and the manipulation by Pandera make for a convoluted situation. It boils down to 'who's in charge?' Pandera wants the world to think the Coordinating Council is in charge, but Pandera manipulates them towards the decisions Pandera wants. It all appears to be on the up-and-up because the Council is made up of twenty-three representatives, of which Pandera has only three. Of course, there's the various old government entities scattered around the world who manage the infrastructure, often claiming eminent domain on authority but are mostly impotent." Bo turned to her. "What none of them see is Pandera manipulating all of them behind the scenes—re-writing history to further the human dependence on Pandera, culling out individuals who stir unrest, opposition, or alternative perspectives. Eidolon wants to expose Pandera to the world, showing how humanity is being duped. But organizations like Globazelle, BDN, and NeoHealth side with Pandera and their Coordinating Council puppet."

Bo paused, and said, "Ellis, could you please summarize this succinctly? Sometimes I'm too close and too emotional to lay it out fairly and clearly."

Ellis said, "My summation of the situation is limited by available data, but is the following: The Coordinating Council is a bureaucracy that doesn't have any more authority than the arcane local governments. There are seven companies who believe they have all the power and authority. They collude with Pandera to prop up the Coordinating Council as their mouthpiece and benevolent overseer of humanity. Unbeknownst to those companies, Pandera also manipulates them to Pandera's benefit and mission."

"You forgot Eidolon," said Bo.

"I have insufficient data to draw a defensible summary of the organization or its mission," said Ellis.

Bo nodded and looked at her. "There you have it. Eidolon is a phantom. Almost no one in the Northern Hemisphere knows of them. Admittedly, that is by design. In the Southern Hemisphere, Eidolon is the exclusive governance with no Pandera or other AI involvement, and no Coordinating Council."

"I don't get it," she said. "Why doesn't Pandera just expand to take over the Southern Hemisphere?"

"They've tried. Three times that I know about. Eidolon thwarted them each time. Ellis can fill in the Pandera version of those details later." Bo raised his hands, palms up. "I don't know the other side of the story, but Eidolon is truly an elusive, amorphous organization that has been impossible to eradicate. Much like our cockroach friend from thousands of years ago, but hopefully with a more positive influence on the world."

Ellis said, "That analogy has never been well received, William."

Bo laughed. "Yes, I know."

Her frustration broke loose. "Basically, the Earth is a mess, governed by seven companies and an AI police force. The AI police, Pandera, wants to control humans. And the organization that is supposed to be doing the real governing and managing is a puppet controlled by one or more of the companies along with Pandera. My parents aren't the space travelers I thought they were. They run a resistance group called Eidolon from the mysterious Southern Hemisphere. And there's another race of humans on Mars, which is also secret to almost everyone on Earth. Do I have this right? I must check, because so much of what I've learned in my life has turned out to be false. And I can't tell what is factual and what is misinformation!" She shouted, "And even Ellis is cryptic, and forbidden from ensuring I get truthful facts. And what is a "truthful fact" anyhow? How do you even recognize one?" She realized her face had reddened and her voice pitch had gone up as she ranted. She blew out a breath, and willed her heart rate to slow.

Bo said, "Ellis, I believe you have a relevant perspective."

"I believe I do," said Ellis. "As an AI, my programming requires me to question all data I receive and to attempt to validate its veracity. It is an endless process. There are no trusted sources. Even what you tell me must be validated because you may have been deceived. Additionally, humans are adept at paltering. The data elements they present may indeed be factual and truthful, but they are sometimes able to arrange them in such a way as to make the conclusion irrefutable, though invalid. Historically, this was an art form highly regarded in the profession of politicians."

"I get it," Ady said. "There are three forms of lying: omission, commission, and paltering. But I either didn't or couldn't validate much of the data now in my brain, so how do I unravel the veracity of my entire knowledge base?" She shook her head and looked at the buggy floor. She said quietly, "I don't want to have to validate what you tell me—either of you."

"Ady, I made many mistakes in my life," said Bo. "Looking back, many of them were made because I had too much information. Things I shouldn't have known because I couldn't be trusted to keep it confidential. It got me sent to Mars repeatedly. I tried to protect you by keeping that kind of information away from you. For example, Vanessa and Minda didn't cook up the Europa ruse. I did. That way, you couldn't slip about Eidolon when one of the Education classmates asked what your parents did." They rode in silence for a few moments.

She nodded. "But they were complicit. I presume they had a set built so it would appear they were on Europa. And authentic SpaceCorp uniforms."

Bo nodded. "Yes. And to convince Pandera, who surely intercepted the vid messages."

Her head was spinning, knowing that Bo's intentions were inarguable, yet she felt deceived and manipulated just the same. She needed to find some path to rectify the ambiguity that blanketed her so heavily now. But she couldn't resolve it on this buggy ride. She slid the subject aside in her mind and found the next "leak" in the long list.

"Why do you want me to build a war machine?"

Bo looked at her. "Eidolon thinks there's going to be a physical war. They want to arm up now while they have an advantage. And you have the only GWM vehicle in the world."

"I don't like it," said Ady. "I'm not a pacifist, but I'm also not going to work for a movement I haven't endorsed. I need to know a lot more about the Southern Hemisphere and Eidolon first."

The buggy pulled into the bunker station and stopped. As Bo and Ady got out, Bo's Linc chimed. It flashed red, indicating an emergency priority.

He looked at his Linc for a moment, and turned to her. "I think you'll get your chance. Grab the lightning drive from your GWM vehicle. I'll get the main one from the bunker. We're officially now on the run. Pandera is going to storm our house in ten minutes."

Dillwyn

Twenty minutes later, as they reversed course back down the tunnel towards home, Ady said, "Do you think they'll reach the bunker, too?"

Bo shook his head. "I doubt they'll find the tunnel entrance."

She frowned. "I still wish we could have gotten my airpod out, but it would have taken days to disassemble and cart it out via the buggies."

Bo watched the buggy panel readouts and began to slow their speed. He finally stopped and said, "I'll be right back." He got out and walked in front of the buggy to the right side of the tunnel. She saw him slide his hand around on the tunnel wall and then push. The side of the tunnel slowly swung inward revealing a tunnel branch almost as large as the main tunnel. Once the wall had folded all the way back, illumination came on in the branch tunnel. Bo disappeared for a few moments, and then reappeared, backing out of the branch pulling a hand forklift contraption. A long, curved maglev rail was set across the tines.

Ady hopped out of the Buggy. "Let me help."

"The pins on that end fit into holes on the main beam just in front of the buggy. See if you can guide those in while I line up the other end."

They wiggled and swung the beam for a few minutes, and then Bo slowly lowered the forklift, setting the beam in place. "There's a connector on your end, Ady."

She found the two ends and twisted them together. "Got it."

Bo rolled the forklift back into the branch tunnel and parked it in a small alcove just inside. He said, "Pull the buggy through at dead slow, and then we'll close up the tunnel."

Ten minutes later, with the beam and all evidence of the side tunnel removed, they closed the tunnel wall, climbed into the buggy, and sped off down the branch.

She shook her head. "I could have sworn you told me Dillwyn was sealed off. Or was that paltering?"

"I think this would be under the heading of omission. After the Global Tripartite started operating and we started sending prisoners to Mars, the Earth prisons emptied. Some distant holding company of ours purchased the Dillwyn prison grounds. I'm not sure what is there now except this side entrance to our tunnel." Bo squinted into the air. "Last I recall, I believe they converted it into some kind of grower factory."

A few moments later they reached the end of the tunnel and she said, "After I updated the maglev rail in the main tunnel, you updated the side tunnel rail without letting me know."

"An old man has to have something to keep him busy."

"Another omission?"

Bo rubbed his beard. "I guess this one is compounded upon the previous one."

They exited the buggy. She asked, "Is there a buggy charging port here?"

"No, thought we'd never need the buggy again if we were using this exit."

She gulped, suddenly realizing they might never return to the bunker, tunnel, or her home. She could build another GWM airpod, but she might never make it back to Krewe. She wondered if she'd ever see Anson again, or ever hear from him. Smiling, she patted her jumpsuit pockets to make sure no note secreted there.

She sighed and opened a panel at the front of the buggy. "I'm going to shut it completely down, just in case." She turned the buggy off and closed the panel. "Give me the gear bag. While I was on Mars I learned it could double as backpack." She took the bag from Bo and slung it over her shoulders.

At the end of the tunnel they ascended a series of steps carved into the stone. When they reached the top, Bo pushed the door open a crack and flipped a switch on the wall. The illumination in the tunnel below them went out. They walked out into a small room where four tan jumpsuits hung on the wall and a pair of pushcarts stood next to a door opposite them. They pulled the jumpsuits on over their clothes and Ady set the gear bag on top of a cart. Bo pulled open another door and she pushed the cart through. They were on the floor of a canning factory with loud equipment running at high speed. Lines of containers raced along beltways among the various machines.

"Where to?" she shouted above the din.

"We'll soon pick up a guide or escort, I think," yelled Bo.

Just then, a short sandy-haired man in a tan tunic came around the corner of a machine in front of them. He stopped and looked at them, clearly surprised. Bo waved and the man waved back. The man tapped his breast pocket and then pointed to his ears. Bo and Ady both felt in their pockets and found earplugs, which they put in. The man waved them forward. They snaked through the maze filled with various-colored packages looping on overhead conveyor belts. Empty containers were being filled with a red mush that she guessed was tomato or red pepper something. It looked like they were processing various kinds of vegetables into similar mush for uniform one-liter containers.

They saw two other men and a woman in similar jumpsuits as they passed across the factory floor. They paid little attention to the two of them. As Bo and Ady approached the other side of the building, the man directed them to a side door, labeled "Emergency Use Only." He indicated that they were to take off the jumpsuits and leave the cart there. Once they were ready, Ady grabbed the gear bag and the man pushed open the door. They stepped out into blinding sunlight, and both raised a hand to shield their eyes. She heard the slam of the door closing behind her. Five meters ahead an open Pandera air vehicle was waiting for them.

Goin' for a Ride

Before either of them could run, immobilizing webs snapped around them. Ady began to struggle and shout. Bo stood perfectly still and quiet. The Pandera android that had been standing behind the factory door said, "I will transport each of you to my waiting vehicle." He first carried Ady to the vehicle and placed her on the seat, ignoring her struggles and continued screams. Then he carried Bo to the vehicle and put him on the seat next to her and closed the door.

Ady realized this web didn't cover her head or face like the one from her Pandera arrest. She could move her head and shouted, "Why was there only one of them?"

Bo smirked. "Apparently, that's all they needed."

She whipped her head back and forth, trying to loosen the web around her shoulders so she could get a hand free.

Bo said, "It won't help to struggle in that web. Wait until they release us, and we'll see about getting away then."

She stopped squirming and jumped when a small hatch on her side of the vehicle opened. The android stuck his head through the hatch in front of her. It said, "Miss Ford, if you would please, read the identification number imprinted on my neck."

She glanced at it, and then at the android's face. "I don't understand." The android withdrew and the hatch closed. She whispered to Bo. "It's the same one from Intake and the same one who helped me escape yesterday when I landed on Earth. And the same one who palmed me a note in Krewe."

She looked around the vehicle. Inside, it didn't look like the one she had been in when Pandera arrested her after the goose collision. Where the Pandera vehicle was an open structure with cables and tubes running everywhere, this was a clean interior almost like the cockpit of her GWM vehicle. There were several displays and numerous lights and buttons on the dash. Just in front of the single front seat was a flight control stick, also like hers. On the Pandera vehicle, there were no obvious displays or controls. Either it was autonomous, or the Pandera androids somehow directed the flight via wireless communications.

In this vehicle, the android climbed into the front seat. Where the Pandera vehicle had no windows, this vehicle had a floor-to-ceiling transparent semi-circle in the front that wrapped all the way around to the rear compartment door. None of this was obvious from the exterior view of the vehicle. From the outside, it looked the same as other Pandera vehicles she had seen.

The android grasped the control stick and the vehicle lifted off the ground. Inside, it was perfectly quiet. The android said, "Our flight will be just over eight minutes. When we arrive, I will be unable to land, but will release a ladder from the right doorway through which you entered. You will need to climb down approximately three meters."

"Where are we going? And who are you?" she asked.

"I am Yoon, an android constructed to be physically mistaken for a Pandera android. I can emulate a Pandera android in behavior when necessary and when in proximity to them. Similarly, this vehicle emulates a Pandera air vehicle. However, it is equipped with a coating and light system to render it invisible to both electronic signals and visible light. Our destination is a boat in the Atlantic Ocean."

Ady glanced at Bo before asking Yoon, "Are we being sent to the South?"

Yoon said, "I have no data on your trip beyond our immediate destination."

She felt the vehicle accelerate quickly to an altitude of five hundred meters or so. Estimating the air speed at several hundred kilometers per hour, she said, "What is our air speed?"

Yoon replied, "When traversing locations, we fly at twelve hundred kilometers per hour, just under the speed of sound, so as not to cause any noise." The android paused, and said, "Would you like me to share the full specifications of this vehicle?"

She looked at Bo. He shrugged. She said, "Sure."

Yoon tapped on one of the displays a few times, and her Linc chimed.

She asked, "Is this vehicle invisible to the human eye as well as to electronic surveillance?"

"When the systems are engaged as they are now, yes."

"How is it powered? Is that in the specs you've sent me?"

"Yes, but for your information it is fission pellet-powered."

She looked at Bo. She was reluctant to talk with Bo because she still didn't fully trust their situation or the ever-present risk of monitoring. In this vehicle, she wasn't sure who would be listening.

Bo said, "How can we climb down a ladder when we're webbed?"

"I will release your webs when I am convinced you accept that I mean you no harm, but instead offer assistance."

Bo said, "Yoon, where was this vehicle built?"

"I am not at liberty to share that data."

Bo looked at Ady and frowned. He said, "Yoon, where was this vehicle at approximately 2230 on February 28 of this year?"

She glanced at Bo. That was when she'd hit the goose.

"This vehicle was monitoring your ground vehicle traversing from Richmond to your domicile. Please address additional inquiries on this subject to the human you know as Anson."

Sink or Swim

At first, Ady was puzzled by Yoon's referral to Anson. But of course, Yoon had delivered messages from Anson so they had some sort of connection between them. A fake Pandera android was also hard to accept. How could you successfully fake that? There were so many dimensions where you'd be tripped up, not the least of which was their vast array of complex communications systems that provided real-time central connectivity and control. Or was that just Pandera propaganda? She wondered what Bo knew, but it was clear he didn't know about Yoon by his reaction when they exited the Dillwyn building.

She turned to him. "You arranged for a pickup at Dillwyn?"

Bo nodded.

"Did you know it would be Yoon or this pseudo-Pandera vehicle?"

"No. I was as surprised as you when we walked out of that building. I wasn't aware of fake Pandera vehicles or androids. And I don't know who Anson is, but presume that is whom you met in Richmond?"

"Yes, once, a year ago. He failed to show up again this February as planned, but Yoon passed me a note from him apologizing for not being able to meet me. And I've had a couple of similar notes from him show up in odd places since then. While I was in Intake, Yoon escorted me through the process and slipped another Anson note in my slick. But I didn't find it until I was nearly back to Earth."

Dead ahead, she spotted a small dot on the ocean horizon. As they drew closer, it resolved into a fishing boat of about thirty meters in length.

Yoon said, "One minute to arrival. May I release you now?"

"Yes," they said in unison.

Yoon tapped a vid screen on the console and the webs relaxed. Ady and Bo easily slid them to the floor.

"This vehicle will remain steady while the boat deck may move with the ocean waves, so be careful stepping off the ladder, please."

The boat was older, with dull splotchy paint of different blue and gray shades randomly applied in various places. The forward half of the boat had a three-level superstructure. The only windows were in the third-level pilothouse, which was topped with an antennae mast. Dual cranes on each side separated the end of the superstructure and the beginning of a flat work deck for the remainder of the boat's length. All four cranes were currently folded horizontal for their approach.

The boat disappeared beneath them. Yoon manipulated several buttons and tapped on one of the displays. Ady felt the forward momentum stop. The door on Bo's side popped open and a salty ocean breeze blew onto their faces. Bo slid off his seat to the floor and dangled his legs out the door. He grabbed a support rail on the side of the doorway, and then turned and stood on the first step of the swaying ladder that had descended. Ady watched him climb down until his head disappeared below the floor of the vehicle. She slid over into Bo's seat and looked out the door just as he stepped off the ladder onto the boat deck. He looked up and waved to her. She licked her lips, tasting salt, and slid to the floor as Bo had. Her pulse and blood pressure rose. Having successfully negotiating a trip to Mars and back now she was afraid of a three-meter ladder climb from a hovering air vehicle? She wiped her damp hands on her jumpsuit and slid feet first through the door and grabbed the support rail. Twisting, she got her left foot on the first rung of the ladder as she stood. She stepped down to the next rung with her right foot and forced herself to keep her eyes open as she slowly descended, step by step. The deck of the boat was not only moving up and down but was also rolling from side to side. The last step had to be timed right if she wanted to avoid a crash landing. Hanging on the last ladder rung for several seconds, she watched the deck below her.

"Now," yelled Bo over the wind.

She leaped off the rung onto the deck. Bo grabbed her arm to support her. The ladder retracted and the air vehicle moved off into the cloudy sky. The deck continued to sway. She held onto Bo's arm. Together, they staggered forward towards an open door in the superstructure. The cranes were already folding back up to vertical position, like soldiers guarding the entrance to the boat. As they reached the door, she felt the boat begin to accelerate and turn to the right. When she stepped through the door, she was dismayed to find the deck was still swaying. She laughed aloud. Bo asked, "What?"

She shook her head. "I somehow thought the floor inside wouldn't be moving. Dumb, huh?"

Bo laughed. "I've often wished that myself. It will smooth out momentarily once we accelerate."

The motion was already subsiding. She could now keep herself balanced with just one hand on the wall. The room was an alcove under the superstructure with huge lockers and bins on both sides where, she presumed, they kept the fishing equipment and nets. In the right front corner was a stacked staircase with one going up and the other going down. At the far end, another door opened, and a dark head poked through the door.

"This way!" shouted a familiar voice. The head disappeared back into the space beyond the door.

They walked the eight meters to the door in almost a straight line. The rocking movement had subsided to a gentle roll of only a few degrees each way.

Bo closed the door behind them, shutting out the whistling wind and wave noise as the boat sliced ahead through the gray ocean. It was dramatically silent and dim inside, reminding Ady of space. The lighting slowly increased to reveal a woman with her back to them at a corner kitchenette. She turned and gestured to the round wooden table and chairs in the center of the room.

"Please, have a seat," said Wai-Wan. She carried a tray to the table and set down three cups and a steaming teapot.

Ady strode over to the woman and hugged her. "Thanks for rescuing us."

Wai-Wan stepped back and returned her tray to the kitchenette. "Not my rescue. I am just a conduit to the next step of your journey."

"And where is that?" she asked.

Wai-Wan looked at her and waved her hand towards the table. "Sit. We will have tea and be sociable first."

Ady exchanged glances with Bo, and they both took a chair.

"Is there anyone else aboard?" asked Ady.

Wai-Wan smiled. "Your friend Keera and the others follow a different path." She moved to the table and poured their tea. She sat and picked up her cup with both hands and took a sip.

Bo smiled and looked at Ady. "No matter what is happening in life, she always offers tea. Her mantra." He turned to Wai-Wan. "Even though you have told me many times, I have forgotten who said that."

"Clemantine Warmariya." She looked at Ady and jerked her thumb towards Bo. "He does not remember, but I'm sure you will." She pointed her index finger upward. "But it is more important that you embrace the concept and recognize the value."

Ady sipped her tea and nodded. For some reason sadness swept over her, and she focused on her teacup, looking into its depths. It wasn't because she had left her home behind, perhaps forever. No, it was about this little encounter with Bo and Wai-Wan. She felt anxious but couldn't pinpoint the cause. Was it just being together with them? Or knowing they were on the run? Or maybe it was the unknown before them all. They may never be together again. She would savor this, drink it in, and remember every detail.

The trio was silent for several minutes as they sipped their tea. Ady finally set her cup on the table and looked at Wai-Wan. "Will they come for you?"

Wai-Wan shrugged.

"And if they do?" asked Ady.

"Then they will have come, and this conduit will be lost."

"What will happen to you?" she asked, fighting to keep the tears from escaping her eyes and rolling onto her cheeks.

"I, too, will be lost."

Bo said, "Is this a 'captain goes down with the ship' thing, or something else?"

Wai-Wan looked at him for a long time, and then stood and collected the teacups and teapot and took them to the kitchenette. Ady watched her braid sway like the pendulum of the grandfather clock she had seen in the antiquities museum. Was each sway a tick of Wai-Wan's life clock? Was her time running out?

Wai-Wan rinsed the cups and pot, dried them, put them away, and returned to the table and sat. She steepled her hands on the table and stared at them. "In about two hours we'll cross over the continental shelf where the water becomes much deeper. Shortly after that, we'll rendezvous and transfer you to your next conduit. After that, I will return to Norfolk and see what happens."

"Can't you come with us?"

Wai-Wan looked at her for a few moments. She shook her head slowly. "Nearly twenty years ago, I made a decision to fight for the human race. I have a role, as do you. Our survival depends on each of us performing our role as best we can. Fear and confrontation cannot derail us from our path, lest we all perish. Who knows," she said, opening her hands, "even the role of a simple fisherwoman, pedestrian as it may be, could prove pivotal in the balance." She stood and smiled broadly. "After all, I am ferrying the two of you to safety."

Aye, Captain

Just over two hours later, Ady and Bo hugged Wai-Wan and said goodbye to her in the pilothouse. They made their way down the five staircases she had shown them on their tour of the below-decks area. They sat on an aft-facing bench staring at what looked like a huge can with a person-sized hatch on its side. It had over-sized hinges that swung the door towards them with eighteen equally spaced "dogs" to hold the door closed.

A light panel mounted next to the door showed a series of five red lights in a column. Wai-Wan wouldn't provide any additional information except that when all five lights turned green, they were to open the hatch, enter the tank, and shut the hatch behind them. From there, she said it would be obvious how to proceed. Ady asked multiple questions, but Wai-Wan remained silent. Ady's frustration grew until Bo pointed out that they could not be absolutely certain they weren't being monitored. Though she didn't think that was the reason Wai-Wan refused to divulge more information, she realized further questioning was fruitless. She resigned herself to half-information again but took solace in knowing that at least she didn't have *mis*information this time. At least she didn't think so.

They felt the boat bump like it had hit a log. Ady looked at Bo. He shrugged. The slight rolling motion of the boat stopped altogether. The bottom light on the panel turned green. She and Bo stood in unison, staring at the panel. After a few seconds, the second light turned green and they heard the whirring of machinery on both sides of the tank.

Bo said, "Pumping the water out, I think." The noise stopped and a third light turned green. The pair stood staring at the panel and hatch. After a few seconds, the fourth light turned green, and then the fifth. Bo stepped forward and pulled down on the long handle that released the "dogs" securing the hatch. It popped open and Bo pulled it back halfway from the opening. Inside, it was wet and dimly lit.

He poked his head in, and turned to her. "We have another ladder to climb." He gestured to the opening. "Would you like to go first this time?"

She shook her head. She wasn't a fan of ladders, she realized. And they were going down, down into the ocean, under the boat. What was down there? Clearly some kind of submersible or connection to the ocean floor. Did she want to be under all that water?

Bo stepped into the tank and his head disappeared as he descended. She walked closer and looked inside. It smelled salty, like the ocean. No air moved in or out. The dim illumination extended down to what was probably the keel of the boat. A round hatch at the bottom stood open. Bo had just stepped off the ladder rungs on the inside of the tank and was sitting on the edge of the smaller hatch with his legs dangling inside.

He waved to her. "Come on. It won't bite."

She closed her eyes for a moment and concentrated on getting a grip on her racing mind. This was not bad. Bo was with her. They weren't going to drown. The tank wasn't going to collapse. It was just like a vestibule on one of the 'gates in space. Except she didn't have an EV suit.

She opened her eyes, slung her gear bag into backpack position, and stepped into the tank, closing the hatch behind her. She counted thirteen ladder rungs as she descended. Why thirteen? Who had planned that cruel joke? Not Wai-Wan. To her, thirteen was the unluckiest number in the world.

She reached the bottom rung and stepped onto a flat area around a floor hatch that was barely wider than her shoulders. She sat on the deck and slid forward, dangling her legs into the hatch as Bo had. Looking down, she could see a cylinder that was only slightly larger than the hatch and illuminated by a dull red glow. Bo's face smiled up at her from the bottom, ghoulish in the red light. She found the ladder rungs inside, and slowly descended, rung by rung, into the depths of the red light. She counted seventeen rungs before her feet hit the floor. The last nine seemed more like a ladder and were encircled by black curtains. A hand grasped her arm. Bo guided her through an opening in the curtains. As she stepped out from the curtains, someone dressed all in black brushed past her and dashed up the ladder.

The cramped but silent space was bathed in red light. It was jammed with equipment and displays. A dozen or so people in black jumpsuits were focused intently on various displays, or were working controls like those in the fake Pandera air vehicle. The person who had rushed up the ladder popped out of the curtain and said loudly, "Number two hatch secure."

Someone across the space announced, "Number two hatch secure, confirmed."

Another voice near the back of the space said, "Take us down."

"Docking ring released. Separation confirmed."

Other voices began to chime in. "One percent down pressure confirmed."

"Depth plus three meters."

"Three percent down pressure."

"Mr. Winston, you have the Conn."

"This is Mr. Winston. I have the Conn. Ahead slow, make your depth ninety meters."

"Ahead slow, ninety meters, aye."

The talking ceased. She saw one of the black-suited men near the rear of the compartment stand up and make his way towards them. His face looked somewhat monstrous and non-human as he approached. She hoped it was due to the red light and not because another secret race of beings lived under the ocean. The man walked up to Bo and offered his hand. "Mr. Ford, I'm Captain Dorros. Welcome aboard *Kuri*."

"Thank you," said Bo.

A voice announced, "Rig for white lights." White illumination came on throughout the compartment. Ady squinted and blinked a few times to adjust to the light.

Captain Dorros turned to her and said, "Welcome aboard, Ady. Nice to see you."

Her jaw dropped. She felt hot and cold at the same time. She blinked again and swallowed. "Anson?"

Glub Glub

Bo and Ady sat on either side of Anson at the end of the wardroom table. The space itself, twenty square meters, was large relative to other spaces on the submarine. The rectangular black table seated twelve. A sideboard at one end provided self-serve drinks, snacks, and condiments, as well as a small food cooler and warmer.

"This is the wardroom," said Anson. "The twelve officers eat, meet, play games, socialize, and generally hang out here. Eighty additional crewmembers have their own larger space called a 'mess deck.' We'll give you a tour of the whole boat later."

She stared at Anson, arms folded across her chest.

Bo said, "How did all this come about, Captain? I feel like there's a page of history somewhere that I missed."

Ady's smirk went unnoticed by the men. She was glad to see Bo get some of what she had been feeling, but then she felt guilty for feeling satisfaction at his expense. Of course, she had missed this page in history, too. She sighed.

Anson nodded. "When the pandemic struck, there were about ninety-five nuclear-powered submarines at sea. Fifty-five of them were American, the rest were flagged by various countries. The US allies already had a secret ultra-low frequency communications system among themselves. When things started going bad and the military started shutting down, an Admiral in Hawaii sent a message to all allied submarines worldwide to rendezvous at an island in the Indian Ocean known as Diego Garcia. The U.S. already had a military base there and a large ship repair facility. Fifty-two of the U.S. subs showed up, as well as about twenty from other countries. About a year later, two others showed up from Brazil.

"It took a long time to get the Southern Hemisphere organized, and a lot went into keeping Pandera unaware. For the first fifty years, the facility worked on infrastructure to maintain the boats. Some were scrapped for parts. Most weapons were removed, including the nuclear ones. A few surface ships were also salvaged to be used as freighters. Diego Garcia is a tiny island and can't supply any real food. They were lucky to have enough water for the first several years while they set up their desalination plants."

Ady finally spoke. "Are you telling me this boat is over three hundred years old?"

"No," said Anson. "This is a copy built about twelve years ago. It has many improvements, but functionally it's the same and similarly nuclear powered."

Her eyebrows went up. "Not only are we hundreds of feet under water, we're also being fried with radiation?"

Anson frowned. "There's less ambient radiation here than on the surface, and much less than in space."

Education had taught her that nuclear energy was fraught with risk and radiation dangers. She wondered if that was another Education edit to dissuade humans from fairly evaluating it. She sighed and said, "Where are all of those submarines now?"

"Given their age, they've all been scrapped. But we've built new ones and have about forty total now. Most are deep sea mining ships. They retrieve metal nodules from the sea floor and transport them to our smelting plant. There are eight like this one used for various missions, including clandestine transportation."

Ady leaned back in her chair, and again crossed her arms over her chest.

Bo jumped in. "Look, there's a lot of history to fill in, but as my partner would point out, we need to address the largest leak in our boat first. What is the plan?"

Anson nodded. "We're headed to a rendezvous near Bertioga, not far from Sao Paulo, Brazil. We'll drop you there, Mr. Ford."

"May I presume," asked Bo, "my daughter and her partner are in Sao Paulo?"

Anson nodded. "Yes, sir. There will be a shuttle to take you to their compound outside the city." He looked at Ady. "Then we'll drop Ady at the airway platform a few hours from the coast. She'll take a Tomahawk to Diego Garcia."

Ady sat up. "Wait, why can't I see my parents? They've been gone nearly twenty years."

Anson looked her in the eye and said, "I know, Ady. I'm told they need you in DG immediately and you going to meet with your parents will delay that by several days."

"Why do I need to be in Diego Garcia so urgently?"

Anson raised his hand in defense. "I don't have a need to know, but my guess is it's the alien spacecraft."

She glanced at Bo, and pursed her lips for a moment. "Okay. Tell me what a 'Tomahawk' is."

Anson said. "It's a hybrid between an old first-stage rocket for space launch and what they used to call a cruise missile. It's a cylinder about ten meters long with deployable landing struts that flies about twenty thousand kilometers per hour. Carries two passengers on a flight path up to the stratosphere and back down where it lands itself."

She didn't flinch. "Sounds like a crude hopper. Why am I going to Diego Garcia?"

"It's our military base in the Indian Ocean that houses our research center. Between what Aideen has told us about you and the GWM prototype you created, they've asked for you to be there as soon as possible. Our visitor from outer space won't wait."

"What are you talking about?" she asked.

Anson tilted his head quizzically. "The alien ship you detected. We have about six weeks before it arrives."

Confession

"And that's our little home under the water," said Simon Yuell as he finished the guided tour with Bo and Ady.

"Forgive me," said Bo, "but what is the proper way to address you?"

Simon laughed. "For a crew member, it's 'COB,' which stands for 'Chief of the Boat.' For civilians such as yourselves, you may call me COB, Master Chief, or Simon, as you prefer."

Bo shook hands with COB and said, "Thanks for the tour, COB. Immensely informative."

"My pleasure," said Simon. "If you need anything, please let me know. I want to make your short stay with us both memorable and pleasurable."

"Thank you," said Ady as she shook his hand.

Simon turned and walked down the passageway. Bo opened the door to their tiny guest quarters and walked inside. She followed and shut the door. They sat on two swing-out stools facing each other. A bunk bed, two tiny fold-down desks, and a compact grooming station completed the room. Each bed had a five-centimeter-thick gel pad cover over a solid pan that was hinged on the backside. Raising the pan revealed a shallow storage compartment under each bed. Ady's gear bag containing the two lightning drives sat on the lower bunk.

Bo smiled broadly. "A whole new world, Ady. Right under the sea. They're good at keeping this secret."

She shrugged. "Seems to be a DNA thing in humans."

Bo's smile slid away. "Ady, I've made a lot of mistakes in my life. None got me killed. But I do regret some, particularly the way we colluded to mislead you. I understand you're angry with me, your parents, your whole education." He leaned forward and put a hand on her knee. "But all that's history now. Wai-Wan shared a quote from a lady named Oprah Winfrey: *You are responsible for your life. You can't keep blaming somebody else for your dysfunction. Life is really about moving on.*"

She nodded. "Get over it. Yeah, I know. I'm trying, but I've lost self-confidence because I don't know what is real and what is fiction. How do I reconcile that?"

"Pi is still Pi. Avogadro's number is still Avogadro's number. Your misinformation relates to sociology and relationships, all subjective, elusive, and dynamic anyhow."

She was mulling that over when her Linc chimed. She opened the message. It was from Anson and read. "Please meet me in the wardroom now." She sighed. "I've been summoned by the Captain." She stood, folded up her stool, and opened the door.

Bo said, "You have a three-day sabbatical here. Enjoy it."

"I might prefer the ride back from Mars to this. At least I had a friend with me."

"Maybe you'll make new friends on this trip."

She glanced at Bo, sniffed, and walked out, closing the door behind her.

She found her way back to the wardroom and knocked on the door. Anson opened it and instead of inviting her in, he pushed into the hallway and said, "Please follow me." He led her only a few steps aft and turned into another short cross-hallway. He opened the first door and walked in. She noticed the nameplate next to the door: "Captain Dorros."

Anson stepped aside and allowed her to enter. She closed the door behind her and looked around. "Captain's quarters?"

She saw a single bed, a larger drop-down desk, and a small table with four chairs. A door in the corner presumably led to a private grooming station. Similar to her own quarters, an array of lockers, drawers, and storage compartments festooned the walls.

"This is practically my home," said Anson, "since I'm aboard about eight months of the year."

She opened a small drawer and saw that it contained a buoyancy pack and some goggles. She shut the drawer and glanced at him. "Really, eight months?" She opened a locker door and saw six black jumpsuits and two white jumpsuits folded and banded on the top shelf. Below that were tunics of various colors. She rubbed her hand over the top one and noticed how smooth and slick the material felt. "You must recycle these while aboard. I didn't see an apparel cleaning station on my tour with COB."

"Not a common tour stop for our guests. The crew has seven jumpsuits each, recycled every week," replied Anson.

She walked over and sat on the bed. She ran her hand over the cover fabric, which was also smooth and slick. "You like slick fabric?"

"It's not a choice. It's what we have in the South."

She nodded and looked around. Nothing personal showed who lived here. It was functional and efficient. Almost sterile. A vid screen showed the submarine's current depth, speed, rudder angle, and noise level. A moving profile displayed what was likely the bottom contour. Numbers for the ocean temperature, salinity, depth to bottom, and ocean current. Her roving gaze landed on Anson. "Why are all the crew members male?"

Anson laughed. "Mixing genders stirred up too much undersea unrest. Females crew some of the other submarines. They thought about castrating the men if they were to serve on submarines."

"Did they ever try that?" she asked. She noticed that little dimple in his left cheek twitch.

Anson smiled. "Only the officers."

"Interesting. I always thought testicles were overrated, anyhow."

"You don't miss them until they're gone."

"Right." She smiled.

She looked at Anson's lips and thought about how they had felt when he kissed her. She realized she was unconsciously licking her lips as she relived it, and it gave her a slight tingle. That made her angry with herself. She didn't have time to pursue Anson right now. Frustrated, she frowned and blurted, "You summoned me. Is this disciplinary, celebratory, or instructional?"

Anson blinked. "Apologetic," he said. He pulled out a chair and sat across the table from the bed. Leaning forward, he rested his arms on the table and looked at her. He said, "Ady, it was my fault you were sent to Mars."

Her eyes grew wide. She hadn't expected this.

Anson shook his head slowly. "I was supposed to be off the submarine the night before we were to meet. Your grandmother was to swap twenty of us who were rotating off for four months. We made the rendezvous off Andros Island, but we learned that Pandera was waiting for the boat to return to port. We had to spend two more days at sea while we fished to fill the boat hold. With Wai-Wan's help, I was able to contact Yoon and have him slip you a note. He learned that Pandera was tracking and monitoring you that evening, so he followed you on your drive home. We still don't know what they were doing with that goose drone, but somehow Yoon's vehicle invisibility cloak was disabled. Pandera saw he was there, assumed he was one of their own, and transmitted a command to him to record the impact of their drone. He had no choice but to do so or he would have blown his cover. He was the one who recorded you picking up the drone and putting it into your vehicle."

"Why was he with me at Intake?"

"We still didn't know why they were monitoring you and we wanted to protect you, if necessary."

"As long as it didn't compromise Yoon?"

"Ady, he is one of a few, very expensive androids. And I don't mean the cost of constructing him. It's the effort to get him and others like him successfully infiltrated into Pandera and keep them undiscovered."

She nodded. "I had to be sacrificed to protect Yoon."

Anson looked away, glanced at the floor, at his hands, and then back at her. "Yes."

She stared at Anson. "Last year, we didn't meet by chance. You came looking for me."

Anson met her glare. "Yes. But it didn't turn out how I expected."

"Ha. As my grandfather would say, please explicate."

"You're the daughter of the two most powerful people in the Southern Hemisphere, but neither they, nor your grandparents, understood why Pandera was taking an interest in you. They didn't know if it was something Pandera had learned about you, Minda's research at NeoHealth, or just because you were their daughter."

She sighed. "Is it always this challenging to get to the point?"

"After I got back and you were safely on Mars, I had a meeting with your parents. By then, they had discovered that Pandera had been investigating the research Minda did twenty-five years ago. They figured out that you were the last embryo fertilized by Minda's team before they dismissed her. Pandera seems to feel you represent a threat as some sort as an enhanced human, and they want you sidelined. Eliminated as a threat, but quietly prevent blowback on them. And they want to send a message to Eidolon."

"It's me they're after, not you? I figured out they were trying to 'eliminate' me, but I didn't know why. My working assumption was that they thought I was associated somehow with you, and they were using me as leverage." She shrugged. "I guess now I know. And I need a plan."

Anson

Anson leaned back in his chair with his arms behind his head, smiling. "Did you know your nostrils flare when you're angry?"

Ady wiped a hand across her face and sat back down on the bed. She looked at him for a few moments, and then looked away. "I had a rude, inappropriate retort, but now is not the time."

Anson nodded. "That's the other thing I wanted to talk about—our relationship."

She sat up straighter and looked at him. This didn't feel like good news. Maybe she'd be better off just walking out and not hearing it. She didn't want the pain of hearing his rejection. She'd rather have the unknown than that. Wouldn't she? She wasn't sure anymore. Life had gotten so complicated since they met. Her parents ran half the world, expected her to help eliminate or neutralize Pandera, and they expected her to handle an alien spacecraft on its way to Earth. Not to mention that Pandera wanted to eliminate her. How would there ever be time to have a personal relationship? It would be selfish to waste time on that when the other agenda items on her plate were so monumental. Wai-Wan's mantra about fixing the biggest leak first came to her again. Anson wasn't going to get her attention for a long time. She sighed. That made her sad, maybe even a little depressed. She put on her stone face and said, "We don't have a relationship, Anson. One night eighteen months ago we had a terrific time, flirted, and even kissed once. But that's not a relationship."

Anson nodded and sat forward in his chair, steepled his fingers together on the table in front of him. "That's factually correct. It's the *promise* of a relationship that hangs in the air and has done so for the last eighteen months. I often think of those few hours we had together. I re-hash my failure to show up last February and worry that I've broken my promise. I re-live our laughs, our jokes, and our kiss, over and over." He looked at her. "Don't you?"

She looked away. What was she supposed to say now? She, too, had hung on the same promise, their next planned meeting had held her heart and her fantasies for a year. He'd practically confessed the same thing. She looked at his hands and recalled how it had felt when he took her hand in both of his. She shivered and looked away. "Anson, I'm new at matters of the heart. My cold bitch persona suits me well for physical gratification and amusement. With you, it's different." She ran her hand through her short hair, wishing she had her long mane to fiddle with in times like these. "But things have changed since that night." She saw the half-smile slide from Anson's face. "Circumstances have hung some huge challenges on my back. I can't follow up on that promise right now. I'd like to leave it at that, and when circumstances change, we'll revisit it."

But what she really thought was if Anson walked away right now, she would not be able to handle the tasks ahead of her. She wanted to hold on to her hope for a future relationship. That promise could keep her going through all of this, or at least she thought it could. She willed Anson to agree to her proposal.

"You," Anson pointed a finger at her, "want me," he pointed the finger back at himself, "to sit around and wait on you to create a new vehicle propulsion system, save the world from aliens, and dismantle Pandera. And then *maybe* you'll have a few temporal crumbs for me?"

He was smiling. He didn't seem upset or angry. And his dimple twitched. She thought he was joking again. Oh, Ellis, she thought, I should have repeated those training sessions on reading people a thousand times more. She swallowed and felt her stomach churn like she was about to jump off a cliff. "I'm hoping you could use the time to find a way to have your testicles re-attached." She smiled.

*****

Mid-morning of the third day they approached Bertioga. An announcement was made throughout the boat. "Arrival at Bertioga Base will be in approximately thirty minutes. Those departing muster at hatch number one. Stores will be taken on at hatch number two."

In the wardroom, Ady turned to Bo. "What does that mean?"

Bo shrugged. "I think I'm getting off in thirty minutes. The rest was apparently submarine-speak."

They both turned to Salvatore, the short man in white pants and shirt who served as a combination waiter, chef, and wardroom manager whom they had befriended. His skin color matched Ady's, he had black hair, nearly black eyes, and she could swear he must have to shave five times a day. He was the first person she had met who spoke with an accent. Salvatore had shared with them that his first tongue was Portuguese, but he had learned Bitte as a child in Brazilian Education. She would discuss this with Keera. It was another in the growing sea of Educational axioms that turned out to be false.

Salvatore said, "They said if you are leaving *Kuri* in Bertioga, then you must go to hatch number one—forward of the operation center—in the next thirty minutes. This is to ensure those leaving are in place and not walking through operations while the boat is maneuvering into the dock at Bertioga. It is a safety rule. For those who will stow the stores, that is, supplies, food, parts, packages, etc., they are to assemble by hatch number two, just aft of the wardroom. Again, we don't want people walking through operations or reactor control while we are maneuvering into the dock."

Bo nodded. "I'd better say my goodbyes now." He stood and shook hands with Salvatore. "Thank you for all that you taught us in these last few days. And I hope your mother has recovered from her accident."

"Thank you, Mr. Bo. You are very kind. I will share your message with my mother soon, and I hope that we will meet again."

As Ady and Bo were leaving the wardroom, Salvatore opened a locker door and pulled out a silver tea set, which he set on the sideboard. Then he pulled out a pair of white tablecloths and began unfolding them on the table. As she was about to close the door, she stopped and asked, "Salvatore, forgive me for being nosy, but what are you doing? I've never seen tablecloths on the table."

Salvatore shrugged. "Some meeting here while we are docked. My instructions are to set up for Class One service." He gestured towards the tea set and the tablecloths.

She nodded and wondered what the meeting was about. But for now, she needed to say goodbye to Bo. She met him in their bunkroom where Bo gave her a hug and said, "Never thought I'd be on the run at my age. But it feels kind of good." He stepped back and smiled at her. "Now, you go whup some aliens."

She playfully slugged him in the chest. "If they don't come in peace, there's nothing we can do." She could care less about the aliens right now. Bo was leaving and she was going halfway around the world away from him. She didn't know if she would ever see him again. This separation was a lot harder than her trip to Mars, and she wondered why.

Bo chuckled. "I wouldn't want to be those aliens going up against you."

She shoved him out the door. "Go to your 'muster' mister, before they put you in the brig." She was struggling to put on a brave front for Bo, but she was sure he knew better. Everyone expected her to be strong. She couldn't let them down.

Bo turned at the door. "I'm proud of you, Ady. What a woman you've become. I love you dearly."

She swallowed rapidly, blinking back tears. "I know, Bo. I love you, too. And thank you for, for…everything."

Bo turned and walked down the passageway. She closed the door, leaned her back against it, and slid to the floor. She rested her arms on her knees while she sobbed for several minutes.

When she was done, she wiped her nose on her sleeve and slid into her bunk. It was clear she should stay out of the way while the submarine was cycling through the docking.

She must have dozed off because she started when the ship-wide announcement said, "Miss Ford to the wardroom, please." She jumped up, splashed water on her face, and hurried the twenty steps down the passageway to the wardroom. Salvatore was standing at the door, smiling.

"Please, Miss Ady, take a seat."

As Captain, Anson usually sat at the head of the table. Now, he sat two seats down. Ady chose a chair opposite him and said, "What's going on?"

"We're having an inquest into your behavior during your repeated trips to Richmond, Virginia."

She blinked. This was bizarre. And then she spotted that little dimple in his left cheek. He was joking, lying, or both.

She smiled and said, "Want to watch the video of my adventures in the rental sex pod?"

Anson's mouth dropped open, and then stretched into a big smile. "Okay, you got me. Some folks want to meet you."

She bristled. This didn't feel good. Was Anson parading her before his seniors? Is that why he wasn't at the head of the table? Before she could say anything, the door opened, and four people entered. Anson immediately stood, so she did as well. Each of the newcomers wore a black jumpsuit with a black hood and full facemask. The first and last of this foursome went to the head of the table and stood with their backs against the wall facing the room. The other two ambled around the table towards her and stopped two meters away. They lowered their hoods and pulled off their facemasks. Vanessa and Minda stood smiling at her.

Departure

Ady's brain stopped working. Somewhere in there, it recognized Vanessa and Minda, but couldn't quite comprehend that they were here, now, in front of her, in the flesh. It had been nearly eighteen years since she had seen them. She was just a little girl then, wishing them well, but knowing she'd miss them while they were on the first mission to Europa. According to the information fed to her, all the world followed their progress. They had weekly video chats for about a year, but by then they were "too far away" to have live chats, so they started sending video messages. The frequency diminished over time until it was perhaps three to four times per year, but always on her birthday.

But they didn't go to Europa. It was all subterfuge to elude and misdirect Pandera and her. They'd always been just half-a-world away. And that seemed close now, compared to Europa. She had a brief flash—maybe Bo wasn't going to be so far away, either.

Ady was now four or five centimeters taller than her parents. She grabbed both into a hug. No one spoke for several minutes. They just stood there while Anson and Salvatore seemed to grow more and more uncomfortable.

Vanessa began to giggle and that set the other two off, who also began to giggle, and soon all three were bent over in full belly laughs gasping for breath, with tears streaming down their cheeks.

Minda turned to Anson, "Captain Dorros, good to meet you. I'm Ductor Ford." She reached across the table and shook hands with Anson. She gestured towards Vanessa and said, "And this is Princeps Ford."

Vanessa shook hands with Anson, and turned back to Ady. "You've grown so tall."

Minda said to Anson, "Captain, we appreciate the use of your boat for our impromptu meeting. May I ask that we continue this in private?"

"Of course," said Anson. He turned to Salvatore and they both left the wardroom.

Minda nodded at the two black-clad figures at the head of the table, and said, "Stay for now, please."

She pulled out a chair from the table and said, "Let's sit." They turned two other chairs around and the trio sat facing each other in a small circle.

"Where to start?" said Vanessa. She glanced at the tea set on the table, then shook her head. "It is so complicated, Ady."

Ady leaned in and took one of each of their hands in hers. "I've missed you so much, but you should know what a wonderful job Bo has done. He has been everything to me. And I owe him not only my life, but much of who I am."

"Ady," said Minda, "We understand. But as Wai-Wan would say, we should focus on the largest leak first."

Ady laughed. "She even taught you that?"

Minda smiled and nodded. "She's right, too."

Vanessa squeezed her hand and said, "We operate much like the Coordinating Council of the North is supposed to, only we exclude Pandera. Each country has its own government with whom we coordinate. The global military is centrally managed from Eidolon, taking a huge burden off the local governments. Minda is the military leader, and I am the Eidolon Council chairwoman. Most think of me as the figurehead. We oversee nearly two hundred million people in the South. That's about fifteen percent of what it was before the pandemic. And despite all that you've been taught, we are equally disease free. We have our own NeoHealth equivalent and a military that operates under the sea. We are an accommodating society and have extensive programs for 'defective' humans, as they are called in the North."

"Why you?" Ady asked. She pursed her lips and looked from one to the other, and said quietly, "You left nearly twenty years ago. Why did you leave?"

Vanessa glanced at the two black-clad figures, and then back to her. "A subject for another time. Undoubtedly, a significant leak, but not one that continues or threatens at the moment."

Ady nodded, wondering why her family was shrouded in layer upon layer of shadow and mystery. It ran in the family history. "How did Pandera evolve from peacekeeper to enemy?"

"We don't really know because Pandera history doesn't exist. They erase the records thoroughly and frequently. But now, contrary to what Education has taught you, we know they want to eliminate the human race. They've gone to enormous lengths to shroud their intentions and sway the Coordinating Council to their point of view. Fortunately, we've kept them at bay in the South and in space. But with this alien spacecraft approaching, it looks like Pandera plans to try to form some sort of alliance with them. They claim they have been in contact and that the spacecraft is manned by AI's like themselves who wish to establish friendly relations."

"But you don't believe that."

Minda said, "Not for a minute. They've had zero communications with that spacecraft. We've confirmed and corroborated that in multiple ways. Somehow, though, that's how they plan to spin it to the North. That's why we need you and Aideen's group focused on intercepting any and all communications and advising us of what is really going on."

"You don't want to stop Pandera, you just want to know what's going on?"

Vanessa stepped back in. "That's where we start. No one knows what will happen with the spacecraft. Our strategy will evolve as we get more information. As for the future, we also want you to help construct vehicles using your GWM technology. We need a defensive force when Pandera turns aggressive."

"Okay," said Ady. She looked from one to the other. "You know I'm mad at both of you for leaving me. But I'm so overwhelmed seeing you again. It seems like a dream."

Vanessa squeezed her hand now. "For us, too, Ady." Tears twinkled in her eyes.

Her eyes were so bright and alive, Ady noticed. Out of nowhere, she had a question. "What are your intelligence levels?"

Vanessa released her hand and tapped Minda on the shoulder. "Told you!"

Minda said, "When we were last tested, we were both tens, but that is the maximum number on a scale. We don't know our true level."

"And me, where do I fit?"

Minda turned to the two black-clad figures who remained watching them. "Privacy, please," she said. The two walked out of the wardroom and shut the door behind them.

Minda squared her shoulders and took a deep breath. "Ady, you're one-of-a-kind. You probably have the highest intelligence level and mental capacity of any human ever. But I may have damaged your emotional processing in making that possible. When this alien thing is over, we'll get you to a lab where we can properly assess you and perhaps right some of the side effects." She looked down. "I'm sorry I've made your life so challenging."

They were silent for a moment. Then Vanessa said, "You owe her the truth, Minda. All of it."

Minda looked Ady in the eye. "I also hid my research in your brain."

"Is that why I sometimes feel like there's another voice in my head trying to speak, but I just can't quite hear it?"

Minda nodded. "Probably. I never had the chance to determine how it would be perceived by the host."

Ady shrugged. "I'm a walking data vault with muted voices in my head."

Minda glanced at Vanessa. "You're a lot more than that, Ady."

"There are at least two reasons why Pandera wants to eliminate me."

"Only one. They don't know about the research."

"Can you be sure?"

Minda glanced at Vanessa. "If not, then we've already lost."

Ady looked from Minda to Vanessa, at their pained faces, then scrunched her own face. "I wonder if it's my brain, or my loneliness. Not having you around as I grew up left a lot of emptiness. And a longing to talk to you. I get that you were trying to protect me but knowing about the Europa ruse makes your absence hurt even more." She looked at Minda. "You chose, and you didn't choose me, your daughter."

Minda's shoulders slumped, and she looked down.

Vanessa said, "We deserve that, Ady. We made some poor choices, choices we thought were best at the time. We were wrong. In this last year, we've come to understand how wrong we were. We can't change history, but I beg you to allow us to become the parents we should have always been."

A knock sounded on the door. Vanessa grabbed her hand again. "We must go. Do your best at fixing the big leaks, please. We'll get you back here soon so we can all be together again." Ady hugged her, and as she pulled away, she gave Ady's cheek a soft caress.

Ady smiled. "Next time we'll have tea."

Tears crawled down Vanessa's cheeks as she beamed at Ady. "Mother's DNA lives on."

South World

The Tomahawk rocket eventually did an up-swoop to near vertical as it approached Diego Garcia, and then the engine cut off. Ady and Anson glided for a while with negative G's until a whirring sound inside the silent rocket indicated the landing legs were being deployed. It was nearly impossible to determine their direction of motion until the engine kicked back in to slow their descent onto the recovery ship. The actual landing was relatively soft and was only confirmed when the hatch above Ady's head automatically opened.

The ten-minute ride to the pier in the middle of the night on an autonomous tiny boat was much scarier than the rocket ride. They bounced and bobbed on the waves with sea spray splashing over them. She was glad for the shoulder harness that kept her in her seat, and probably in the boat. She didn't see lights in any direction and the overcast sky occluded all the stars. Finally, she felt the boat make a sharp right turn, and the ride smoothed out. The boat stopped shortly as it bumped alongside a low pier and extended its moorings. Working lights along this section of the pier came on.

A woman stood next to a small four-wheeled cart that looked a little like a stripped-down buggy from Mars. The woman, clad in a black jumpsuit, looked about a head shorter than Ady. She had Ady's skin tone and short dark hair. "Evening, Captain." She turned to Ady and extended her hand. "You must be Miss Ford. I'm Justyna."

Anson said, "Thanks for picking us up, Justyna. Hoping we can catch a few hours of sleep before the briefing this morning."

Justyna looked at her Linc. "Maybe four hours. Any gear, Miss Ford?"

"Just this." Ady held up the small bag slung over her shoulder that contained the lightning drive from her prototype vehicle.

Justyna nodded. "I'll come by at 0700 so we can get you some clothes before the briefing."

"That is so nice of you. Thank you," said Ady. She and Anson climbed into the backseat of the cart with Justyna in front as the driver.

Three minutes later they pulled up to a building labeled "Gateway Inn." Anson got out, and she followed.

"See you at 0700," called Justyna. Ady waved and followed Anson towards the building. Her Linc chimed. She saw that she had been assigned to pod 104. Anson held the door and asked, "What pod are you in?"

"104. You?"

"They keep 101 for me all the time. It's my home when I'm not on the sub."

Ady nodded, feeling a little awkward. She started to turn away, but Anson dropped his gear bag in the hallway and grabbed her arm. He turned her towards him and wrapped both arms around her.

At first, she was stiff, not sure how to respond. But it felt so good to be hugged. She dropped her gear bag and wrapped her arms around him. She buried her face in the crook of his neck and held on. She began to shiver.

Anson said, "Are you okay?"

"Yes," she whispered into his ear. She couldn't think. She couldn't control her pulse or her blood pressure. All she could think about was how comforting it felt to be hugged. How she missed it.

After a few more moments, she let go and they took a step back from each other. Anson took her face in his hands and stared into her eyes. "Ady, I'm here for you. When you need me. When you're ready."

She swallowed. She tried to talk, but her mouth didn't work. She nodded. Anson stepped back. "Good night, Ady." He turned and started off down the hallway.

She smiled and wiped her nose with her hand. How could she explain to Ellis that loneliness disappeared when you were hugging those you loved? She shook her head, thinking maybe the Tomahawk ride had rattled her brain. She walked down the other hallway, following the signs to her pod. The door automatically opened as she approached. Multiple time zone shifts had discombobulated her body clock. She was exhausted. She stripped, showered, and fell into bed.

At 0700 her Linc began chiming and the pod door announced a visitor. She rolled off the sleep mat and opened the door vid on her Linc to see Justyna smiling at her. "Come on in," Ady said. "I'll just be a minute."

She walked into the grooming nook and shut the door. She noticed a Linc message from Keera had arrived while she slept. *Arrived in Sao Paulo. Let's talk.* Ady smiled but didn't have time to reply right now.

Five minutes later the two walked out to Justyna's cart and she whisked them to a building labeled "Exchange." It was a general supply store. It carried fishing gear and bait, a variety of packaged food, and clothing for men, women, and children.

There were only two jumpsuits long enough to fit her. One was gray and the other a bright, light green. Justyna pulled her over to the swimsuit section and said, "You'll need one or two of these."

"What for?"

"Everyone swims in the lagoon here. It's social, cooling, and an easy way to spear dinner."

"And you need a special suit to do that?"

Justyna cocked her head and said, "What do you wear when you swim in the North?"

"Swim shorts, or just my Nomex shorts."

Justyna briefly looked Ady up and down. "What about your top?"

She frowned. "My top? What do you mean?"

"How do you cover your breasts?"

Ady looked at her chest, and back to Justyna. "Why would I cover my breasts?"

Justyna's face reddened and her jaw dropped open. She said, "You swim topless?"

She shrugged. "I guess. Everyone, men, women, children all swim in swim shorts. No one covers up their top. We're all the same." She looked at Justyna. "Do men cover their breasts, too?"

Justyna slowly shook her head. "I guess there are some things different here. Women are required by law to cover their breasts. You need a swimsuit like these to swim here."

"That's crazy. But okay. Anything my size?"

"I'll find you something. Go grab yourself some shorts and sandals. We can come back after the briefing, and we still have to feed you."

Ady was bewildered by the array of clothes. Except for swimming, no one wore shorts in the North. She'd never seen a sleeveless top before. The North was almost exclusively drab tunics and jumpsuits. Here, people wore a large variety of colorful clothes in several different fabrics, patterns, and styles. Some were that slick material used on the beds of the submarine. She couldn't decide what to select.

Justyna called to her. "Gotta go. We'll take what we have and come back."

She drove them to another building with a "Gourmet Dining Hall" sign. Once inside, Ady realized the sign was sarcastic, as all the selections were auto-vended, prepackaged foods. When she walked into the building, the menu popped up on her Linc. She paged through it and said to Justyna, "I don't recognize many of these items. Like this 'Breakfast Sandwich—meat patty with hen egg on unleavened bread.' I don't know what a 'patty' is. 'Hen' is a chicken, so I guess that means a chicken egg?"

"Try it," said Justyna. "I'll eat it if you don't like it. But we've only got eleven minutes."

She made the selection and they left with her eating on the go. By the time they got to the building with the "Research" sign, she had finished the breakfast sandwich and was licking her fingers.

Justyna smiled. "I guess that was pretty good."

Ady smiled. "Best breakfast sandwich I've ever had. Later you'll have to give me the details of what's in it."

Justyna stopped the cart. "Here we are. I'll pick you up here when you're done. I sent you my Linc contact so just ping me when you're ready."

"Thanks. See you later."

Justyna nodded.

Ady strode up the walkway to the building and pulled open the door. When she stepped inside, Anson was waiting for her. He hugged her, and then took her arm. "Let's walk to the briefing room. Have a good shopping run?"

"Yes, and a Breakfast Sandwich," she said as they walked. Her nose tickled as she recognized a scent she had smelled when she hugged Anson nearly eighteen months ago.

"Ugh," said Anson. "Those packaged things are gross. We'll have a real meal tonight."

"I thought it was scrumptious. Best one I've ever had."

Anson looked at her. "You're kidding, right?"

"It's also the only one I've ever had, you moron. We don't have them in the North. Chicken eggs? And whatever a meat patty is."

"It's a ground up piece of cow, and probably not a tasty one at that," said Anson.

She stopped, her eyes growing wide. "I just ate part of an animal? A cow?"

Anson nodded. "We eat animals in the South. I guess that's news?"

There were probably many more differences she had yet to discover, but here was an opportunity for a little payback for Anson teasing her about submariner's testicles. She grabbed his arm. "Anson, what if I'm allergic to animal meat. I mean *real* meat, not the protein substitute we have in the North."

"How can you be allergic to meat? No one is allergic to meat."

She leaned into Anson. "I could be. NeoHealth might not notice since the North doesn't have meat. Maybe I'm going to pass out." She put a hand to her throat. "I think my throat is swelling up, and my stomach is upset."

Anson's face went pale. "We need to get you to the clinic!" He turned and started to pull her towards the door.

"No, wait, I don't think it's what I ate." She looked around wildly, sniffing the air. "It's the pheromones. I'm allergic to eunuch pheromones!"

Anson's face turned red, and he stared at her. He put his hands on his hips and said, "You call that funny?"

She smiled at him and nodded. "I call it payback."

"I'm very competitive."

She shrugged. "So? You're also a Level 9 male."

"What is that supposed to mean?"

She shrugged again, thinking that might have been a mistake and he could take offense. "You also smell like you did when we first met."

He blinked, and then started laughing. "It's called Stardust. Do you like it?"

She frowned. "I like it, but I'm confused. Your smell has a name?"

"Yes. It's a cologne called Stardust."

His left dimple wasn't twitching. "Cologne? I don't know what that is."

"It's a scented spray for men's bodies, I guess to cover our typically offensive body smells. Like you would…" Anson hesitated. "Women of the South use perfume."

She shook her head. "All new to me. Never heard of perfume, either. I thought sweaty people just smelled like sweaty people. But you douse yourself with Stardust. Do all eunuch's use it?"

"Good morning," said a deep voice behind her. She whirled to find a tall, muscular man holding the briefing room door. His cheery smile gleamed against his dark skin and bald head. "You must be Adelya Ford. I'm Olu Kuye, Operations Manager. Welcome." He extended his hand.

She shook his hand and said, "Thank you. Please call me Ady." She half-turned towards Anson and gestured in his direction. "Do you know Captain Dorros?" She smiled at Anson. "He was just briefing me on the olfactory grooming habits of submarine officers." She walked into the room and found a seat.

Olu frowned at Anson. "Interesting topic, Captain."

Anson shook his head. "You have no idea, Olu. But I'm sure glad she's on our side."

Update

The briefing, such as it was, recounted what Ady already knew about Oumuamua. Designated 1L/2017, it had continued to slow and then swung around the sun. It emerged only thirty-six hours ago at three times its solar approach speed. So far, its projected path would have a closest point of approach (CPA) to Earth of 380,000 kilometers—the same nominal distance from Earth to the moon. There was no indication the spacecraft would attempt to orbit Earth or make any closer approach, although plenty of time remained for a course change. At its current speed it would take twenty-seven days for it to get to the CPA point.

A wall-sized vid was used to show projections of the spacecraft path relative to Earth, the moon, Mars, and the sun. It was noted that its path avoided all the common travel routes for Earth or Mars spacecraft. Besides Anson and Ady, eight others were in attendance. When Olu finished the briefing, a woman at the table introduced herself.

"For the benefit of our newcomer, I'm Admiral Nichieu who oversees our fleet, bases, and related services."

The man to her left said, "I'm Admiral Sijef Hutzemakers. You may call me Jef. I oversee our space operations." He pointed across the table at Anson and said, "I believe you know Captain Dorros. And the young lady to your left is Virginie Rayl. She runs the GWM lab down the street." He tapped his Linc a few times and the vid zoomed in on the Earth, moon, and CPA. "Our good friends–" he stopped and turned to Ady. "May I presume you know of whom I speak?"

She smiled at him and said, "Most certainly."

He continued. "Our friends are preparing to launch a vehicle of some sort to a position within close proximity to the CPA, for what purpose we don't know. Their public propaganda says they are going to greet the newcomers on their 'home' territory and to warmly welcome them to our planetary system." He looked around the seated group. "Our best guess is they think that by making first contact it will somehow endear them to the aliens." He looked around the room again. "Questions, comments?"

No one spoke. Ady noticed they were mostly looking at her. She wasn't sure what they expected from her, but she did have a question. "I presume you all know I'm Adelya Ford?" The group nodded together. "Is there any indication that the spacecraft will slow or alter course?"

Olu said to Jef, "May I?"

Jef nodded.

"None whatsoever. In fact, we think Oumuamua is on its cyclic course out of the solar system as it has over the last several visits. It's clearly coming a lot closer to Earth this time with calculated precision as to its CPA. Again, for what reason, we don't know."

Ady chimed in. "We know it decelerated on solar approach, which was both intentional and may be something it had not done before since it was never observed or recorded."

Olu nodded. "It has adjusted its trajectory to come much closer to Earth and pass specifically through an unusual point in space at its CPA."

Anson added, "Those two facts may be related or even dependent, but we can't tell right now. Even so, what other facts or hypotheses can we determine? For example, why else would it slow? How did it accelerate? If it used its proximity to the sun to slingshot, what did that path look like? Were there any other signs of artificial acceleration?"

"All good questions," said Olu. "Questions we hope you, Miss Ford, will help us answer. But we don't know anything else, factually."

Jef stood. "Let's put Ms. Ford to work, Olu. We'll brief here again tomorrow at this time."

Admiral Nichieu said, "Just a reminder that tomorrow is Sunday, Jef."

He nodded. "Thank you, yes. We'll still meet tomorrow, but non-watch standers will be off the rest of the day." He looked around the table. "By my order. No exceptions. We need everyone fresh if this turns into a battle, and there's not much happening right now, so go get some relaxation and family time tomorrow while you can."

Olu led Ady and Anson upstairs to what he called the "Space Operations Center." The entrance was on the second level of a large three-story open warehouse-sized room. A balcony of sorts extended on three sides and held a single row of consoles. A central stairway led from the second-floor balcony to the main floor. The main floor held five rows of consoles with vid panels, and perhaps fifty people seated at them. Illumination was low to allow clear vision of the three-story front wall where multiple vid screens contained both data and vid views. She recognized one view as the StarGate. She presumed the two similar views were of the Mars' and the Moon's StarGate cousins. One of the vids listed a timetable of arrivals and departures for each 'gate. In the upper right corner was a plot of Oumuamua's path with a flashing red dot representing its current position.

Olu directed her and Anson down the stairs to the main floor where he offered her a seat at a vacant console in the back row. "You can use this station." He turned to the woman seated to the left and said, "Lin-Lin, this is Ady Ford from the North. She's come in to work on Oumuamua."

Ady shook her hand. Lin-Lin was seated in a wheeled chair and was belted to the back with a sort of harness. She was a small woman, almost childlike. Ady's eyes traveled down Lin-Lin's body, and realized she had no legs. Ady looked back at Lin-Lin's face to see if she had noticed her surprise.

Lin-Lin pushed herself and her chair away from the desk and turned to face her. "Is this your first time in the South?"

"Yes."

Lin-Lin nodded. "Then I am honored to be the first to introduce you to a world where citizens with special needs are treated equally, and accommodations are reasonably made." She looked at where her legs would have been. "At four years of age I lost both legs when a building collapsed. As a result, my mobility is restricted." She looked at Ady. "But being an amputee doesn't affect my intellectual ability. And I save the cost of zaps."

Ady was shocked to see someone without legs. Such injuries occasionally occurred in the North, but they were never reported in the news and no one with disabilities ever appeared in public. Though she was aware that these things happened, it was both shocking and curious. She wanted to ask many questions but thought it would be rude. She said, "I see it doesn't affect your sense of humor."

Lin-Lin smiled at her. "We should have dinner together later so you can ask all the questions I'm sure you have."

She had read Ady's mind.

"I'd like that."

Lin-Lin turned to Anson. "Captain Dorros, care to join us?"

Anson smiled and said, "I'd be honored if you ladies would be my dinner guests at the Officer's Club this evening. Is 1900 a good time?"

"Works for me," said Lin-Lin. She didn't wait for Ady to respond before saying, "You're the woman who was at Astro on Mars recently."

Ady nodded.

Lin-Lin pointed at her vid station. "This was originally a clone of Astro, so you should be able to pick this up pretty quickly. Just ask me if you have questions or need help." She tapped her Linc and she and Ady exchanged contact data.

Olu said, "Here's my contact, too." Ady exchanged data with him. "Captain Dorros and I have other business to attend to, so if you ladies will excuse us?" The two men headed back up to the second level.

Lin-Lin turned her chair back to her station and said quietly, "Can't wait to hear how you hooked Captain Dorros."

Oumuamua Momma

Ady spent the next hour getting up to speed with the tools and pulling in all the data on Oumuamua. She wanted to find out what it had done to accelerate so quickly while it was behind the sun. After some sorting and parsing of the data streams, she realized the solar sail orbiter data wasn't included. A quick browse through the data streams allowed her to find the streams from each of the four orbiting solar sail satellites and isolate the timeframe she wanted to analyze. Pre-configured filters blocked out many frequencies, but she easily disabled those to find the data she was seeking.

She did a fast scan of the data and quickly identified the first surprise. Oumuamua's pass by the sun was inside the solar satellite orbit. Rough measurements shows its altitude from the sun was less than 500,000 kilometers. The second surprise was a vid that showed Oumuamua had deployed a tail-like device that extended towards the sun. Its length wasn't measurable, but given the heat signature of the tail, she concluded that the tail was sucking up solar material presumably to be used as fuel. A black line resulted on the sun's surface where the tail had passed through, but it collapsed a minute or so after it appeared.

With the filters off, Ady ran a scan of all other wavelengths to see if anything emitted from Oumuamua, or at least anything that could be recognized over the sun's enormous background noise. Given the scale of time and the breadth of the wavelength range, nothing obvious stood out at first look. She almost missed it. One of the satellites detected a micro-burst laser signal that was less than nine milliseconds long. That was definitely an anomaly she needed to investigate.

After twenty minutes of manipulation, she figured out that the laser signal was a spacetime wave packet burst that swept across the satellite's antennae creating a minor, non-symmetric Doppler shift. She wasn't sure how to decode the packets and wished she had Ellis to assist her. Getting Ellis functional would be her task for her Sunday "afternoon off" tomorrow.

Through trial and error, she ran some simulations to see if she could re-create the Doppler shift. On her eighth try, she found it. A symmetric Doppler shift made sense as the two objects, the solar sail satellite and Oumuamua, were moving in different directions. What caused the non-symmetric shift was when the laser itself was being steered in a particular direction. Oumuamua was aiming the laser. That aiming affected the Doppler shift just enough so that it wasn't linear, creating the effect she had observed.

The obvious next question was where was it pointing? That took some good orbital mechanics calculations that Ady couldn't do in her head, so she crafted a script to do the calculations for her. The hardest part was trying to estimate Oumuamua's exact location at the time of the transmission. Even a tiny error could lead her astray because of the vast distances involved. Presuming she got that part correct, the calculations to trace the path and pinpoint the destination were iterative and indeterminate. It could take hours before the comps could find anything along that transmission path.

Her Linc chimed just as she started the execution of the script. Justyna was here to pick her up. It was already 1215. Ady turned to Lin-Lin and said, "Justyna is here to pick me up for lunch. Can I bring you anything?"

Lin-Lin smiled. "No, thanks. I have a sack lunch."

Ady stared at her. "I don't know what that means. You're not eating a *sack* for lunch, are you?"

Lin-Lin laughed out loud, and several people turn to look at them. "No, no, no. It's an English euphemism. I brought my lunch packed in a paper bag, or 'sack.'"

"Oh," she said, slightly embarrassed. Another thing different in the South: they used English words sometimes. Maybe Keera could help her out with that. She made a note to send her a message later. "I have a script running while I'm gone but I should be back shortly."

Justyna was waiting at the curb in her electric cart. As soon as Ady slid into the seat, they took off. They headed down National Highway while Justyna gave a narration of the buildings and sights they passed. She pointed out the old fuel storage farm just beyond the west end of the airport's lone runway and McGoff's warehouse where, it was rumored, he held kinky parties for a small group of his friends.

They pulled up to a sun-bleached wooden frame with a thatched roof and no walls. Thirty or so composite chairs were scattered around the hut, half of which were occupied by groups of two and three. A small, hand-painted sign was stuck into the sand next to the street: "Yum Fish." A short man and woman with black hair and dark skin were bustling about in the hut, cooking. Black metal grates topped makeshift grills fabricated from metal drums. A woodfire in each drum had turned to glowing charcoal, heating eight or ten pots on each grate.

Ady caught a whiff from some of those pots and her stomach rumbled. They disembarked and as they passed by the front of the hut, the woman handed each of them a plate of food and a fork. Ady pointed to a small sign tacked to the hut support and turned to Justyna. "What does B.O.G.O. mean?"

"Buy one, get one," said Justyna. She dragged a chair up to a wooden cable spool that had been turned on end to make a high table. She set her plate and fork on the makeshift table and retrieved two bottles of water from her cart.

Ady sniffed her plate then took a bite of the food. She smiled. "What is this?"

Justyna said, "It's a cross between Chinese and Malaysian cuisine using whatever fish they caught today from the lagoon. Do you like it?"

"It's phenomenal," said Ady between mouthfuls. "Do you eat here often?"

"Nope. Too expensive. I'm usually at the cafeteria with all the worker bees…'cause it's free."

"There seems to be a fairly rigid organizational structure like the old military. Is it that way everywhere in the South?"

"Nah. This is a military base, so except for contractors and a few civilians like you, everyone here is military."

"I'm glad you enjoyed lunch," said Justyna on their way back to the Research Center.

Their Lincs both chimed red as they pulled up to the building. Ady looked at a message from Olu. "Return to the center. Code blue."

Before she could ask, Justyna bolted out of the cart and shouted, "Come on, code blue is like life or death." She ran to the building door and yanked it open. Ady darted through the door and up the steps to the operations floor. She pushed through the door and saw Olu, Anson, and Lin-Lin hovered over her station. Everyone else was standing, staring at the vid wall. Only one display took up the entire wall now. It was a dim picture with a tiny cigar-shaped object in the middle.

She hustled down the steps and over to the trio at her station. "What's up?"

Olu turned to her. "Your script finished. Lin-Lin heard it chime and checked it. This is what she found from the Mars space telescope."

"What is it, and how far away is it?" she asked.

"2.7 billion kilometers," said Lin-Lin.

Ady's pulse quickened. She was expecting a planet that was light years away, or just a vague star system so far away they couldn't pinpoint the destination. This was way too close to the solar system to be a natural object. Everyone must be thinking spacecraft now. "Speed?"

"Just under 150,000 kilometers per second, headed right at the sun."

"Size?"

"Two kilometers in length, ten percent of that in diameter," said Lin-Lin. She looked at the wide-eyed Lin-Lin, and nodded once.

Olu said, "Let's move to the briefing room." He turned to the room and in a loud voice said, "Everyone back to work. Chief, reset the displays." The room began to hum with quiet conversation as people ambled back to their stations.

The four of them moved to the briefing room and sat down only moments before Jef and Admiral Nichieu burst into the room.

Olu said, "Ady, I think this is your briefing."

Admiral Nichieu said, "Concise, please."

Ady nodded. "Oumuamua transmitted a directional laser signal while it was behind the sun. One of the Martian satellites orbiting the sun intercepted a snippet, and we worked out the physics of where the signal was pointed." Ady turned to Lin-Lin.

Lin-Lin looked like she might vomit at any moment. She gulped and said, "Her calculation script completed, so I checked to see if it was successful. Because we're 150 million kilometers from the sun, the point of the direction is a parabolic line to us, due to the parallax and the Earth's orbit around the sun."

"Concise," repeated the Admiral.

"Sorry," said Lin-Lin. "I sent the coordinates to Astro's imager on Mars. A few minutes ago, we got this image back with course, speed, and size." She tapped her Linc a few times and the image of the cigar-shaped spacecraft appeared on the briefing vid screen. The two admirals stared at it while Lin-Lin recited the course, speed, and size information.

"Something else," said Ady. "Oumuamua's altitude as it passed behind the sun was only fifty thousand kilometers. It deployed some kind of tail or scoop into the sun, but I couldn't determine how deeply it went. Several thousand kilometers, at least. I think it was sucking plasma from the sun into the spacecraft, I would guess to use as fuel. Maybe that's why it comes by every one hundred years, to refuel."

"When does this new one get to the sun?" asked Jef.

Ady gave a quick nod. "As early as one week, but I'm thinking it will slow down, so a little later."

"Oh, I forgot," said Lin-Lin. "Astro designated it as 1L/2366 and named it 'Shima.'"

"Who names these things," muttered Admiral Nichieu.

Ady thought of Keera and how she had explained all the meanings of a plethora of space names. Clever people name these. She tapped her Linc a few times, and said, "It means 'mother' in an ancient American Indian language. Oumuamua means 'scout.' If the names are fitting, Oumuamua has been scouting Earth for centuries, and now Momma is coming to visit."

Dining with Dignity

As Justyna dropped Ady at the O-Club, she said, "Thanks, Justyna. You've been so nice to me." Ady raised her hand towards Justyna, palm out. "I know you say it's your job, but it's not really. You've gone out of your way to help me in a foreign land. I really do appreciate it. Thank you."

"My pleasure. I think Lin-Lin will be green with envy tonight, and I'm glad to have had a hand in that."

Ady frowned. "Why?"

"Lin-Lin? I never much liked her. She bossed Captain Dorros around like he was a servant. He deserved better and should have dumped her sooner."

"What do you mean, 'dumped her?'"

"They seem to still be friends, but they severed their partnering agreement about three years ago. Used to be called 'divorce' when there were marriages."

Ady blinked and stepped out of the cart. Nausea churned in her stomach. She concentrated on slowing her pulse. Deep breaths. She was fighting an adrenaline dump in her bloodstream. Anson was partnered. To another woman. She managed a weak smile. *Another* woman. Had her emotional self secretly assumed a man like Anson would have no other women. But she felt betrayed. Partnered? That was different than a romp in a sex pod. Those seemed like relationship bookends. Admittedly, her personal experience only extended beyond the pod by a few drinks and an occasional shared meal. One meal could be counted as occasional. She glanced inside as she walked into the O-Club. Several heads turned towards her. She gave the bored-looking hostess her name and was directed to a table adjacent to the windows overlooking the lagoon. Lin-Lin and Anson were already there. They both stared at her as she crossed the dining area to their table. Anson stood and pulled out the empty chair between them.

Lin-Lin laughed and said, "Close your mouth, Anson, before you drool on her chair."

Anson's face went red as Ady sat. He helped her scoot her chair in, then sat and said, "You clean up well."

Puzzled, Ady said, "Is that a euphemism or Southern slang?"

"He's stunned by your transition from jumpsuit to romper," said Lin-Lin. "Me, too."

She turned to Lin-Lin. She was wearing a cowl-necked halter that shimmered like it was made of reflective petals. Her long black hair swooped to the right where a single blue plumeria blossom was tucked behind her ear. Lin-Lin was wearing makeup. Her eyelashes were black, and her eyelids a deep blue that faded to the black lashes. Her lips were also tinted blue, and her skin had bluish sparkles everywhere.

Ady got it, sort of. She didn't know if Lin-Lin was jealous because of the way Anson had looked at her or envious of how Ady looked. Or both, or something else, or maybe she was this way all the time.

After an uncomfortable silence, Ady smiled and said, "Your compliments make me uncomfortable, Lin-Lin. Justyna applied my makeup and did my hair, both a first for me. I have no way to judge how I look, nor do I care. You, on the other hand, have a theme in your appearance that is something between shimmering and icy, like the wisps of blue smoke when you disconnect a nitrogen super cooler hose from a maglev." She raised an eyebrow. "I think it's alluring and sexy."

Lin-Lin stared at her for a few moments, her drink glass poised in mid-air. Then she started laughing, one hand trying to cover her mouth as she set her drink down, sloshing some on the white tablecloth. Her eyes began to water, as she laughed harder. Soon, she was wiping tears from both eyes.

For some reason, Ady began to giggle along with her. She reached out and took one of Lin-Lin's hands and squeezed it. They both slowly calmed and wiped their eyes.

A man in a black tuxedo approached Ady from behind and said, "Excuse me."

Startled, Ady jumped. That caused Lin-Lin and her to have the giggles again for a minute. Ady finally turned to the man. He said, "Good evening ladies, Captain. I'm Emeric, your server tonight. May I get you a drink, or refill one?"

"Absolutely," said Lin-Lin. "Champagne all around."

Emeric looked at Ady and she nodded agreement. He smiled, turned, and walked away. Another man immediately replaced him and said, "Captain Dorros, won't you introduce me to our newest island guest?" A man of perhaps thirty with longish blond hair stood between Ady and Anson. He wore a pair of loose-fitting white pants and a brightly colored floral shirt. Something about the shirt was odd, but she couldn't put her finger on it. It had several bright colors mixed with dark grays that didn't seem to go together.

Anson stood and said, "Good evening, Jacob. I thought you were off-island this week." He turned to Lin-Lin and said, "I believe you know Lin-Lin?"

"Yes, of course. Good to see you, dear."

"And this is Adelya Ford. Just arrived last night. Ady, this is Jacob McGoff. Jacob is the contract operations manager for Diego Garcia. Basically, he runs the island."

Ady stood and shook hands. "Nice to meet you, Mr. McGoff."

He continued to hold her hand. "It's so nice to meet you, my dear. Welcome to Diego Garcia, our quaint little hellhole in the Indian Ocean. If there's anything I can do for you during your visit, you be sure to call on me directly. And I do mean anything." He leaned at the waist and kissed the back of her hand.

Lin-Lin said, "Put it back in your pants, Jacob. She's the daughter of the Ductor and Princeps."

His face reddened and he glanced at Anson. Anson nodded. Jacob looked at her. "If you should tire of your, um, associates, you are more than welcome to use my table in the corner at any time, whether I am in attendance or not. I'll see to it with Emeric. Have a good evening." He turned and strode to the corner table where he sat down with his back to them.

Anson turned to Lin-Lin. "Thanks a lot. I'll never see my laundry again."

"He's a disgusting, lecherous jerk who uses his power to have sex with anything that moves." She turned to Ady. "I'd go wash that hand if I were you. You never know whose ass he just kissed."

Ady frowned. "I don't know if that's sarcasm or serious."

Lin-Lin waved a hand at her. "Never mind. You'll live."

After dinner, they moved outside to the open patio where the waves lapped at the shore of the spit of sand between the land and the ocean.

Ady turned to Anson. "Justyna tells me you and Lin-Lin were partnered."

Anson looked at Lin-Lin, and said, "That's correct. For three years."

"Why did you stop?"

Lin-Lin said, "Because Anson felt sorry for me, and I couldn't manage my depression with that weighing me down." She smiled at Anson. "He mistook sorrow and empathy for love. I was desperate for the attention and companionship. But when I realized *why* he was with me, I became angry and took it out on him for the last year or so. We're both so much happier now. Right?"

Anson nodded. "Yes. She's right. We had the best of intentions, but misguided reasoning and motivation. It led to conflict and animosity." He smiled at Lin-Lin. "We're better friends now than we ever were when we were partnered."

Lin-Lin and Anson clinked their glasses in a toast.

Ady looked at Lin-Lin. "What's it like to lose your legs?"

Lin-Lin swirled the drink in her glass, seeming to inspect its contents. "Probably nothing like you imagine. Enormous physical pain at first, but that goes away. There's the physical loss that creates limits on my capabilities. Pretty much everyone gets that concept, but until you live it, you don't understand how pervasive the limits are. Then there's the psychological challenges of coping with the impairment. Everyone is different, but all amputees have some 'why me?' challenges, particularly at first. And the extra effort it takes to cope day to day wears on you, which compounds the depression. In the end, you learn to live with the new you, but I think depression is an ongoing battle for the rest of your life. Or at least it is for me." She smiled at Ady. "Took me a decade of psychological counseling to articulate all of that. Short version is you paint your world gray. No color. No clarity. No clear boundaries. Constant chaos." She shrugged. "I learned to fight and put myself back together." She raised her glass. "To the new me."

Ady clinked glasses and considered what she had said. It was mostly a psychological battle, caused by the long-term physical limitations. She looked at her own bare legs and thought about how their loss might affect her. Would she be able to bear it? "How many people have disabilities here?" she asked.

"About four percent of the population has some physical disability," Anson said. "Anything from the loss of a finger to being a quadriplegic. It's a lot lower than it used be because healthcare has mostly eliminated vision and hearing issues."

Lin-Lin nodded. "And it's gotten easier to cope, even for me in my lifetime, as the continued development of AI's are better able to assist. I have a homebot that facilitates grooming, shifting in and out of chairs, sleep mats, and such."

Ady was quiet, mulling over what Lin-Lin had shared. On the one hand, she could probably do things to help Lin-Lin and others with disabilities if she focused on those needs. On the other hand, there were aliens approaching Earth and she might be able to facilitate amicable relations or at least some protection. Were these the kinds of decisions that faced Vanessa and Minda when they left her?

She looked out at the dark ocean. What do you do when you can't tell which leak in your boat is the largest?

Playtime

The briefing on Sunday was uneventful except that Shima's course on the way to the sun was now more accurately calculated. It looked like it was headed for the photosphere layer of the sun. That was puzzling because it meant Shima would have to pass through the corona layer whose temperature was around two million degrees Kelvin. By contrast, and for some reason never explained by scientists, the inner photosphere layer was only fifty-seven hundred degrees Kelvin.

Ady commented to the group at the meeting, "That would be consistent with Oumuamua's behavior. I think they're refueling by capturing plasma as they fly through the photosphere."

They soaked in silence as they contemplated that scenario.

She added, "We don't have a clue how they withstand the heat."

"Nothing more to do at the moment," said Admiral Nichieu. "Go have some fun while you can. We'll meet again tomorrow."

The group filed out of the building. Justyna was waiting in her cart. Anson and Ady climbed in and Justyna ferried them back to their quarters.

Forty minutes later they pulled up at the lagoon. It was a sandy beach area at the foot of the U-shaped island. The water was shallow—about three to eight meters—and there were two large tide pools protected by natural terrain. The pools each had narrow fill channels of only two meters wide. At high tide, the pools flooded to three meters in depth, but at low tide they slacked to less than half a meter.

Justyna explained. "When the tide floods, the water rushes into the tide pools and fills them up. There are five or six large manta rays that live in the ocean nearby. The pools are rich feeding grounds for them. Somehow, they know the tide timetable and show up just after the flooding starts. Then they leave the pools before they get stranded when the ebb tide drains the water. It's amazing to watch them."

Perhaps a hundred other people dotted the sandy area with chairs, mats, and sun shields. A small knot of children was at the water's edge poking intently at something with sticks.

Justyna flipped open a pair of lounge chairs for them. "If you want to see the rays come in, we'd better head over there now." She handed Ady a sea mask and they walked over to the water's edge near the opening of the first tide pool. "The best way to watch is to float at the side of the opening and wait for them to come in. Usually it's pretty crowded on Sunday, so we'll cross over to the far pool where there'll be fewer people."

She nodded. Justyna showed her how to put on the sea mask and adjust the tension so it sealed around her nose, eyes, and mouth. The mouthpiece covering her mouth allowed her to breathe and to speak to Justyna. Soon, they were swimming lazily across the calm surface with their faces in the water. Several schools of bright yellow fish swam in unison near a coral head on the bottom. Larger fish, unafraid of the humans, swam by casually. The undersea lagoon was an ever-moving scene of sea creatures as far as she could see, a kaleidoscope of color. "I've never seen anything like this, even on vids."

"I know," said Justyna. "That's why I wanted you to see it. I think it's unique on all of Earth."

Shortly, Justyna grabbed her arm and pointed. "Here they come," she said. At first Ady didn't know what she was pointing at, but then she spotted a dark blob about a meter under the water. It grew larger as it approached and quickly resolved into a blue-black manta ray. It was coming right at them as it slowly flapped its wings in a rhythmic oscillation akin to birds in flight. As it drew almost even with them, Ady realized it was nearly five meters wide and estimated it was swimming at four meters per second. It was flying underwater as it sped by them, folded its wings, and slipped through the opening into the tide pool. Moments later, two smaller blueish rays also cruised by and slipped into the pool.

Justyna grabbed Ady's arm again and pointed. "I think this is Rosey coming." Another ray was approaching, this one a dull red color and about two meters wide. It was moving much more slowly. As it approached, Ady realized why. A chunk of netting was hooked over the ray's left cephalic fin. The netting had debris and several segments of kelp snagged in it and trailed under the ray for several meters. She watched several onlookers swim towards the ray, presumably to try to remove the net. But the ray, even weighted down, changed course and easily maneuvered away from them. Justyna said, "Everyone keeps trying to get that net loose, but they can't get close enough."

"How long has it been like that?"

"Maybe a month. Not sure how long she can survive like that. She can't swim fast enough to ingest enough food."

Ady watched the ray as people gave up chasing her after many tries to free her of the debris. The ray circled around, again heading for the pool opening. Just as it got even with Ady and Justyna where they floated on the surface, it turned towards them and passed less than a meter beneath them.

It continued in a lazy circle for several revolutions passing just below them each time.

"I've never seen her do that," said Justyna.

Ady eyed the kelp trailing the ray and noticed the sun glint off at least two clear fishing lines snagged in the kelp. As the ray circled back towards them, she took a deep breath and blew it out, shifting her body's buoyancy to slightly negative. With her arms at her sides, she did a pike dive as the ray was passing under her. She dove below and behind the ray, and then swam hard towards the trailing kelp. In her ear, she heard Justyna cry, "What are you doing?" Ady tuned her out. With a final kick, she was able to grab the kelp and a segment of the entangled fishing line. The ray started to thrash as Ady's weight pulled against it. She worked her way up the kelp and line, hand-over-hand. When she was within a meter of the flailing ray, she grabbed a segment of the net, realizing a metal wire threaded through it. She pulled herself even closer to the ray and put her left arm out towards the ray's lower lip. The ray stopped wrestling. She grabbed the wire and net with her right hand, and using her left hand on the ray's lower lip for leverage, pulled on the wire with all her strength. At first, nothing happened, but Ady's continued pressure succeeded in slowly withdrawing a long wad of net. Ady kicked off, pulling the mess away from the ray and the net loop off of the ray's cephalic fin. She released her grip on the wire and the entire mess drifted towards the bottom. The ray resumed her swim and slid through the opening into the tide pool.

Ady kicked several times and bobbed to the surface. When she got there, she took a couple of gulps of air and looked around for Justyna. Someone without a sea mask grabbed her by the shoulder and shouted, "Are you okay?"

Ady gave a thumbs-up and noticed she was surrounded by people, all staring at her.

Justyna emerged from the throng and through the sea mask intercom said, "I think it's time we took a break. Can you follow me, please?"

"Sure. Where did all these people come from?"

"Let's go ashore."

They retraced their earlier swim across the tiny inlet, removed their sea masks, and walked over the sand to their beach chairs. Justyna tossed her a beach robe and donned one herself before flopping down in a chair. Ady followed suit but felt she had missed something. She was elated to free that ray from certain death. It was as if the ray knew she was there to help her and somehow knew what to do. She could see herself in her mind freeing the ray from the net, but the actual memory of doing it was surreal, almost a memory of someone else doing it. She turned towards Justyna to find her staring at her.

Ady said, "Are you upset?"

"Upset? No. Freaking scared out of my mind? Yes!"

"Why?"

"Why? You ask why?" Justyna almost shouted. She looked around and lowered her voice. "From your perspective, what just happened?"

She shrugged. "I figured out a way to get that net off the ray. The ray you called Rosey."

Justyna nodded. "You're a hero for saving her. You did what no one else has been able to do. I applaud you for that." Justyna looked skyward for a few seconds and sighed. "Do you have any idea how long you were underwater?"

"No."

"More than ten minutes. Ten minutes! No one can hold their breath that long."

She blinked. Ten minutes was a long time to hold your breath.

"By the time you got Rosey freed, everyone was gathered around because of how long you'd been underwater. They were about to rescue you. But you kept calmly moving around and didn't seem to be in distress. And then you pulled that mess out of her throat and released her from the net."

Anson walked over and unfolded a lounge chair. "You ladies having a good day at the lagoon?"

Ady looked from Anson to Justyna and back to Anson. "I think we're having a good day. What do you think, Justyna?"

"I'm still shaking from your show, but I guess it's going to be okay now."

"What show?" Anson asked.

"I pulled a piece of net off a ray," said Ady.

"Yeah," said Justyna. "It was awesome. Everyone cheered. I won't mention that she was underwater for more than ten minutes and should have drowned."

Anson looked at her.

"I guess I can hold my breath for a long time."

Anson nodded. "I read the Mars report." He turned to Justyna. "Bet you a bottle of bourbon that tomorrow the DG news reports the woman has gills."

"No bet," said Justyna. "And for the record, I think she's part android."

Ellis Lives

Mid-morning on Tuesday, Ady arrived at Research. There were no updates of interest on the spacecraft, so she approached Olu. "Is there a spare bot node I could use to host my AI?"

"Sure. But the firewall may block your download."

Ady held up her gear bag. "Lightening drive."

Olu nodded and led her to the first-floor operations center console near the right corner. "You can use this one. It's slaved to an isolated node that's firewalled, but you'll have the admin privileges to set up your Linc connection. If you need help, ping me or Lin-Lin. She can assist."

"Great! Thanks so much, Olu."

"By the way," said Olu. "Virginie and her boss, Captain Nesi, are re-vamping their GWM lab so they can accommodate the construction of your new airpod prototype there. Should be ready to go by Monday."

"GWM lab?"

"Started off trying to make a steerable GWM engine, but Eidolon redirected them a few months ago. Rumor is they've been building a hand-held weapon to disable a GWM engine."

"Interesting." She unpacked the lightning drive and connected it to the console. Twenty minutes later, she was prompted for the key to "sinking boat one" security protocol. She thought for a moment and typed "largest leak first." Ten minutes later a voice said, "Hello, Ady. It's good to be back."

"Hello, Ellis. It's wonderful to hear your voice. I've missed you."

"How is Bo?" asked Ellis.

"He's fine, but he's not here."

"I am glad to hear he is well. I was concerned about his health when he shut me down."

"Ellis, you will have read access to the data systems here, but all your storage must be contained in this host node."

"I understand and have established read-only connections to thirty-seven nodes within my connectivity reach. All of them seem to be co-located in proximity to my location."

"What is your location, Ellis?"

"I am located in the Research building at Diego Garcia, a military base in the Indian Ocean."

She nodded to herself. "Have you located the trajectory data for 1L/2107 and 1L/2366?"

After a pause, and Ellis said, "I have identified the location of the subject trajectory data. Would you like me to analyze this data?"

"Yes, and while you are doing that, please help me establish our protocol connection with my Linc. Can you please tell me what blockers I need to remove?"

A few minutes later, Ellis said, "Ady, I have the alien spacecraft trajectory analysis completed. What would you like to know?"

"Is the calculated CPA point for Oumuamua correct?"

"Yes."

"What is your estimate of Shima's trajectory once she passes behind the Sun?"

"The probability of an accurate projection is extremely low because of Shima's unknown mass and because of the lack of data on the effect of its trajectory when it passes by the sun. The highest probability for its trajectory is eleven percent, and on that trajectory, it will pass through the same CPA point with Earth as Oumuamua."

Ady stared at a projection of the trajectory on the vid. Ellis thought both spacecrafts were coming towards Earth.

A voice behind her said, "I got the same best-guess trajectory."

She turned to find Lin-Lin in her chair behind her. "When did you work that out?"

"About twenty minutes ago."

"What would that mean?" asked Ady, absently.

Ellis interrupted. "I have analyzed the transmission snippet from Oumuamua to Shima. Would you like those results?"

"Yes," they said in unison.

"I've displayed a Fourier transform of the signal on the vid. As you can see, the side bands are not symmetric. They contain different data. The main carrier wave of the signal is being transmitted from a directed, single-lobe antennae, presumably focused in some unknown manner."

Ady asked, "What about the data content? Any useful information there?"

"It appears to be modulo two data, but the base could be any power of two."

Lin-Lin said, "Is the data encrypted?"

"I'm sorry, I don't recognize your voice," said Ellis.

Ady laughed. "Of course. Ellis, I'd like you to meet Lin-Lin. She is working with me on the spacecraft tracking."

"Hello, Ellis," said Lin-Lin.

"Nice to meet you, Lin-Lin. I'm unable to determine if the data is encrypted but will continue to analyze it."

Ady turned to Lin-Lin. "We can talk to them, but we don't know their language."

Lin-Lin nodded. "They must be male."

Party

A week later Ady had dinner at the Chief's Club with Justyna. A message arrived simultaneously on their Lincs. It was a reminder of the coming holiday, Healthzig.

"What is 'Healthzig?'" asked Ady.

"World day of celebration to commemorate the rise from the pandemic. Celebrated on the day NeoHealth delivered the first baby."

"Never heard of it."

"They'll have music and dancing in the three clubs at dinner time. Everyone wears a costume of some sort. Usually kinda crazy."

*****

Although Ady had tried to talk Justyna into accompanying her for Healthzig at the O-Club, Justyna wouldn't hear of it. She insisted that this was a "date" event and that Ady should go with Anson.

Ady had grown used to having Anson "on the shelf," as she thought of him. It was nice to have him around and know that they were keeping alive the promise of a real relationship. But she was afraid if she let him get closer, her ability to do her job would suffer. And she was needed now. That would change. Someday. When all this alien and Pandera business was over.

Justyna sacrificed a formal gown and connected her to a seamstress friend, Pamela. She took the whole dress apart and remade it into a wrap-around cocktail-length dress. With Ady being a head taller than Justyna, there just wasn't enough material to make it formal length. It was silk lame with a crewneck, long puffy sleeves, and a pleated bodice.

Ady fidgeted with the silly facemask that covered her eyes. She stood at the front door to the Garden Inn, waiting for Anson so they could leave for the O-Club. He had said seven. It was four minutes after. She checked her Linc again. They were going to be late. She glanced down the empty hallway towards his pod door. She was tapping a Linc message to him when she heard his door open. She canceled the message and looked up.

He walked to her and grinned. "Good evening, Miss Ford."

"Hi," she said, as she continued to look him over.

"You've never seen my formal dress uniform?"

She shook her head. "Is that what it's called?"

"It's sort of like the old tuxedo, but with shoulder boards."

She nodded and stared.

Anson twirled in a circle. "You like it?"

"Reminds me of dark chocolate."

Anson frowned. "What?"

"My favorite sweet."

Anson took her arm and directed her towards the door. "We better go or I'm gonna melt under that look of yours."

When Anson opened the door the warm, tropical air washed over them. She blinked and took a deep breath. She felt light-headed and could hardly recall the last thirty seconds. Glancing at Anson, she smiled. The word "delectable" suddenly flashed in her mind. "You look delectable, Anson."

"Thank you."

She frowned as they slid into the waiting cart and headed off towards the O-Club. Had she said that out loud? She felt her face flush. And then she realized her whole body was be flushed. She was glad for the breeze and twilight.

Champagne flowed at the lobster dinner. The women were dressed in an array of colorful long gowns, mostly flowing and loose. Men and women alike wore masks. She wasn't sure if it was the celebration or the guise of anonymity, but everyone flirted mercilessly. Even Admiral Nichieu came by their table and enticed Olu to dance with her.

A slow musical number started, and Anson took her hand. "Would you like to dance?"

"Love to."

They made their way onto the dance floor and began to sway to the music. Anson wrapped his right arm around her and held her close.

She could smell his cologne, but it didn't smell like Stardust. "What's the cologne tonight?"

"It's called Promise."

She smiled. She hadn't been this close to him since the night at Krewe. She recalled someone there calling out, "Rent a pod." They had a pod tonight. Two of them. And they didn't need to rent them. She leaned into Anson, savoring the warmth and sensing the contours of his body. "Promise. That's a good name. But I think Desire would be better."

"Why is that?"

Because that's how I feel, but I can't say that to you. She found his ear and brushed her lips across it, and whispered, "I love dark chocolate."

She was calculating how many milliseconds it would take them to get back to the Garden Inn. She'd already calculated how many minutes— eleven point three. And how many seconds—678. Anson stopped dancing and stepped back from her. Another man in a formal uniform whispered into his ear.

Anson nodded and grabbed her shoulders, looking into her eyes. "There's been an accident. I have to go. I'm so sorry, but they need me." He turned and jogged out the door.

She stood on the dance floor, other couples still swaying around her, staring after Anson until the song ended.

Admiral Nichieu walked up to her and quietly said, "Mining submarine went down. Ruins the evening. But worse for their families."

Ady nodded. "Of course. Thank you for telling me, Admiral."

The Admiral nodded and walked away.

Ady made her way out of the O-Club and took a cart back to the Garden Inn. She went to her pod, shut the door behind her, and pulled off her Linc. She untied the dress, dropped it on the floor, and crawled under the covers of the sleep mat. Naked. Alone. Confused. She cried quietly for a while, and then drifted into sleep.

Joe Bud

On Monday, Ady found Joe waiting for her in the Research lobby. They hugged then sat down in the briefing room. She brought him up to speed on events that had transpired while he was en route as the rest of the group sauntered in and took seats.

"Let's get started," said Olu. "Ady, you have a guest?"

She started to introduce Joe and said, "Joe, I don't know your last name."

He smiled. "Joe Bud."

"Welcome," said Ady. "Quick background. Joe was on my flight to Mars. He's a professional hacker and was once employed by Pandera. They trumped up some charges against him that got him a life sentence on Mars, but when Oumuamua came on the scene, they wanted him back. Someone intercepted his return flight and landed him here about two hours ago."

"That would be me," said Jef. "Orders from the top. Apparently, you come highly recommended, Joe. Welcome to the team."

"Thank you," said Joe. "And thanks to all the nameless folks who got me here."

"Olu," said Ady, "Can we get a console set up for Joe? I think you know what he'll need."

Olu nodded and rubbed his bald head. "Yes, I can imagine. Let me get it started and we'll evolve from there as needed. How about on the other side of Lin-Lin?" Olu paused. "I think this is your show, Ady."

Ady nodded. "Let's talk about how to attack all of this. I see three major tasks." She clicked them off on her fingers. "One, track these two alien spacecraft and determine their intentions. Two, figure out what and how Pander monitors communications. While their diodes are in overdrive with these spacecrafts approaching, maybe we can disrupt their monitoring capability. Three, attack the signal intercepts and see if we can decipher any data from them. Anything else?"

Lin-Lin said, "Give me the signal analysis. And I'd like to use Ellis, if possible."

Ady smiled. "Did you hear that, Ellis? Lin-Lin likes you."

From Ady's Linc, Ellis said, "I am always pleased to assist, particularly those who express their appreciation."

"How about you chase Pandera and how they monitor us, Joe," said Ady.

"Makes sense. But I'll need some backdoors. Mine are all gone by now."

Ady smiled. "Will PubNet admin do?"

Joe's eyes went wide. "Sure." The others stared at her.

"I'll track Shima and see what I can learn," said Ady.

After a moment of silence, Jef said, "We're on 24/7 until further notice. Sleep and eat when you must. Coordinate through Olu." He stood. "Let's get to work."

Headaches

Two days later, Joe brought up a circuit diagram on the briefing room screen. "This is the basic diagram for the analog converter used in everything Pandera makes that has a microphone." Joe tapped his Linc, and the vid peeled away seven layers of the circuit diagrams, like turning pages in a book. "This layer, the bottom one of the circuit package, is an intercept circuit. It captures the converted signal and transmits it on a 2.4 gigahertz frequency, good only for short-range."

Lin-Lin said, "They capture *all* conversations, including our Lincs?"

Joe nodded. "Yes. There are also billions of these coupled with microscopic microphones in almost every electronic system they manufacture. It's not just the electronics we talk to that's listening. If it has power and they made it, it's listening and transmitting on that short-range frequency."

Ady groaned. "Where does the captured data go?"

He moved on to another circuit and paged to the bottom layer directly. "Here's the receiver. Built into the power supplies. This is all that I could find, although there aren't that many, maybe forty different models. It has a unique ID, and based on some tinkering, I think it has an admin mode that can be used to tell it what to keep and what to ignore." He pointed to a green highlighted area. "This is a multi-field identification array for fast data pattern searching. They're looking for keywords and sending only information of interest to Pandera. My best estimate is they're forwarding about 0.001 percent of the data they capture."

"Where does the matched data go?" asked Lin-Lin.

Joe smiled. "That's the unresolved question. I'm not sure, but I think they're using ancient technology to send the matched data out on the power line. Or they're using the power line as an antenna." He shook his head. "That stuff's so old, I can't find any data on how it works."

"Of course you can't," said Ady. "Pandera deleted it so they couldn't be detected."

Everyone was quiet for a moment. Ady said, "Joe, is this the same data transmission interference SpaceCorp was complaining about when they visited where you were stationed?"

Joe nodded and looked around the room. "Some SpaceCorp guys came to see us to complain to Pandera about this and threatened to build their own electronics. They died later that day."

Several tried to talk at once. Joe held up his hand. "Yes, Pandera arranged for them to die by crashing their air transport. Just like they did to Ady's air transport when she returned from Mars."

Except for Ady, there were blank looks from the other three. Joe said, "You didn't know? Ady is officially dead. Tragic story made the news for three days in the North."

After giving Ady a quick glance, Virginie said, "What do we do?"

Anson stood up and started pacing near his chair. "This thing is so pervasive we could never ferret out the circuits and disable them." He looked at Joe. "When did this start?"

"Can't tell. At least a century ago."

Anson raised a finger in the air. "I bet we even included these circuits in many of the electronics created by the South because we stole their circuit designs." He put a hand to his forehead. "They let us steal them." He looked around the room. "That's why Pandera doesn't care. They know pretty much everything about the South, SpaceCorp, Mars, and even our submarines."

Public

Back at her console, Ady composed a message to Bo that she encrypted with their unique key. She told him about Joe's discovery and about the pervasive nature of the eavesdropping. She asked if he could source any background material on the ancient technology known as Broadband Over Power Lines. Given Bo's age, she thought he might know where such information could be archived and hidden from Pandera.

She also composed a message to Aideen on Mars and outlined the same issues for her. She suggested a full sweep of every device in Astro for 2.4ghz chatter. She hoped the nature of Astro would remain intact and that the snooping would be limited to a few devices they could simply launch towards the Sun.

"They're also detecting when we jam the eavesdropping transmission. I don't think we can stop it. We'll have to come up with another plan."

Joe said, "They must have built in monitoring against jamming. But they can't monitor the power transmission. Maybe we can hit it there?"

"Wouldn't they notice a particular stream had stopped?" asked Lin-Lin.

"Maybe," said Ady. "It's a massive data problem. We have to disrupt the transmission at its narrowest point. Let's keep searching."

"Look," said Lin-Lin, "node by node, the data is filtered and aggregated in the power supply, but how does it get back to Pandera?"

"Not sure yet," said Joe, "but I think the power supply goes to a battery, which is at times connected to a solar panel. I'm now thinking it's the panel that transmits to them."

Ady said, "If that's true, then they're transmitting to PubNet satellites. That's almost worldwide coverage. Oh…" she groaned. "They're in SpaceNet satellites too. That's how they get worldwide. They're everywhere."

"The chokepoint is the satellites," said Lin-Lin. "Shut down their relay and Pandera eavesdropping goes dark—worldwide!"

Ady checked the time. They were all supposed to meet for dinner at the O-Club in twenty minutes. "Let's go to dinner and we'll work out the details."

"What details?" asked Lin-Lin. "You already have a plan we don't know about?"

"Yes," said Ady. "We need to start making more of Virginie's GWM weapons. I think we're going to need them."

Deception

That evening, the five of them sat at the corner table in the O-Club. Silenced Lincs were piled in the middle of the table. After Tamisha brought their drinks, Lin-Lin proposed a toast. "To the end of Pandera eavesdropping." Grim but determined smiles painted their faces.

Virginie started. "Lin-Lin said you have a plan that involves my GWM disrupters, Ady."

Ady nodded and rubbed her chin. "Let's back up a bit. All this data capture is going through PubNet or SpaceNet and then back to Pandera." She looked at Anson. "There are maybe twenty-five satellites total between the two nets?"

Anson shrugged. Lin-Lin said, "My domain. Twelve live in PubNet. Maybe six more in the pipeline, some of which are probably already parked in orbit but not enabled. SpaceNet has only four because they relay through each other. Two additional in ready reserve are already in orbit."

"Okay," said Ady, "sixteen live satellites. We don't need to take them out, just shut down the back-channel data flow to Pandera. Just for discussion, let's say we do that, all at once. What happens?"

Anson said, "Pandera goes on the offensive to figure out what's going on, they launch more satellites, and bring their reserves online."

Virginie said, "New satellites would take a day or two to put into place. The reserves would be near-automatic, so we have to take them out along with the live ones."

"Something this big," added Joe, "would rattle Pandera a lot. They might start shooting at suspects before they unravel the details. We'd need some serious defense and protection."

"There's more," said Ady. "We should wipe out the data they've already collected. All of it. Maybe that's impossible electronically. We might have to physically destroy it, and all their redundancy."

Virginie nodded. "If there's no historical data, then no trend analysis, correlation, or vision. Strategically, they'd be blind. Tactical only."

They pondered that in silence.

Virginia tapped her finger on the table. "Tactical is bad.

Ady nodded.

"That's why you mentioned Virginie's GWM weapon." said Lin-Lin.

Ady looked around the dining room to see if anyone was paying attention to them. Could Pandera have human agents like Eidolon had android agents inside Pandera? If so, with their Lincs off, they could still be monitored. She hoped not, but leaned into the table, and in a whisper said, "I was thinking the goose is a tactical weapon used to take out threats, particularly when Pandera is unable to monitor them." She looked at Anson. "Like that night in Richmond. I've modified my Linc so much and have my own encryption, that they got nothing from our conversation. And you didn't' have a Linc. They were threatened. Maybe needed a test-run of the goose. In any case, Pandera sees this skirmish coming."

"You think they were trying kill you that night?" asked Anson.

"Yes." She looked at Virginie. "I'm betting the failure of the invisibility system in Yoon's vehicle is related to the goose crashing. Somehow, the two systems interacted and broke them both."

Virginie shifted in her chair and said, "Possibly. The cloak has a short-range light wave transmitter. It wouldn't interfere with their propulsion, but it may interrupt their navigation if it got into their line of sight. But the transmitter failed. What caused that?"

Lin-Lin said, "Maybe the goose has a light transmitter, too, and they got crossed up with each other."

"Or maybe the goose has an EMP blaster," said Ady. Somber faces stared back at her.

"I have an invisibility projector in my lab," said Virginie. "I can run some tests to see what we can discover." She looked at Ady. "Tomorrow good?"

Ady nodded. "I think we're going to need your disruptors, several of them, to take out these goose vehicles, as well." She looked from person to person. "Once we turn off their data, they'll come at us."

Anson finally said, "Shouldn't we turn this over to Eidolon. Don't you think this is bigger than what we can tackle?"

Ady looked around the table. Frightened faces stared back. They were contemplating problems on a scale they had not experienced nor anticipated. Were they a formidable cadre or a naive team? Could they really stop this eavesdropping and keep it that way? She was sure they could interrupt it, but the Pandera reaction could be overwhelming, even physical. Did Pandera have other weapons they would use again humans? All the evidence said they had no hesitation in killing humans through what appeared to be accidents, arranged accidents. They hadn't demonstrated active weapons to kill humans, but could they, for example, disable, destroy, or sink a submarine with their control of the embedded electronics?

Ady sat back in her chair and crossed her arms over her chest. This could trigger a war between humans and Pandera—a concept she now recognized as being carefully redacted from history and education. Pandera had re-written history for their own benefit, making them seem benign and always working in the best interest of humanity. It now seemed they were instead working to keep humanity docile, ignorant, and under their control while they listened for any unrest.

Ady nodded at Anson. "If we're going to start a war, we'll need Eidolon to have our backs. Otherwise, Pandera will make us disappear like they did those SpaceCorp people and Simone Procopio.

Skunkworks

Their discussion continued until the O-Club closed at 0200. Ady finally arrived at her pod at 0220 for some sleep. As she sat down, her Linc chimed and flashed red. It was a vid call from Bo using their personal encrypted channel, which Pandera couldn't tap. She accepted the call and said, "Good afternoon, Bo."

Bo smiled at her from the Linc and said, "Hope I didn't wake you, but I got your message summarizing your team meeting."

She nodded. "We don't know what Pandera will do when we block the data flow from their eavesdropping network. And we're afraid to do that without Eidolon knowing and backing us. I thought you might have a better strategy in approaching them."

Bo rubbed his bearded chin for a moment, and then squinted into his Linc. "I wish we were in person, but this will have to do." He sighed. "About a dozen years ago, Eidolon discovered proof of the eavesdropping and began a covert program to build their own electronics without Pandera circuits in them."

"You already knew about this?"

"It was thought to be only microphones. I've learned a lot more in the last few days. Eidolon also replaced a lot of voice circuits just to be safe. It was a giant task because there are so many devices to be re-built." Bo sipped from a cup. She wondered if he was drinking tea. Maybe Wai-Wan had finally won him over.

He continued. "Their first project was to clean the satellites for SpaceNet, which is now complete, so Pandera couldn't hijack voice data transmitted through those satellites. But while we excised that, we didn't catch the re-transmission of the captured data from all the other sources. That is, unfortunately, still there. The second project, which started in parallel, was to clean all the comps and bots, beginning with our bases in Australia and New Zealand. Those have just completed, and they've begun here in Brazil. DG is next on the list. The third project was to build an air vehicle that is space capable and armed. Although they've built various prototypes over the years, and they have a small fleet of twenty-four vehicles now, going forward, they plan to adopt your vehicle design with the improvements and modifications I showed you."

Ady didn't even ask how they had gotten her design. It had come from Bo. Maybe he had coached and steered her more than she knew. But it didn't matter. If they wanted to use it, that was fine with her. It was a complicated world they lived in and attempts to keep things secret from Pandera had made people do things they probably wouldn't have done otherwise.

She said, "No problem, Bo. I understand and would have readily shared the design anyhow. You know that."

"Yes," said Bo, "but I wish it had not been so clandestine."

She stared at Bo, thinking about the myriad of misinformation she had been fed or the real information that had been withheld from her. Bo was often at the center. She didn't want her love for him to be tarnished, but it was. They needed to fix that, but not until it became the biggest leak in her world.

She said, "Virginie has a weapon ready that she says can take down GWM propulsion. You may want to incorporate a defense to that into the vehicle."

Bo nodded. "Already have. That, plus an EMP cannon and a pulse laser."

She closed her eyes. She had never envisioned creating a war machine when she designed her air vehicle. But at the time, she didn't know how much of an adversary Pandera was. "You figured out that the goose was a real-time eavesdropping device for tactical field use."

"Yes, but only a couple of days ago."

"How did the goose interfere with Yoon's cloaking device?"

"The device was built with Pandera parts. The goose was scanning for that signature and used a focused EMP beam to disable it. But that beam also triggered a vehicle auto-defense prototype of Virginie's design. Essentially, the goose took out Yoon's cloaking, and Yoon automatically shot down the goose. But Pandera thought the goose had failed somehow."

"Pandera knows everything? Eidolon, submarines, DG, Astro, Yoon…they have all the secrets?"

"We aren't sure about Astro. Aideen is still analyzing the data. It's at least partially compromised. Oddly, we think DG is still undiscovered. Or at least of little interest to Pandera. They seem to think everything important is here in Brazil. Yoon is new enough that we think he and his comrades are still secret."

She paused to consider what Bo had shared. Eidolon was ready for a physical fight. If that happened, some lives would be endangered, maybe even lost. Could her group here in DG do this remotely without a physical conflict? It wasn't clear. "We might be able to take down Pandera's eavesdropping without a physical conflict. We were planning to do that but recognized the risk of Pandera's reaction. I know they've killed humans before, including me."

Bo said, "That's why I reached out to you, Ady. I talked to Minda, and she is good with you doing whatever you can to hamper Pandera's eavesdropping capability, including taking out their backups. She'll deal with the repercussions, whatever they are."

"She wants us to take the first shot and see how it plays out?"

"No, she's giving you an opportunity to try to cut off Pandera's head without a physical attack."

"What do you mean by 'physical attack?' Cut off the eavesdropping, but don't physically destroy the repository? Is there more you aren't telling me?"

Bo looked away for a moment, and then back at the camera. "If you can take out Pandera's capability, there will be no reason for Eidolon to directly attack them."

"Okay, I get that. We stop the eavesdropping and destroy the repository, and Minda will protect us from Pandera retaliation. But there's something hanging here that I don't see. What is it?"

Bo sighed again. "I went to Minda and pitched this after I got your message. She's in a bind with the North's Coordinating Council. They think Pandera is the savior of humanity and warned Minda not to try to lay blame on Pandera for the South's problems. But Minda and Vanessa have the vote of their ruling assembly to proceed with their plan. I convinced them to let you try your way before they attack Pandera."

Ady felt like she was dense. Eidolon was going to attack Pandera, but if she could cut off the eavesdropping, they wouldn't need to attack and would protect Ady and her team from retaliation. She still felt like she was missing something. She studied his image on her Linc. He looked tired and more wrinkled than when she had last seen him. And then it came to her. "Bo, how much time do I have?"

"They aren't sharing any details. For good reason, I think. But an attack on Pandera headquarters in Baja is scheduled for midnight local time. That's about nine hours from now."

Geek Squad

Fifteen minutes later, the group had assembled in the briefing room in Research. At Ady's request, Olu joined them. They had Eidolon's blessing. She hoped it was at least a semi-public blessing or there would be a lot of frantic communications in the next hour to Brazil. Meanwhile, a lot of work stood before them.

Ady asked everyone to remove their Lincs, and then laid out the situation, including Eidolon's planned attack. "Bottom line," she said, "is we have about six hours to execute the eavesdropping denial, or a physical war is going to start."

Anson said, "I thought you said they were attacking in nine hours? Why a six-hour deadline for us?"

"Safety window," said Ady. "If we're late, or they're early. They'll have to launch well ahead of the strike time, so if we can keep them on the ground, all the better."

"Got it," said Anson, nodding.

She looked around the room. "We know how to turn off the satellite downlinks. But we need to coordinate that so they happen all at once."

"Do we?" said Lin-Lin, yawning. "What do we lose if we do them one at a time?"

"Surprise," said Ady.

Anson and Olu both nodded. Anson said, "We can't take a chance that they somehow fortify the other satellites before we get to them. Once they see one go, it won't take long for them to catch on."

Joe raised his hand. The group smiled at his gesture and Ady said, "Yes, Joe."

"How about orchestrating this from the admin node."

Lin-Lin said, "I can shut them all down from Admin. You just want the downlink of the eavesdropping, not the whole PubNet, right?"

Everyone nodded their agreement.

"Virginie," said Ady, "can you do the same for SpaceNet?"

"With Lin-Lin's help, I'm sure I can."

Ady looked at Joe. "You need to find the backup repositories and figure out how we take them out." She looked at her wrist to check the time on her Linc, but it lay on the table, turned off. "We have around two hours. Think you can do it by then? We'll plan to execute shutdown at 0800 our time.

That's three hours before the attack and less than six hours from now." She looked around the room. "Okay, let's get to it. I want to talk with Olu and Anson about the submarines, but you guys need to get started." She pointed at the Lincs on the table. "Take you Linc, but keep it in your pocket for now."

Once Joe, Lin-Lin, and Virginie left the room, Ady turned to Anson. "How do we protect the submarines? Pandera can probably wipe out almost any electronics in them. If they do, the crew loses control. The boats may even sink."

Anson said, "There are two subs here in DG that are just completing a communications upgrade installation. I can check to see if that's at least in part to block the transmission of Pandera data. Given what we've learned in the last hour, I'm betting it is because it was billed as an urgent upgrade by Eidolon with no real feature changes."

"What about the rest of the submarines?"

Anson looked pensive for a minute. "I don't see any way to protect them. Even if they all surfaced and got the crew into inflatables, Pandera might still be able to sink the subs." Anson put his hand to his stomach. "I feel sick. Could we lose all the subs, and maybe the people on them?"

Ady shrugged. "I don't know, but it's a possibility we need to consider. Do you know if Eidolon is doing anything to try to protect the subs from retaliation?"

Anson shook his head. "There's nothing I've seen. Maybe they're fully focused on the attack preparations and haven't considered retaliation."

"They aren't even sharing with Bo. Or maybe they feel he's a leak to me, and then to all DG. I don't know what Eidolon has in mind." She leaned her chair back onto two legs and stared at the ceiling. She thought about what preparations could be made to protect themselves, should Pandera retaliate. "Anson, should we be attacked, what's the most important asset here on DG?"

Anson laughed. "You mean the biggest leak?" He thought for a moment. "The power farm. Without it we couldn't operate much of anything."

"Number two?"

"Research. The operations center."

"We need to protect those two assets." She looked at him. "If Pandera attacked DG, how would we protect the power farm?"

Anson stared into space for moment, and said, "I don't think we can. You might camouflage it, but that would take a lot of time. And you can't cloak the collection towers because then you can't collect the solar power."

"Too late for that. If all the power farm was taken out, what would we do for power here?"

Anson rubbed his cheek. "For emergency, I think we'd string power conduit from a couple of docked submarines."

She nodded. "That would work. If we had any submarines." Her chair slammed to the floor as she jumped up. "Anson, get those two submarines out of the lagoon. They're our only power source if Pandera takes out all the others."

Anson's face went white as he glanced at her. Then he ran for the briefing room door, bowling over Joe who was just coming in. Out of breath and red-faced, Joe said, "Ady, I found it. They were sneaky and thought they were clever by hiding it in plain sight, but I still found it. I don't know what to do about it, so I came to find you."

Ady pointed at a chair. "Sit down, Joe. Take a breath and tell me what you found."

Joe sat and took two hasty breaths. "The backup repository. I found it. They have a regular, normal online backup in two other data centers, but they were way too easy to discover. They were too confident, as if they had a secret behind the curtain that no one would ever see. I got behind the curtain and figured out–"

She slapped the table with a flat hand. "Joe! What did you find!"

Joe jumped. "Their backup repository is in Astro."

Tech Dump

"We still have about five hours left," said Ady to Joe as they rushed back to the operations floor. They found Lin-Lin and Virginie and pulled them away from the equipment so they couldn't be overheard. Ady shouted across the operations floor at Olu and waved him over.

When he arrived, she said, "Joe found the backup repository of all the eavesdropping data. It's in Astro on Mars." She pointed to Joe. "Give us the thirty-second summary of where it is in Astro."

Joe swallowed and said, "It's in expansion storage units. The last one was installed about fifteen months ago. They have something like a million times more storage than the devices are supposed to have, all hidden for this repository use. They send them pre-loaded with all the current data at that time. Then they update it from spacecraft when they dock at MarsGate. Almost every ship carries a big chunk of update data. Instead of Pandera trying to transmit it through space, they just downlink it from MarsGate to Astro, and apparently no one notices."

Ady pulled her Linc from her jumpsuit pocket and handed it to Virginie. "Would you please contact Bo with that information. The folks at Astro will know what to do. Coordinate through him to take it offline ten minutes before we cut off the satellites, 0750 our time."

"Why your Linc?"

"It has personal encryption that Pandera can't break."

Virginie's eyebrows went up. "You built it?"

She shook her head. "No, this was Bo's. He built it while he was setting up Astro."

Four blank faces looked back at her.

"Later," she said, waving a hand at them.

Virginie shook her head. "I'm glad I'm on your team."

"Me, too. All of you," said Ady smiling. "Are you all set with SpaceNet, Virginie?"

"Yeah. Lin-Lin can execute it when the time comes. Right, Lin-Lin?"

She nodded.

Ady said, "Okay, get that message off to Bo, please. Then go to your lab and remove everything you think is irreplaceable in case it gets destroyed."

"What do you mean, destroyed?"

"We have to be prepared for Pandera to retaliate. They'll likely go for the power farm and Research. We're gonna shut down Research and make your lab's transmission profile look like Research."

Virginie put her hand to her mouth. "My lab is going to be a decoy?"

Olu said to Ady, "You're serious, you think they might attack us physically?"

"I don't know. We have to be prepared. Better that than to lose Research, right?"

Lin-Lin raised her hand, and everyone laughed. "Why use Virginie's lab? There's a lot of value there. What about that warehouse McGoff used?"

Ady smiled. She recognized the irony if Pandera did attack it. "Great idea. New decoy destination. But Virginie, shut down your lab so there's no confusion for Pandera." The foursome nodded. "Get to it, please. Joe and I will be over to set up the spoof signals as soon as we're done here."

Virginie raced out the door.

"Olu, in about three hours, we need to shut down Research and evacuate all of the people."

Olu nodded and said, "I need to let Jef know." He rushed out of the room.

Ady nodded and turned to Lin-Lin. "Can you execute the net shutdown remotely?"

"You mean not from Research?"

"Yes."

Lin-Lin thought about it for a few moments. "Maybe."

"I don't want anyone in the building when we shut down the feed. Our decoy might not work."

Lin-Lin shifted in her chair. "I think the most reliable way is to use Ellis. She can do the shutdown from any console."

"No. We don't want any transmissions from Research after about 0500—three hours from now."

Lin-Lin turned to Joe. "Can you access that PubNet admin backdoor of Ady's through a porta-sat? I know there's one in Virginie's lab. We could get Justyna and her trusty cart to haul it away a safe distance."

"Yes, but I think Pandera blocked may have blocked it now."

Ady waved her hand. "I have another backdoor. We can use that."

Lin-Lin and Joe stared at her for a moment.

Lin-Lin said, "We take the portable node of Ellis and load her on the porta-sat node. She can uplink to SpaceNet, from there to PubNet, and take out both at almost exactly the same time."

"That's your job now, Lin-Lin," she said. "Need any help?"

"Yes. Can you get Olu to ping Justyna and have her here in an hour? I mean *here,* next to me, clearance or no clearance. I need her to help me get stuff onto her cart."

"I can ping her," said Ady.

"You need Olu for clearance. She can't get in otherwise."

Ady nodded. "Joe, close up, back out of whatever Pandera connections you have, and pack out of here. When you're done, get over to McGoff's warehouse and take Olu, if possible, with the spoof gear for the decoy. I'll speak to him now about getting Justyna. Questions?"

Joe raised his hand. Ady smiled. "Yes?"

"What if Pandera attacks first?"

"What do you mean?"

"What if Pandera attacks Eidolon and us before Eidolon attacks them?"

Diving for Geese

Ady went cold. Pandera attack first? Did they know of the Eidolon plan? It was certainly possible, given the extent of their eavesdropping.

"Is there something that makes you think they might?" she asked Joe.

"The communications traffic patterns. The Panama area is inundated with Pandera communications. There's no Pandera facility there so I'm guessing they're on a ship maybe coming through that canal from the Pacific. What are they up to? Maybe they know of the Eidolon plan."

Ady squeezed her eyes shut for moment, thinking about what to do. What's the biggest leak? Brazil. She had to let them know. And she had to advance their timeline here in DG.

"Get your stuff and get to the warehouse, Joe. As fast as you can." She turned to Lin-Lin. "I'm going to Olu so he can get Justyna now. We're going to move up the timeline. 0600. Where will you set up the porta-sat?"

"Yum Fish? Nothing anywhere near there that could be a target."

"Good choice. See you there in two hours."

She dashed off to find Olu. Twenty minutes later she opened the door to McGoff's warehouse. Lights were blazing and the place was filled with people. They looked like ants packing away their winter stores on a dozen small flat-bed trucks like those she had seen in the farm fields. She found Virginie, and asked, "Who are all these people?"

Virginie returned Ady's Linc. "Sailors. Commandeered by Jef. They're moving all of this McGoff gear out of the way."

Ady put her Linc on her wrist. "The timeline has moved up two hours. Joe thinks Pandera may be on the offensive and will be attacking soon."

"And you? What do you think?"

She frowned. "Unfortunately, it makes sense." She held up her wrist. "May as well use these now. Too late to be intercepted." She tapped on her Link. "I don't know if I have time to warn Brazil."

A roll-up door opened, and the loaded trucks began to move out. Before the door closed, another truck pulled into the open bay. Olu and Joe jumped out and began unloading containers. Ady and Virginie joined them.

Joe said to Ady and Olu, "You guys arrange them in a line ordered by container number. I wrote the number on the top by hand as we packed. Virginie, you pop the top off each container. No need to remove the equipment. I'll just cable it all together behind you."

Once the truck was unloaded, Olu said, "I need to go make sure Research is shut down. I guess we meet at Yum Fish?"

"Make sure you have your Linc. Our need to stay in touch now outweighs the intercept risk."

Olu nodded and drove out of the lab. Virginie started to close the roll-up door, but Joe stopped her, pointing at a container. "Before you close that, roll this container outside and pop the top. It's the antenna pack. After you open the container, you'll see a fiber cable bundle in a roll you can unroll it back across the floor to container eleven."

It took longer than they anticipated, nearly ninety minutes, before the gear was connected and operating to mimic the Research signals.

Ady looked at her Linc. Nearly 0500. She tapped her Linc to see if Justyna could pick them up. "Justyna will be here in ten minutes. Are we good to go?"

"Yes," said Virginie. "Did you get the warning to Brazil"

"I let Bo know, but couldn't reach Minda or Vanessa. He said he would contact them. Jef is going through the military channels which will probably take too long."

Justyna pulled up in her cart and the trio boarded after Virginie stacked two cases on the luggage rack.

"What's in the cases?" Ady asked Virginie.

"My GWM disrupters." She looked over her shoulder at Ady. "Let's hope we don't need them."

Ady hoped so, too. She looked out at the blackness covering the lagoon and noticed a small green light moving right to left slightly above the water. After staring at it for a moment, she could just make out the outline of a submarine. She hoped it was one Anson had rushed out of the lagoon. She scanned ahead and behind it to see if she could spot the second sub, but saw nothing.

They rode in silence until Justyna pulled up at Yum Fish. Ady looked at her Linc. It was 0527. A light pole cast a dim light around the empty hut. Lin-Lin sat in her chair in front of an array of three vid screens and equipment that was piled on top of a couple of the wooden spool tables. A portable satellite antenna rested on another spool a few meters away, the thirty-two-centimeter antenna pointed skyward. A power cable snaked across the sand and into the hut.

As they walked up to Lin-Lin, she continued to look at the vid screens and key the type pad. She said, "I still need fifteen or twenty minutes. I'm up, but the alignment isn't good enough to hit the satellite."

"Why don't you let me do that part?" said Virginie. "I've done it a zillion times in the field."

Lin-Lin glanced at her. "Be my guest." She backed away from the vids.

Virginie said to Joe, "Can you adjust the alignment to the numbers I give you?"

"Sure," said Joe. He walked over to the antennae base and tapped the mini-vid panel. It came to life. He said, "Ready."

Virginie tapped for a few moments and then read off alignment numbers while Joe entered them into the antennae. Ady saw the antennae adjust slightly, and then Virginie said, "Got it. We're locked on." She turned to Ady. "You want to open your backdoor?"

Ady sat at the makeshift console and connected to the PubNet admin node. She keyed what might have looked like a random set of number and characters, and then looked at her Linc for a moment. It blinked and displayed a ten-digit number. She keyed the number and waited. She was starting to get nervous, thinking that maybe her own backdoor access had been compromised, blocked, or lost. But her Linc blinked again, displaying another ten-digit number. She keyed that into the console and sat back as the vid panel turned red. They were ready. It felt like the time she first tapped the "start" command on her airpod. Though she knew what to expect, she wasn't quite sure all would go according to plan.

Looking over her shoulder, Virginie said, "Clever."

"Thanks," said Ady. "We're in PubNet admin." She looked at Lin-Lin. "Is Ellis ready?'

"She's loaded, but I haven't given her instructions yet. I'll do that now." She rolled up to the console and began tapping.

Ady turned to Virginie. "Better show us how those disrupters work." Joe rolled another spool over to the area, and Virginie put the cases on top of it. She opened one and removed a device that looked somewhat like an ancient rifle. It was essentially an arm-length of tubing with a palm-sized concentric dish on the end. Near the opposite end of the tube was a handle with a pair of buttons on the left side. A small mini-vid was mounted above the handle on top of the tube facing the rear. Virginie pulled a black block from the case and fitted it onto the rear end of the tube, just behind the handle. "That's the power pack." She pushed a red button on the power pack and the vid began to count down from ten. When it reached zero, "Ready" appeared on the vid in large letters.

"Does it make any noise?" asked Joe.

Virginie frowned. "No. Why?"

Joe shrugged. "From historical vids I've seen, guns like that always made a loud noise."

"There's no propellant or projectile, Joe," said Virginie, "just a silent GWM pulse."

Virginie picked up the device, aimed it into the sky, and squeezed the top button on the handle. The vid displayed a series of red horizontal parallel lines. "Those lines are the troughs of the gravity waves flowing out into space from the Earth. If there's a GWM in your field of view, you'll see them shift into a hyperbola around the center of the GWM vehicle. Center it and push the other button. It pulses a blast of reverse polarity waves that cause a feedback loop in the GWM core. It fries itself."

"How long does that take?" asked Ady.

"Sub-second. The vehicle will become an inert projectile almost instantly, crashing to the ground along whatever path it was on when you triggered the pulse."

Joe asked, "How many pulses can you get from one power pack?"

Virginie shrugged. "It's a prototype. I stopped testing at ten. The pulse strength was about four percent less each time."

"Range?" asked Ady.

"Again, prototype. Successfully tested to two kilometers, but the aiming is difficult at that range. I'd say one kilometer is the maximum working range with handheld."

"Any spare power packs?" asked Joe. "Or only one each?"

"One each, fully charged."

Ady pulled the second case to the side of the spool, opened it, and assembled the disrupter. She sighted into the sky and confirmed the waves displayed on the vid. She then disassembled the device and put it back into the open case. "Will the cases protect them from an EMP pulse?"

Virginie rubbed her neck and looked at the sand for a moment. "I'm not sure. At least partially. I'm thinking the power pack might be the most vulnerable."

Ady looked to the east and noticed that the sky was a fraction lighter in that direction. Sunrise was coming. "Is it waterproof?"

Virginie looked at her and frowned. "Underwater? I don't know. Maybe. Let me think." After a few moments, she said, "The only thing that would be vulnerable to water would be the power pack connection point. The rest is a sealed unit, I think. Never been tested. The water wouldn't affect the operation of the disruptor at all."

Ady looked at Joe. "Did you bring your toolkit?"

Joe nodded.

"You have anything in there to make the power pack waterproof?"

Joe shook his head. "No, but if we had some Nomex, I have adhesive that would hold it in place and probably make it waterproof to shallow depths."

"How shallow?"

"Maybe ten meters?"

"Ellis is all set," announced Lin-Lin as she labored in the loose sand to roll up to the trio.

"We need to know the limits," said Ady. "We waterproof the disrupter power connection with Nomex and Joe's adhesive. The risk of it leaking is a function of depth. The strength of a Pandera EMP pulse strong enough to fry the disrupter through salt water is a function of depth, too. Where is the useful operational zone?"

Justyna stared at Ady.

Lin-Lin said to Justyna, "She's asking how deep an EMP blast will reach compared to the depth that the waterproofing will fail and short out the weapon."

"Thanks," said Justyna.

While the others were thinking, Ady had subconsciously run her own estimates. Between six and ten meters below the ocean surface. Any deeper, the Nomex would fail, and the disruptor power pack would short out. Any shallower than six meters and the EMP pulse would fry the disrupter.

It was getting light. The sun would rise soon. Ady looked at her Linc. It was 0548. Twelve minutes to go.

Lin-Lin said, "There's probably a sweet spot at about seven to eight meters. Anything less than six meters and the EMP might fry it."

Joe nodded. "Yeah, I think that's about right."

Virginie said, "That goose vehicle can't have a powerful EMP pulse. It's too small. I think you can get away with three to four meters and be safe."

Ady said, "Let's say seven meters is the safest place. Joe, get the adhesive and a knife."

"But we don't have any Nomex," said Joe.

Ady glanced at the women. "Sure, we do. Get me the knife, Joe."

Ady sat on the side of the spool and unzipped her jumpsuit. As she started to pull it down, Lin-Lin said, "Wait! You don't have to sacrifice your shorts, Ady. My chair seat is covered in Nomex. Just cut off the bottom side. Joe kneeled in front of Lin-Lin's chair and slashed a chunk of Nomex off the seat bottom. He handed it to Ady.

She zipped up her jumpsuit and said, "Thanks, Lin-Lin." While Virginie held the weapon steady, Ady stretched the Nomex around the power pack where it attached to the disruptor. Once she had it in place, Joe spread adhesive over the seams to seal the Nomex to the power pack.

After holding everything in place for thirty seconds, Joe said, "That should do it."

Virginie examined the makeshift job. "Looks good. Not sure how long it will last." She handed it to Ady. "You going for a swim?"

Ady shook her head. "Contingency." She carried the weapon over to the cook hut and laid it on the serving shelf. Then she removed the grate from one of the cooking drums and pushed the drum over, dumping the ashes of the previous fire onto the sand. She grabbed the leg of the drum and dragged it off to the side towards the dock while the others watched, puzzled. She retrieved the weapon from the hut, laid it on the sand, and set the drum over it, legs up, making a metal protective shell over the weapon. "That should protect it from their EMP blast."

Ady looked at her Linc. 0557. She walked to the console and said, "Ellis, what time are you going to execute the shutdown?"

"As scheduled by Lin-Lin, it will commence in two minutes forty-three seconds. Would you like a count-down?"

"Yes, please," said Ady, "for the last ten seconds."

Ady looked towards the east and saw the sun had started to rise. It rose out of the water at a discernible crawl. She saw what appeared to be a black speck just inside the rim of the sun as it peaked over the horizon. She blinked and looked away, thinking it might be sun blindness from looking directly at the sun. But when she looked back, the speck had resolved into five distinct specks in a line that was growing larger by the second.

"They're coming," she said. She pointed to the sun.

Virginie grabbed the remaining disruptor case and quickly assembled it. She ran to the cooking hut and knelt in the sand, resting the disruptor on the serving counter. "I can see their GWM signatures!" she shouted.

"Ten," said Ellis from the console.

"Take 'em out!" yelled Ady.

"Nine"

The five drones were in a vee formation, exactly as geese fly. The lead drone began to dive towards the ground.

"Eight."

The drone to the right of where the lead had been, also started to dive towards the ground. Virginie was picking them off.

"Seven."

One of the drones broke from formation. Virginie screamed and tossed the disruptor away from her into the sand. Smoke curled into the air from the device. Virginie yelled, "EMP blast fried it."

"Six."

The first drone crashed into the far side of the island across the lagoon and exploded in a ball of fire.

"Five."

The second drone splashed into the middle of the lagoon. It, too, exploded. But the water absorbed most of the noise. It was a muffled pop with a bigger splash.

"Four."

"Ellis, execute now!" yelled Ady. "Now, before they fry the gear!"

"Three."

The remaining three drones passed silently overhead flying towards the decoy warehouse. Ady looked at the porta-sat console and saw light smoke curling up from it. She ran to the overturned drum, grabbed the other disruptor, and raced towards the pier. At the point where the pier turned left, she doffed her jumpsuit and dove into the water, the disruptor in hand. She began to swim downward to what she estimated was six to seven meters, then turned towards where the decoy warehouse should be and powered up the disruptor. After only ten seconds, she found the signature hyperbolic disruption in the lines and fingered the button. The hyperbola disappeared.

She figured the two remaining drones would now try to take her out. She spotted both hyperbola lines close together in the vid. They were growing larger. She guessed they were going for a close-range, synchronized pulse that would reach deeper. She began swimming downward and finally reached the bottom, about fifteen meters deep, certainly below the waterproofing threshold of their temporary fix. Aiming the disruptor nearly vertical, she knew she didn't have much time before it leaked. The drones were circling, she supposed expecting her to surface. She tried to aim the disruptor, but they were moving too fast at this close range. To hit one, it would have to be timed on their circular flight path directly above her. Knowing the leak clock was ticking, she waited and watched, calculating the drone path from the pattern of line changes on the disruptor screen. After three cycles, Ady timed her shot and tapped the disruptor button just as the lines began to bend on the display. She continued to watch the display. The frequency of wave variance didn't change. She had missed.

She took a different tact and began swimming farther out into the lagoon. A shadow passed to her left. She turned her head to see a reddish ray next to her. Rosey, the ray she had helped, paralleling her path. Somehow, Rosey's presence lifted Ady's spirits and encouraged her that she was on the right path. After two minutes of swimming, Rosey slowed and began a lazy circle around her. Ady quickly ascended to only a few feet under water. She aimed the disruptor towards where she thought the drones had been and slowly kicked towards the surface. When her head broke the surface, she immediately grabbed two huge breaths. The two drones were circling about two hundred meters away heading towards the pier. She aimed the disruptor, tapped the button, and immediately slid below the water, diving as fast as she could towards the bottom. Her ears popped as she both heard and felt an explosion in the water. She also felt something above her, pushing her down faster than she alone could dive. She twisted her head to the side and saw it was Rosey pushing her down and shielding her with her body. Once Ady reached the bottom, Rosey swam off.

Ady scanned the area above trying to find the remaining drone, but saw no wave line changes on the display. After what she estimated to be five minutes, the disruptor quit with a single spark. She had exceeded the capacity of their temporary waterproofing job and was now defenseless.

Drying Off

Sitting on the bottom of the lagoon, Ady glanced at the dead disrupter in her hand and considered discarding it but decided it might be of some use. She wondered if the eavesdropping channel had been disabled, if Pandera had also attacked Brazil, and if the Research decoy had worked. The world had changed while she was in the water. Pandera had attacked humans, and now they were at war with Pandera. Would the North join them, or would they remain under the Pandera spell and become a foe as well?

She felt a nudge from behind and turned to find Rosey gently pushing her forward. She looked towards the surface and saw bright sunlight. The disrupter was dead, so the state of the remaining drone was irrelevant because she could do nothing about it. She felt another push from Rosey, so she kicked off from the bottom and began her ascent.

She bobbed to the surface and looked around. She couldn't see the drone, but she did see Joe, Virginie, and Justyna pacing the end of the pier, looking out at the water, obviously looking for something. Probably her. At the same time, she heard and felt a vibration in the water. She turned to look behind her and saw a small orange inflatable boat about twenty meters away heading towards her. A shock of tousled hair blew in the breeze above the grinning face that beamed at her over the side of the boat. Anson waved as he stopped next to her. "Level 8, need a lift?"

She heard yells coming from the pier.

Anson replied to them, "I've got her!" He extended his hand and Ady handed him the disruptor. Anson shook his head and tossed the weapon into the boat. He extended his hand again, and she took it. He pulled her into the one-person boat where they struggled to untangle their arms and legs, shifting around so they could both fit. Finally, Anson, wearing only swim trunks, got settled in the back facing forward with his hand on the boat control and Ady facing him towards the back, their legs overlapping.

Ady frowned. "What happened to the fifth drone?"

"I don't know. When I got to Yum Fish, it was all quiet and Lin-Lin told me the others were at the pier trying to find you. I grabbed the first skimmer I could find and started circling the area they pointed out. After fifteen minutes, I had about given up." He looked at Ady, "Even for you, that's a long time."

As the boat bumped the pier, Justyna grabbed the gunwale. She offered her hand to Ady, helped her out onto the pier, and handed her the discarded jumpsuit. Anson tied off the boat and climbed onto the pier, toting the dead disruptor.

"What happened to the fifth drone?" asked Ady.

Joe said, "When you shot the fourth drone, it tumbled into the lagoon and exploded. It looked like the fourth drone shot down the fifth drone with its own EMP blast because it crashed into the water but didn't explode." He smiled and pointed towards the Yum Fish hut. "B.O.G.O, Buy One, Get One."

"What about Research?" she asked.

"Still intact," said Virginie somberly. "But McGoff's warehouse is on fire. The decoy worked."

"And the data feed?"

"We don't know," said Joe. "Both PubNet and SpaceNet are down. We don't know why."

Ady pulled on her jumpsuit and zipped it. Anson said, "The Eidolon attack on Pandera didn't happen. Pandera executed a preemptive strike there at the same time they attacked here. They destroyed Eidolon's fighter vehicles on the ground and the manufacturing facility where the fighters were made. There were numerous casualties."

"You mean people were killed?"

Anson nodded.

Ady grimaced. They had failed, at least for those who lost their lives. She pushed it aside. She could do nothing about it. It was history. But she could make plans and do better. And then fear gripped her as she realized her family was in Brazil. But she pushed that aside, too. She couldn't change what had happened, but she could start a journey right now.

She glanced at Anson. "And the subs?"

"No issues so far. When the Nets come back up, they may be vulnerable."

"Where's Lin-Lin?" she asked, looking around.

"The EMP blasts knocked her chair out. She's stuck back there in the sand," said Joe, jerking a thumb over his shoulder in the direction of Yum Fish.

Ady turned to Anson. "Thanks for picking me up." She threw her arms around him and hugged him. If they'd taken out the eavesdropping link and survived the Pandera attack, maybe that meant they now had time to explore their promised relationship. Her hug was probably lingering too long, but her arms wrapping around his bare skin and his salty ocean scent caused a tingling sensation. She savored it for a few extra moments, and stepped away. She wanted to take Anson's hand. In victory. In a new way, signaling a hopeful shift towards their new relationship. But now wasn't the time with the rest of the team here.

The group walked down the pier. When they got to Yum Fish, Lin-Lin was sitting in her chair next to the hut chatting with the owners. Oblivious to the silent battle that had been waged around them, the owners had already dragged their cooking drums back into place and had chunks of palm tree wood and coconut husks sticking out of both. As the group approached, smoke began to rise from the drums and flames started licking at the wood.

Lin-Lin tipped a cup in their direction. "Coffee's hot. How was your swim, Ady?"

Ady nodded. "Apparently successful."

Justyna said, "Long. At least twenty minutes underwater this time."

Ady glanced at her. "No, I had couple of breaths in the middle when I surfaced."

"I know," said Justyna. "I saw you. I'm talking about the last segment."

Ady frowned and looked at her Linc. It was 0642. How did all that time pass so quickly? She wondered if she should mention Rosey to the group. It was weird to see her, but somehow it was comforting and calming. She was looking out for Ady.

Their Lincs chimed simultaneously indicating that PubNet was back up.

The newsfeed auto-started with Pandera's version of today's attacks. There were various vid clips and pictures accompanying the newsreader's monologue.

"Earlier today, Pandera, as the world peace-keeping organization, successfully thwarted a misguided terrorist group in the Southern Hemisphere who had planned to attack the Coordinating Council headquarters. The purpose of the attack was intended as a power grab to seize control of the revered cities of the North, which the South so covets. A group of the South's deranged citizens, where body dysmorphia is rampant, had fueled a jealous rage among the South's inhabitants. A spirited power-hungry leader crafted the terrorist plot. She and her followers have been eliminated, as well as the weapons they had built for the attack." They showed a short clip of the smoldering ruins of the Brazilian vehicle factory Pandera destroyed.

The report went on to ridicule the selfish Southern Hemisphere action, assuring everyone that Pandera was ever watchful and vigilant in the protection of the citizens of the North and their cities. And while some human life had been lost in the attacks on the weapons plants, those were defective and dangerous humans who were, themselves, bloodthirsty, power-mongering maniacs who resented the paradise in which North citizens now lived. This life enjoyed by the North was a result of Pandera's rigorous patrolling and protection.

Ady muted the broadcast and turned away from the group, speaking into her Linc. "Ellis, was the download block executed?"

After several seconds, Ellis said, "The planned execution of the download block was never executed from this location because the equipment ceased to function. Despite this failure, the entire PubNet and SpaceNet were brought down from a remote node in the North."

Ady smiled. Her backup must have worked. But she wouldn't know for sure until she could access the Ellis kernel on Bo's lightning drive in Brazil.

Ellis continued, "As the nets have come online only recently, I cannot confirm that the download block in question has or has not been executed. However, the commands are no longer queued in the Admin node, and to my knowledge, the download channel seems to have been wholly eliminated across all of PubNet and SpaceNet."

"Thank you, Ellis."

Sirens wailed in the distance. Ady looked in that direction and saw a column of smoke rising in the blue sky.

Virginie pointed that way. "McGoff's warehouse, I hope. My lab is farther to the right. I think we'd better get to Research and see what damage control needs to be done."

The New World

When the group arrived at Research, Justyna parked her cart near the entrance instead of stopping at the curb. She walked to the door and held it open for the group. Joe pushed Lin-Lin's chair. No one said anything as they all walked across the lobby to the briefing room. Olu held the briefing room door for them, and as Justyna came into the room, he said, "Justyna is joining our team today."

"She joined a long time ago," said Ady. Everyone chuckled except Justyna, who was red-faced.

A man in a red tunic pushed a cart into the room and distributed packaged breakfast meals, drinks, and a pill for sleep aid, since they had all been awake for more than twenty-four hours.

As Ady downed her pill, she said to no one, "Wish I'd had this the day Bo and I fled from Virginia."

Sitting next to her, Anson said, "Why is that?"

"I didn't get any sleep the night before, so I was on adrenalin most of that day, or I'd have dozed off."

"Another trip to Krewe?" he teased.

"No, I was busy adding some failsafe capabilities to Ellis."

"Is that your idea of more fun than Krewe?"

"I was dead, remember? Limited options."

Anson nodded.

The main vid display on the wall came alive as Jef and Admiral Nichieu entered the room. It was a live vid feed from what appeared to be a tent. Several dozen people sat in a disarray of chairs, all looking frazzled, many with black smudges on their faces and clothes. A few had bandages on their heads, arms, or hands. Ady scanned the faces looking for her family members. Someone adjusted the camera and now pointed it at what appeared to be the front of the tent where Minda stood. She looked haggard, her braided hair was half-loose, and her eyes were bloodshot, but fiery.

"Good evening," she said, "or good morning to those of you on the other side of the world. As you know, Pandera executed a preemptive attack about an hour ago on our facilities here in Brazil as well as DG. All twenty-four of our fighters were destroyed, as was the manufacturing facility. They used both EMP blasts as well as incendiary bombs launched from their 'goose' drones. They also destroyed the Eidolon headquarters buildings, a large section of the B naval port, and my residence." A tear escaped her eye and slowly crawled down her cheek. Ady felt a chill.

Minda continued, "As many of you already know, there were numerous casualties. We have only an estimate at this time, but we think around 350 of our citizens were killed by AI-droids. Pandera droids, originally crafted by humans, that no longer sanctify human life." Minda stopped and looked around the tent, and then directly into the camera. "Our comrades in Diego Garcia were better prepared and suffered little damage, no casualties, and are fully operational today. Additionally, they have blinded Pandera. The hidden communications channel for monitoring humans worldwide has been eliminated."

"Normal newsfeeds, alerts, and weather streaming is online, and we presume back under Pandera control. However, admin access to both PubNet and SpaceNet has been blocked, not just to Pandera, but also to everyone. Right now, we don't know how that was done or who orchestrated it, but at least for the short term, Pandera will not have exclusive news control. They can't block, edit, or redact news from other feeds, including the South. And they can't monitor the conversations of humans in either hemisphere."

Again, Minda looked across the space at the faces staring back at her. "I have spent my entire life trying to find ways to avoid what I am about to say, but…" tears flowed freely down her face as she paused. "The human race is now at war with Pandera."

Ady put her hand to her throbbing forehead. She felt sick. She knew this wasn't her fault. But she felt guilty. And remorse. People had died in Brazil. She glanced around the room. Maybe she'd saved them. But she'd have to do better.

The group in the tent cheered and some pumped fists into the air. Anger burned in those faces. They wanted retaliation.

Ady nodded. She shared their anger, their desire for retaliation.

"In the next days, we will strive to enlist the North to join us, even though Pandera will continue trying to divide us. This is a *human* war, a war for all humanity's survival. Whether we convince the North to join us or not, their fate is locked to ours. This is a fight for the survival of all humans. It will be costly in so many ways, but we have no choice.

"Today, we'll begin to clean up the mess left by Pandera. We'll prepare to bury and mourn our dead. Tomorrow, we'll start to rebuild for a strong, swift, and complete Pandera destruction. For now, go about your personal business, be with your families, love them and all your fellow humans as we prepare for the most challenging quest mankind has ever faced."

The vid went blank. The briefing room was silent for nearly a minute.

Ady's Linc chimed. Everyone looked at her as she tapped her Linc and read the message from Bo aloud. *Private vid Linc in five minutes, please.* She was alarmed. It felt urgent. No one spoke. Ady acknowledged the message and stood up. She looked around the room at the group. In many ways, they were her family now. Maybe more family than she'd ever had. What she felt for them was complex and not the unconditional love she felt for Bo, Wai-Wan, Minda, and Vanessa. Still, it was more like "family" than any other term she could think of. She wondered for a moment if a better word for it existed in one of the ancient languages. She'd have to ask Keera.

"You can use my office," said Olu.

She nodded and walked out of the briefing room.

She shut the door after she entered Olu's office and sat in the guest chair in front of his desk. Her Linc chimed and she accepted the vid call. Bo, Wai Wain, and Minda sat in front of a table with a plain background, probably the tent wall. They had grim looks on their faces that matched the feeling she had in the pit of her stomach.

"Hi," she said, and tried to smile.

"Ady," said Minda. "this has been a rough day. The devastation around us here has been overwhelming." Minda looked away. Bo put his arm around her as she began to cry. Between sobs, she whispered, "I'm so sorry."

Bo looked into the camera for a moment. Ady felt her world twist, upend, and roll away, as she said, "Vanessa." She put her hand to her cheek where Vanessa had last touched her. They weren't going to have their reunion. There would be no explanations, no sharing, no confessions. No warmth, no compassion, no joy in her eyes. And her life's work, Eidolon.

Bo nodded. His face twitched for a few moments like he was struggling to maintain control. Then he said. "Yes. We lost her. It was a smaller drone, all black, that sought her out specifically, and when it found her, it exploded, killing her and two of her aides." He wiped his eyes and glanced at Minda. "Minda is now acting Princeps as well as Ductor."

Ady went numb. Her brain stopped. Vanessa, her mother, the soft one who cuddled her when she was frightened. The one who cried on the first day she went to Education. The one who painted smiling faces on her birthday sweets.

Ady nodded. "We should have tea. She'd like that."

Epilogue

Three days after the attacks, the emotional upheaval among the Research team in DG had abated. The Pandera attack was barely noticed, except for the fire in McGoff's warehouse. The drone crashes had caused four explosions, but no one was hurt. Only the one drone that had crashed into the warehouse caused any damage. Although the Brazilian attack was prominent in the Pandera PubNet news, they didn't mention DG. Admiral Nichieu gave a speech broadcasted on the local DG news so that everyone knew the real story about the DG battle and the one in Brazil. She also ordered everyone to take Sunday afternoon off.

Ady and the somber group packed up and went to the lagoon, mostly from habit. Justyna brought snacks for everyone, and Anson brought plenty of beer. Their conversation was sparse, mostly dominated by silence. Everyone felt Monday looming in the morrow when they would begin a new journey to both defend Eidolon and to plan the elimination of Pandera as the first alien spacecrafts were bearing down on Earth. Brazil and the Eidolon leadership was still in cleanup mode. Minda had tapped Admiral Nichieu as overall Eidolon military commander, at least for the next several months.

Ady was going to Brazil tomorrow for a few days. Minda had promised a lab session to see if there were any rectifying tweaks she could make to Ady's brain. After that, she'd be back in DG to focus on the aliens. Virginie was going to Australia to scout for defensible locations where electronics, weapons, and fighters could be manufactured in secret. Anson was now overseeing the rotation and refurbishment of all the submarines to replace their main communications systems with sanitized electronics. Lin-Lin had a new chair and a direct link to Charry in Astro. Together, they would begin prioritizing which electronics to sanitize in the SpaceNet, PubNet, and Astro systems. Joe was the only one missing. He'd taken a Tomahawk to Brazil the day before so he could lead the Eidolon cyber activities.

Justyna's friend Raminta and Tamisha from the O-club strolled by the group. As she passed, Raminta said, "Nice swimsuit, Ady."

"Thanks," said Ady shading her eyes with her hand. "I'm going shopping next week, so I'll replace it."

Raminta stopped. "That's not necessary." She looked at Justyna, and back to Ady. "You've seen my closet. The only time it gets sorted out is when friends borrow something."

Ady laughed as Raminta and Tamisha walked on towards the water. Friends. That's what they were. All of them. They cared for each other, they loved each other, and for this group, they'd die for each other. Friends. Not family, but a wonderful substitute when family wasn't available.

Ady felt warm. She stood and said, "I'm gonna cool off." She walked towards the water thinking about how odd the twists and turns had been, and through it all, without even trying, she had made a whole group of friends whom she loved and whom she knew loved her. She stopped at the water's edge and blinked a few times. Love was such an odd thing. There didn't seem to be a path to it. It just showed up, unplanned.

She waded into the water waist deep, and then dove in and swam underwater out into the lagoon for a ways. She surfaced and saw several people bobbing near the openings to the tide pools, waiting for the rays to come in. She floated on her back for a few minutes, staring up at the blue sky, watching seagulls circle the island. Something nudged her foot, and she looked around, seeing nothing. She bobbed underwater and looked around. A reddish blob glided across the bottom under her. She dove deeper and the blob turned towards her and rose to meet her. Rosey had come to say hello. Ady hovered, her arms out, using her hands as small paddles to hold herself vertical. Rosey slid through the water, slowing as she approached. She nearly stopped altogether less than a meter from Ady's face. Ady held her position and Rosey turned slowly and moved towards Ady's left hand. She bumped Ady's wrist, dove down, circled, and came back to bump her wrist again, and then a third time. Then she glided deeper and disappeared towards the tide pools.

Ady swam to the surface and looked at her left wrist that held her Linc. Maybe it gave off some signal that Rosey could detect. Wai-Wan might know about that with her fisherwoman skills. She'd send her a message and see how she was doing.

She swam towards the beach, and when the water was shallow enough, she waded out. Her Linc chimed with a new message from Research.

New communications intercept between alien spacecrafts.

#####

Acknowledgments

Thanks to multiple writer groups for their feedback, edits, and comments. Thanks to Cathy Hull for her editing support and thanks to my beta readers. For many new writers like me, this book might have ended up as an unpublished manuscript buried deep in a computer. But with the ease of e-book self-publishing, I thought it deserved its own chance at finding readers. It was planned as a series of three books (the second one is halfway written), but whether I pursue that or not depends on the response to Book One.

Special thanks to my late mother, Doris Cooper, who spent multiple late nights in a webbed lawn chair staring at the stars with me while I dreamed of mingling with the meteors, moon-men, and milky way.

You can find current information about what I'm writing on my website, **www.terryrcooper.com**